Joanna James' Journal

Trish Henry Green

For Dorothy

Joanna James' Journal

Fifty, fat and fabulous—Joanna James' time has arrived.

Newly divorced, with grown-up children, she can finally embark on a journey of self-discovery back home in the UK. But life is never that simple. A transatlantic relocation, family issues, and dipping a toe into the dating scene complicate her plans.

Settled in her new forever home, Joanna decides to pursue her childhood ambition of making a living as an author. Undeterred by the men who cross her path, she works to achieve her goal.

Joanna isn't averse to romance, but this time, it will be on her terms—or not at all.

'Joanna James' Journal' is a standalone contemporary women's fiction featuring a woman finding her way after her life turned upside down. Laugh and cry with Joanna as you enjoy her journey to ensure her later life is fulfilling and triumphant.

"There's no place like home."

Wizard of Oz (1939)

Contents

INTRODUCTION

I began writing this book as non-fiction to tell the story of my separation and divorce from my husband of twenty-plus years and my subsequent return to the United Kingdom after living in the United States of America. I hoped sharing my story would help other women, particularly those over fifty, feel less alone. Additionally, I wanted to advise anyone wishing to return to the UK in some capacity. So, I hope you'll forgive me for an introduction, usually reserved for non-fiction.

Fiction is my forte, and I found it far more interesting to create the irrepressible Joanna James and then add my story to hers. Hopefully, I've still met the above goals, as fiction can sometimes hold more truths than non-fiction.

Jo isn't me, but we have things in common—she lived in Connecticut, USA, is from Norwich, UK, where her mother and siblings live, and tried writing a novel. However, Jo is a little younger than me, has a different family, and works as an editor.

The most significant divergence is Jo's romantic, and otherwise, interactions with men. Writing these allowed me to comment on dating as a fifty-year-old and some male behaviours. I haven't had those experiences and also didn't meet any famous actors on my flight home to the UK (what a shame).

I hope you like the trips through Massachusetts to enjoy the Fall colours, along the river Wensum to Pulls Ferry in Norwich, around the majestic Norwich cathedral and a brief visit to Norwich's Norman castle.

Whilst I don't claim to be the best poet, writing poetry kept me sane over the last few years and allowed me to work through a few emotions. Some fit perfectly in Joanna's story, so I wrote a few more to work with the remaining chapters.

Finally, please forgive me for using my own historical fiction series, Redway Acres, when I needed a TV show for my famous actor to appear in. A girl can dream.

Thank you and please enjoy Joanna James' Journal.

Trish Henry Green

BEGINNING

*R*eal life is boring.

Not for me was there a heartbreaking discovery of infidelity. No walking in on my husband in a naked tryst with a younger woman or a man, as the movies or TV shows would have it.

Like a candle burning its last, my marriage sputtered to an unremarkable death. The wax gave its all as the fiery wick consumed it.

I was left to be Joanna James, as misshapen and lumpy as the hardened remnant of candle-wax.

NOW I KNOW BETTER

You whisked me away
With your promise of love
Off we flew one day
Into the clouds above
I should have known better

You vowed to be true
And put on a ring
Not let me be blue
And would do anything
I should have known better

I left on a whim
All my family and friends
Stepped out on a limb
Perilous right at the end
I should have known better

You said you loved me
Would say if love were dead
But I didn't see

And you never said
I should have known better

When you left me alone
I clawed my way back
Made a life of my own
Nothing will I lack
As now I know better

ONE

M y husband of twenty-eight years stretched back in his office chair as if we were discussing what to have for dinner. Bruce looked good for fifty-two, and I resented that a bit. Tall, at six feet and still reasonably trim, despite the thickening waist men of his age often develop—his hair dark, with grey at the temples that gradually worked its way through the thick mane. And he had more wrinkles than I, but on him society deemed them attractive. On me—.

I caught my reflection in the squares of glass in the door that lent the room an airy feeling, so calming for an office. Nearly as tall as Bruce, I carried far more weight in my middle and hips. Though my hair was long, I had taken to tying it back since my hot flushes started a couple of years ago. The luscious locks of my twenties had thinned somewhat after three children, and my large boobs were heading south.

I slumped into a nearby chair, then quickly straightened my spine to distribute my figure a little more flatteringly—I hoped. Getting Bruce to communicate his feelings would be more challenging than ascertaining what to have for dinner.

"Can we call this a marriage at the moment, Bruce?" I asked, leaning forward, hoping he might grasp my hand, which I'd reached towards him. Then he would declare he was sorry I had hardly seen him all week, all month, and he would do better.

"I don't know." His eyes ignored my gesture and flicked towards the laptop screen glowing on his desk.

"For goodness' sake, can you close it for a few minutes?" The pain of my once again shattered hopes made me momentarily bitter, and I returned both hands to my lap.

"Okay." He tilted down the device's screen, but I would get no further concession.

"You're hardly ever here; when you are, you're working on that computer. I thought we'd be closer once the kids had grown. Not like this. I can't even remember the last time you touched me."

Last summer, our youngest child of three achieved his mathematics degree. He'd invited his best friend to our family dinner to celebrate, and they came out to us over the desserts. Ethan and Matthew—his boyfriend—now lived together in Boston. Our daughters were married and working hard in their careers in Connecticut. To be honest, I couldn't be prouder of all three of my children.

"Like what?" Bruce, ignoring my last comment about our lack of intimacy, didn't surprise me.

"Barely seeing each other and then having the same conversation over and over again."

"What conversation?"

I sighed at his obtuse comment. "The one where I ask you what you want, and you say, 'I don't know'. What *do* you want?"

"I don't know." He grinned at his 'joke', but I wasn't laughing. At first, Bruce's humour was a big part of my attraction to him. Unfortunately, I was too used to him using it to diffuse an argument he was losing. He spread his hands out in a more serious appeal. "I really don't, Jo."

I took a deep breath, tempted to leave the room and give up as I had done countless times before, but I'd promised myself I would push this to a head. I'd finally reached a point where I was more afraid of continuing to feel alone in this relationship than I was of getting divorced. Even so, thirty years together, twenty-eight of them married, was a lot to throw away. I'd given up my career dreams and future pension to leave the UK, follow him to the USA, and raise our family. He'd worked long hours, but so had I, taking care of the house and kids, and I even got a part-time job editing. Truthfully, it was close to full time these days.

He'd promised to 'keep me in the manner to which I had become accustomed', whatever that meant to him. To me, it meant the fun we used to have when he took me to see the sights of Connecticut, the nightlife of New York City and the history of Boston, the love and affection that had produced three children and the attention we paid to each other at the end of each long day as we cuddled on the sofa to watch the latest 'Law & Order such-and-such' episode. He planned to work until he was fifty-five, pay off the mortgage, and we'd have enough to retire. I'd no idea what he imagined that would look like because we'd only just kept it together during the pandemic—mostly ignoring each other. Where had that couple gone? Used up by life, I supposed, but I hoped we could find them again.

Perhaps he would surprise me, and we'd work on improving what we have now. I'd be willing to make changes, but it's hard to do if the person you want to change for won't tell you why they don't even want to spend time with you. I could ask him if he was having an affair, but that question was asked and answered many times over. When Ethan came out, I even asked Bruce if he was gay.

Blowing out the breath, I tried to make it easier for him, wondering what it must be like to have people around you who wanted to make your life easier.

"Okay, the way I see it, we have three choices." I counted them out on my fingers. "One, carry on as we are. Two, get some marriage counselling. Three get divorced. What do you want to do?"

"I don't know."

Honestly, there are only so many times you can count to ten before ten isn't enough. Bruce always wanted to buy a gun to keep in the house, and he's lucky I dug in my heels because, at that moment, I might have got the damn thing and shot him. *Say, 'I don't know' one more time, Punk!*

"I deserve a better answer than that, Bruce." Clearly, my exasperated expression broke through because he doubled down.

"I don't. I don't know what else to say—I just don't."

How the man directed a team of engineers is beyond me.

"Right, let me make this even easier *for you*. There's no way in hell that I will carry on as we are. So, either we get marriage counselling or we get divorced. What do you want?"

"What do *you* want?"

"For fuck's sake, Bruce, you're the genius here. Can't you figure it out?" That got his attention. It wasn't often I swore, despite being proudly British with a colourful abundance of expletives to hand—or tongue. "If I wanted a divorce, I would say that's what I wanted. WHAT—DO—YOU—WANT?"

"I don't know."

"Why? Why don't you know? Why do I have to spell this out to you?"

"I d—" He had the decency to shrug instead of finishing that sentence, his toe on the floor swivelling his chair this way and that as an alternative to squirming.

"Then I need a yes or no. Will you go to marriage counselling with me?"

I waited just a few seconds, maybe five at most, but my heart beat five minutes' worth.

"No."

Where are the tears? Twenty-eight years, and it ended with a resounding 'No'. I couldn't even cry. I figured I'd shed all my tears each year he pulled further away.

"So that's it then." I stood to walk away and face the end of our marriage alone, just as I would be for the foreseeable future.

He nodded, then stood and stretched his arms out to me. It was the last thing I expected. "Do you want a hug?"

"You fucking bastard," I managed at his offer of the one thing I'd craved from him for so long. Instead, I headed upstairs to the bedroom that hadn't been his for a while—apparently, I snored these days, though he had snored throughout our marriage, and I never slept in another room. At least we didn't need the 'who's sleeping where' conversation.

For good measure, I locked the door. It was just one of those push-in things on the handle that Bruce could easily pop out with the little pointy pin we left on top of the door frame in case the kids ever locked themselves in. I wasn't afraid of him, but I've listened to enough women's podcasts to know about the pity fuck. One last hurrah before we went our separate ways?—No thanks.

On automatic pilot, I used the ensuite bathroom, habit and routine getting me through my ablutions—brushing my teeth and hair, then putting on my pyjamas. I got into bed and turned off the light. I lay there looking at the tray ceiling, opening my mouth in a silent scream, but the tears didn't come. I wasn't sleepy, but I couldn't read or do anything other than lay there—numb.

What will I do now?

A thought crept into my head, and as I gave it access, I panicked a bit, so I shut it down again and closed my eyes. It didn't want to be ignored—tap-tapping on my skull.

Knock-knock.

Who's there?

An idea.

An idea who?

An idea who you can't disregard.

I tried to think of other things, counted sheep, and listened to a sleepcast, but it was a persistent bugger. Finally, I gave it room in my mind and, truthfully, my heart.

What if—what if I went back home to the UK?

***

I'd slept fitfully, but when I woke fully, my first conscious thought was, *What if I moved back home?* Home—that word seemed significant. Though this house, back to which we had brought three babies from the hospital and watched them grow and learn, was our family home, I'd never stopped calling England home, specifically Norfolk. I'd earned my US citizenship a decade earlier, and all our children were dual citizens, courtesy of me.

After showering and dressing, I peered tentatively out of my bedroom door. The spare room, where I presumed Bruce had slept, was visible through its open door—the bed rumpled and blinds still closed. The upstairs bathroom was empty with evidence that he had washed up this morning, and I discovered his office was similarly messy when I ventured downstairs. My soon-to-be ex-husband had gone to work early, so I grabbed a notebook and pen off my desk in the family room and sat at the kitchen counter nursing my first coffee.

At the top of the page, I wrote 'Pros and Cons'—my biggest con for leaving was my children, but they all had their own lives and partners.

I suddenly realized that Bruce and I would need to talk to them about our split. I flipped over the page.

On the top of the second page, I wrote 'To-do'. I started this list with 'Talk to the kids'.

I supposed I should discuss how to go about that with Bruce, so I squeezed 'Talk to Bruce about the kids' between the 'To-Do' title and that task.

Perhaps I would need a separate 'Bruce' list. So, I crossed that out and started another page with questions and actions for him.

Honestly, talking to the kids would probably come down to me, anyway. Still, it felt fairer to ask.

Damn it, I should have done this on my iPad. Now it's a mess.

I added a few more tasks before returning to my pros and cons—what was in our accounts, pensions and investments, plus the house's value (less the small mortgage). Once I had that information, I would know how much I could spend on a home in the UK. I added 'passwords' to Bruce's list to check the balances.

Don't forget the exchange rate. Moving back to the UK won't be cheap.

The biggest on my pro list was spending however many years my mum had left enjoying her company and helping if needed. My siblings were over ten years older than me, so that would be easier for me than for them.

I stared at my top pros and cons. *Yep, when it comes right down to it, the people in your life are the most important.*

Would one of my friends know a reasonable attorney to get the divorce done? Many of our retirement assets were in Bruce's name, but we paid into them jointly. We used my income for our vacations, school trips, and other kinds of extras. I assumed I would still get half of everything and some alimony, given that my potential earnings would be less than his.

Why do we call marriage a contract if we don't agree beforehand on how to divide things if our union dissolves? No one would dream of doing that in a working partnership, would they? Yet, women do that every day, and there's no protection from losing out on work experience and years under your belt. Even if you get your fair share, people see it as 'taking the man for all he's got' or 'getting your pound of flesh'. I added divorce attorneys to my list. I would probably post on Facebook with my friends, letting them know and asking for help.

I would need a new will—another point to add to the list. No way would I risk flying to the UK without changing my will from 'Bruce gets everything' to dividing it between the children—an estate attorney added to the list. I was sure I also needed to update my US passport, which expired soon. Another pro, I didn't need to buy health insurance.

I'd forgotten the biggest pro of all. I wanted to go home.

With the pros and cons showing that moving back to Blighty was my best option, I grabbed my iPad, walked around the house, took photos of everything I wanted to take home, and noted measurements. Most of the furniture would be too big for a British house I could afford.

Would Bruce want to live here alone? I doubted it. I added that question to the 'Bruce' list.

Our bedroom furniture would be a crushing blow to get rid of—our first grown-up furniture set, not even ten years old. I'd scrimped and made do so we could save for Bruce's early retirement, even though it meant going without the best stuff for longer than I should have. He wouldn't get to retire early now. A pang of guilt fizzed in my gut, but I quickly pushed it aside. Yes, I forced this issue, but ultimately, the divorce was his choice. I wonder how many more years we would've stayed married as ships that pass in the night if I'd said nothing?

***

I called my mum while I fixed myself a bite of lunch. It would be post-afternoon nap time for her now.

"Hi, Mum. I'm coming home."

"Oh, lovely. Do you want to stay here? How long is this visit?"

"Forever. We're getting divorced. Things aren't right, and the kids have all moved out. I want to come home."

"Of course you do, Joey. England will be happy and lucky to have you back. Will you live in Norfolk?"

"Yes, I want to be close to you."

"I'm fine, but if that's what you want, I'll be delighted to have you here for however long you need until you're sorted out."

"No. I'm going to get an Airbnb place to stay. I don't want to stress you out. If I need a week here or there, I know I've got you for backup."

"I'm so sorry this has happened, but make sure you get every penny you can from Bruce. Get an excellent solicitor. He might have been the higher earner, but you ran that enormous house for him and raised his three children well."

"He'll be fair, Mum."

"Make sure of it. Get a good solicitor. Don't just take his word for it."

"The way people talk about divorce, it sounds like it's his money for me to take. It's *our* money. We have joint accounts that pay into various investments and so on. I'm entitled to half of everything."

"You're right, Joey. I'm here for you if you need to talk."

"I'm sure I will. I'll keep you posted about what's happening. I'll talk to Elliott, Anne and Susan at some point, but you can tell them when you're talking to them." My siblings would be supportive, too.

"Will you change back to your maiden name?"

"Sherwood? Well, I have always preferred it to Newberry. I don't know. I'll have to give it some thought."

"You do that, my dear."

"I'm off to open a sole bank account, Mum. Talk soon. Love you."

"I love you, Joey. Come on home. It's about time."

I knew what she meant. Bruce had promised we would live in the UK after a while in the USA, but it never happened. Taking kids out of their schools and away from friends is hard and feels selfish.

Then I got into my car and drove to the bank. I would need my first sole bank account and credit card in decades. I messaged Bruce to check that he approved transferring five hundred dollars to my new account. I felt silly. It was my money, too, but it seemed fair to ask, and I wanted to be fair.

Driving back, I opened the windows and the sunroof and loudly played "Enough is Enough" by Barbara Streisand and Donna Summer.

"Get the check, pay the bill, you can do it," I sang. I felt elated and free, and I couldn't help but smile.

***

Later in the afternoon, my boss returned my call. Sophie Clark was my staunch supporter; to be fair, I'd rewarded her efforts with a first-rate work output. I'd often put in extra hours to cover a late submission from an author and meet a tight deadline. After saying it out loud to Mum, the second time I talked of my impending divorce, it was easier.

"Thanks for calling back, Sophie. There's no way to sugarcoat this. I'm getting divorced and moving back to the UK. I'm going to have to put in my notice. How long do you need?"

"Wow, okay, let me think here for a second. First, how are you? I have some time if you need to talk or vent."

"I'm doing okay. I'm keeping busy, so I expect it'll hit me later when I stop." I heard my voice break. *Well, it's about time.* Sympathy and kindness always got me emotional. "Honestly, Bruce and I have been drifting apart for so long, and I think I shed most of my tears already. It'll be hard to leave the kids, but they're all happy with their partners. I don't see them daily anyway, and I can call and text from anywhere. Keeping in touch is much easier than when I first moved out here. There was no social media, no chatting online. Emailing was about our limit."

"That's so hard to believe these days, isn't it?" she agreed. "If you're serious about handing in your notice, I'd need two weeks minimum, but a month would be better if you can manage it. However, I've got an idea that might work and, if it does, will allow you to keep working during your move and beyond. We have a counterpart in the UK that manages UK publishing for us. They could make your salary payments for us. Let me talk to our accountants and see what we can work out. That is, if you're interested."

"Oh, that would be amazing. I'm definitely interested. It's just right now I've a whole lot to do, so if I could work my basic hours only, no extra until I'm settled over there, that would be great."

"I'll tell everyone here not to pressure you for more, Jo. I hope we can keep you, because you're invaluable. You could be our first 'super remote' editor."

"Sounds good to me, Sophie. Thank you so much."

"You earned it, girl. Now, I'll see if it's possible, and you get back to your plans. Let me know if I can help with anything."

***

I stood in the kitchen, considering what I should have for dinner, feeling a little sad. The kitchen and adjoining family room were one area of the house we hadn't updated. I had big plans to rearrange it to improve the layout and natural light and update the doors, handles and countertops. Then, I thought I would feel worse if I had done the big update and now had to sell it. We could give it a spruce up and a new lease on life instead.

Usually, I texted Bruce to see when he was coming home and what he might like to eat. I would cook something for myself and whatever he wanted when he came home later. I reached for my phone without thinking—so ingrained was the habit. Then I laid the phone down on the kitchen counter and made what I wanted to eat. I was proud of myself for realising before sending a text, but it left me with a sense of unease that I'd forgotten something.

Bruce came home late. I don't know what he expected, but I was working a few hours on my computer. The flexibility of editing suited me when the kids were young. I felt I had to earn this new role despite Sophie saying I'd done so already.

"Hi," he said.

"Hey." I didn't look up.

I didn't say anymore as he disappeared into his office to offload his coat and bags, then returned to the kitchen and rummaged through the fridge and freezer. Although I really wanted to help him and ask about his dinner, I stopped myself, putting on a firm lid and twisting it tight. I wasn't even going to food shop for him unless he asked explicitly.

"How long do these pies need in the oven?" he asked.

"Thirty minutes."

"How do I turn the stove on?"

Are you serious right now? "Just turn the middle dial to the temperature you want."

"What temperature do I want?"

"Four-twenty-five Fahrenheit."

"Thanks." He put the pie in its foil container directly on the rack.

I wanted to scream, *Put the pie on a tray so the contents won't overflow into the oven as they bubble up.* I knew who would clean the burnt debris tomorrow. Maybe I would just put it on a baking tray once Bruce had gone upstairs to change. He would leave the tray in after taking out his pie, and the sauce would bake on it as the oven cooled, but I'd use an old tray and could always throw it away if it didn't clean up. Even better, Bruce could have it.

First, the most pressing thing was telling our kids about the divorce. I stopped his progress towards the stairs. "I wanted to ask your thoughts on when and how to tell the children about us."

"Holly texted me an hour ago, so I told her."

"Over a text?" I was horrified.

"Sure. She was fine about it. They aren't little kids anymore, Jo."

"Bellend," I muttered before grabbing my iPad, phone and headset and heading to the privacy of my bedroom, the pie issue forgotten. Here was me being oh so careful of his feelings, yet he had thoughtlessly texted our daughter about it.

Fuck him and all his little minions. From now on, I'll do everything I want to and not consult him.

***

I got comfortable on my bed and started a video chat with my firstborn—Holly.

"Mom," she wailed, "why didn't you call me?"

I touched her wonderful face on my iPad screen, stroking her long hair, which was the colour of her father's, and looking at her eyes—hazel, like his, too. She isn't very emotional, but she might have had a little cry judging by their red rims. A pang of guilt about the joy I'd felt sometimes during my first independent day washed over me.

"Oh baby, I'm so sorry about the way you heard. Your dad can be thoughtless. It was late after we concluded we would divorce, and I went to bed. When I got up, he wasn't there, so I got on with my day. I'd written a list of things to ask your dad, and right at the top was how to tell the three of you. He just got home and told me about your text, so I got straight on this call."

"Why, Mom? Don't you love him anymore?"

"He's hardly ever here, and when he is, he's in our little basement gym or his office. Since Ethan graduated and moved to Boston, it's just been the two of us. I've suggested some vacations or places to go out for the evening, but he isn't interested. I think a marriage should be more than a shared history. I asked him to go to marriage counselling, the alternative being divorce. He chose divorce by not choosing counselling."

"Do you think he thinks you wanted a divorce?"

"No, love. I told him that wasn't what I wanted, but now I see him with clearer eyes. I'm sure I'll have bad days, but mostly, today was good. I'm so angry with him for telling you over a text, but it's too late now. Are you okay?"

"Yes, Michel is here and being his reasonable self, which helps." Holly's husband was French-Canadian and a lawyer. They met on Holly's school trip to Montreal and continued to write to each other for over a year before they both got into Yale. He's very sensible and logical, but he loves the heck out of my daughter, which is his most important quality.

"I'm so glad you have each other."

"Michel says he'll find you a good divorce lawyer if you need him to."

"I don't want to put him in a difficult position. Let me ask a few friends if they know of someone. If I get some names, I'll run them by him if he doesn't mind. Tell him, 'Thank you for offering'. Perhaps he can offer to help your dad, too?"

"Oh, um, well."

"Your dad already asked him, didn't he?"

"Yes. Sorry, mom."

"You don't have to be sorry for anything, sweetheart. Bruce shouldn't have asked him. It's unfair to put Michel in the middle like that."

"You're the best, Mom." From Holly, the apple of her daddy's eye, that was praise indeed.

"Could we add Beth and Ethan to this call? If they're available, we'll tell them together."

"Yes, let's add them, but sorry, Mom, I already told them. I was so stunned and wondered if either of them knew."

"Like I wouldn't tell you all together," I only chided slightly. Bless her. She'd had a shock, and there was more to come. "Never mind, spilt milk and all that. Can you add them?"

Holly got Ethan and Beth on the call. Poor Beth, her eyes were red-rimmed. She always wore her heart on her sleeve. Her colouring favoured me, and her strength reminded me of my mother. I'd seen Beth in action in the emergency room, and nothing I'd known was more formidable. Everyone looked at her as she issued confident instructions.

Ethan looked more stoic, but he showed emotion on his face. In looks, he was almost a carbon copy of his father thirty years ago when we first met—tall and strong, capable and clever. I'd brought him up to express his emotions, but he could be quiet like Bruce was. Luckily, the exuberant Matt brought him out of his shell.

"Do you think you would ever get back together?" Beth asked with a sniff, mopping her nose with a damp, scrunched up tissue.

"No, sorry, Beth. I don't see that happening." My eyes were filling at the sight of her misery.

It wasn't long before they were soothing me rather than the other way around. Like I said, I'm so proud of them all.

"You know that what has happened between me and your dad has nothing to do with anything you kids have done, right? You're all so amazing."

"We know, but what will you do, Mom?" Ethan asked. "Where will you live? You can still stay at home, right?"

"Well, I'd been thinking about that. How would you all feel if I moved back to England? I want to spend some time with your Nana and my siblings. I was hoping to get to know my nieces and nephews better. I'm a great-auntie too. I would love to enjoy those babies until you have your own."

Their thoughts about me moving quickly replaced their loud denials of grand-children. There were exclamations about how much they would miss me and more sobs from Beth.

"What does Dad say?" Holly asked—her dad's staunch supporter, as always.

"Well, honey, it isn't up to him. I'll tell him, of course, but I wanted to ask all of you. Will it be okay if I go? I promise to come back if you need me, and you can visit me there. I'll buy tickets if you want and get a house with a spare bedroom."

Matt appeared on Ethan's screen. "I'm coming to visit you, Jo. I'd love to visit the UK. You know how much I love those little English words that seep into Ethan's language." He kissed the top of Ethan's head, which he could only reach because Ethan was sitting at his laptop.

"Mom, would you move back if we needed you to, for any reason? Would you?" I think Beth will miss me most of all.

"Yes, of course I would visit. Don't forget we're all dual citizens, and we got you all UK passports. You can visit for as long as you want or even move there. I love you all so very much. Thank you."

"We're here for you. We'll be there for Dad, too, but whatever you need to make the move, okay?" Ethan was trying to manage me.

"Your relationship with your dad is up to you and him. I won't be a go-between or ask him to call you or anything like that. You'll have to do that all yourselves. And I promise you all that we'll talk a lot, and I'll share my plans every step of the way. I'll ask for help if I need it—hang on, what the heck is that?"

"Sounds like a smoke alarm."

"Damn it. Your dad left his pie in the oven. We'll talk soon, my lovelies. I have to stop the house from burning down, or I won't be able to sell it. Night, loves."

Why didn't I put that tray under the pie?

CLEAR OUT DAY

Hoarder, collector, saver
A person who can't throw away
A bill, a list, a scrap of paper
Will have to face a clear-out day

Should you go through every box
In case you throw out treasure?
Or trash without looking
And spend more time in leisure?

Be ruthless, but be kind
Sell, or trash, or keep
Throw out everything you can
And find it aids your sleep

Because when you discard
The physical load for you
You'll see to your surprise
Your mind is clearer, too

TWO

My list of things to do before returning to the UK was getting longer by the day. Many of them stacked up one behind the other as they depended on each other. Decluttering the house came before the contractor, who would spruce up the kitchen and paint a few walls, but that would be before the realtor did their staging and chose an open day.

I'd found a divorce attorney I liked very much, and it tickled me to no end when Michel reported he'd informed the attorney he'd recommended to Bruce. I imagined the conversation went like this—

Michel:

I believe Mrs Newberry has engaged her attorney for that divorce.

Bruce's Attorney:

Male or female?

Michel:

Female

Bruce's Attorney:

Okay, as long as it's not Kimberly Masters. Who is it?

Michel:

{Shrugs}

Bruce's Attorney:

> Shit.

Until our divorce, or until we otherwise agreed through our attorneys, Bruce and I continued to deposit our incomes into our joint account. All the bills came out, and we withdrew half of what remained and paid half of any future house problems. I kept one of our joint credit cards to pay for household improvements. Bruce wasn't too happy about it but hadn't argued for anything different. What he had argued over, surprisingly, was my decision to move back to the UK.

Shortly after talking to the kids about our pending divorce, I bit the bullet and told Bruce before one of them mentioned it and got in the middle of any issues. While my kids were adults and coped well with the stresses of the world, like any mom, I would do anything to lessen their burden. Plus, it was an issue between Bruce and me—no one else. He didn't see it the same way.

When he returned from work a couple of days after pie-gate, I asked him to talk to me at the dining table. He took his time, hanging up his coat and emptying his work bag before grabbing a bottle of beer from the fridge and slumping down opposite me, his tie askew and his face grim.

"I want to tell you my plans for after selling the house, Bruce."

"I figured you would move to a smaller place, perhaps closer to Holly and Beth?"

"No. I'm moving back to England."

"You can't do that. What about the kids?" He was suddenly alert and horrified, which perplexed me.

"I've given thirty years to you and the kids. They're all settled and happy in their lives. We've discussed it, and they understand. I'll keep in touch with them every day in one way or another. I want to go home."

"You spoke to the kids before telling me?"

That was rich, considering he'd told Holly and, therefore, all our kids about our divorce without telling me.

"It isn't up to you, Bruce."

"What if they need you?"

"There are these things called planes. I can be here within a day or two; in the meantime, you're here. They're your children, too."

"What if—" he drifted off and gave me a wry smile. It made me think the sentence would end '—I need you.'

I considered the opposite of that—me saying, 'What if I need him?' Then I realised I didn't and hadn't for a while. Men might say, 'You need his money'. To which I would say, 'Until we divorce, his money is my money and vice versa, so shut your pie-hole'—*and now we're back to pies.*

"I don't think you should go," he said instead.

"As I said, it isn't up to you. I'm doing this."

"Have you considered—"

I held up a hand. "Don't bother, Bruce. I've considered all I need to. I have lists, and I know everything I have to do. What I don't need—"

"Is me? I'm right, aren't I?"

"I was going to say, 'I don't need you to tell me what to do'. You didn't want me, Bruce. You made that clear."

"I don't recall it that way. I didn't know what I wanted. Now I do. I don't want you to go to the UK, Jo, and if we need to be together for you to stay, then I want you."

"Too late. I've moved on and am excited to be going. I'm sure you'll find someone."

***

When Bruce returned from work the following evening, I was scanning photos of the children as babies, through school and beyond.

"A colleague of mine has an apartment they're letting me have at a cheap rate until we're divorced and I can decide what I want to do. It's unfurnished, so I'll need to take some stuff with me."

"Okay, if that's what you want. I'd thought we'd stay here as roomies until we sold, but if you'd rather have your own space, that's fine." It meant more bills, I supposed, but we'd manage, and it might be better to sort everything without him underfoot. He stared at me momentarily, making me wonder if he'd expected me to beg him not to leave; then he surprised me with a generous offer.

"I'll put enough money in our account for the mortgage and all the bills here. You can use your money for food, gas, and car upkeep. My health insurance will still cover you until we're divorced, but you'll have to pay your copays and out-of-pocket expenses."

"That seems more than fair. Thank you." I wondered if there was a catch, but gift horses and all that. I didn't mention it. I figured I'd talk to my attorney about it.

"I've booked a van for this weekend."

"I hope you've booked some muscle as well because my furniture lifting days are gone. What do you want to take?"

"Bedroom furniture, I suppose. My office stuff, clothes, and toiletries."

"You can take the spare room furniture and move the sofa bed from the basement up there. We'll need the best stuff left in the main bedroom for staging when we sell. What about kitchen stuff? Does it have plates, cutlery, mugs, all that?"

"I don't think so."

"Get some boxes, and you can take the spare sets of everything."

"I need to take the grill and some of my gym equipment."

"Well, it is yours, so it's up to you, and I never use the grill. Clean up the deck when you move it, though."

As I worked through the kitchen, pulling out his share of what was there, the moment's significance weighed a little more heavily on me. This was it. The last time we would share the same roof after many years of ups and downs. I didn't want to cry, but my eyes weren't cooperating. Nor did I want him to feel sorry for me or try to comfort me, so I kept a watery eye on where he was. When he was outside, I grabbed a couple of tissues to blow my nose and dabbed my eyes, then I crouched back down and continued to pull things out of the cupboards. While at it, I figured I might as well get out all those dusty bowls and small appliances at the back that never got used. I wouldn't be taking them back, and if Bruce didn't want them, I'd run them over to Goodwill. How lucky my friends had all those Pampered Chef parties over the years where I couldn't help but buy something. We had plenty to share between the two of us.

Bruce stepped through the patio doors from the deck and glanced at me. "Oh Jo, don't cry."

"Don't flatter yourself; it's the dust. I've pulled out everything I won't need, so take everything you want, and I'll donate the rest."

"Come on, Jo. Don't be like that." He rounded the peninsula and dominated my space, or he would have done if I hadn't picked up a handy wooden spatula. Honestly, I get why most women would choose the bear.

"You should go, Bruce. Thinking back on it, I've got no idea how we survived the pandemic in this house together."

The truth was, at that point, I still held out hope, but it had all left me now. I grabbed my phone and ran to my room, still carrying my wooden weapon. Once my sniffles were under control, I called one of my best friends, Teena Tramontano. I couldn't do it alone; she was the most organised person I knew. It probably had something to do with her side gig of estate sales. She also got our friend Abby on the call, and after soothing my ills, we arranged a date when they would come and help, including a sleepover night.

It couldn't come too soon.

***

When Saturday came, Bruce turned up with a friend, and they spent the morning loading his hired van. Grabbing one of his boxes, I started loading the papers and sports memorabilia collected in Bruce's office.

"Don't bother with that, Jo. I don't need it at the moment."

"Okay, I'll get a good price for that Jeter-signed baseball."

He groaned, took the box to the van, and returned to continue unscrewing his desk.

As his friend drove off in the van Bruce had hired, I held out my hand for his door key. Bruce slapped it, giving me a low-five and a chuckle. An involuntary shiver ran through me. I loved that sound in his chest, especially when I'd rested upon him as we'd cuddled in bed. Hopefully, he didn't notice, and I put the thought out of my mind.

"No," I said, sounding like I was talking to a child, "I want your door key."

"Why? I said I'll pay the bills," he objected, but I was ready for this argument.

"I still own half the house and would be happy to return to our plan of putting all our money in the bank and splitting it all evenly." I'd worked it out, and he ended up with more of the pot his way if my guestimate of his apartment's expenses was right. "Alternatively, you can give me a key to your other place, or I need your key for here. I'm entitled to my privacy, just like you'll have yours."

Bruce gave up the key, and I agreed to leave it with Holly for emergencies. Knowing how much she loved her dad, she'd have strict instructions on when he could borrow the key—pretty much never. Then I followed his car down the driveway to check the mailbox. There was a large packet for me, and I took it back into the house, curious to see what it was.

Five minutes later, its contents were strewn across the kitchen counter, and I was sobbing—chequebooks for my new solo bank account, with 'Joanna New-berry' across them. I wasn't sure why I was crying, as I'd been so happy driving away from opening the account, but now I wondered at my right to claim that name, Bruce's name. Would I have to go back to 'Sherwood'—my father's name?

Even as more tears assailed me, I felt a sense of being outside my body looking on, but I couldn't stop myself. Grief of the loss of so much time or the post-work future we were supposed to have, perhaps? Relief of being in charge of my destiny after many years? Frustration at not being satisfied with the direction of our relationship and having no way to change it? Ultimately, as my breathing came under control and I wiped my eyes and nose, I had a sense of possibility. This time, if there were to be a significant person in my life, I would carefully choose who they might be.

Recovered, after a cup of strong tea 'English style', I armed myself with a duster, window cleaner, vacuum and floor mop to clean the entire office of the dust bunnies and cobwebs, which were all that remained. Leaving the room bright and gleaming in the afternoon sun, I took apart my desk and shelves in the family room, meticulously wiping down each section and hauling it piece by piece through the downstairs rooms to what would now be my office.

Whenever we got a new piece of furniture or needed some tech set-up, the job would fall to Bruce. Even if I started or offered to help, inevitably, I would get called away by one of the kids, mealtimes, phone calls, bath or bedtime. It never occurred to me to expect Bruce to cover any of those things, and equally, it never occurred to him to offer. Had I insisted on setting something up myself, there would be no doubt that I would get stuck and ask for help. Then he would take over and finish it for me.

"It'll be quicker if you just let me do it, Jo," he would say.

"Then I won't learn," I argued, but now I was paying the price. There was no choice but to do this myself unless I wanted to ask Bruce to pop back over. That was no choice at all.

Once I'd connected all the cables and stacked my reference books in the order I liked them, I wheeled in my comfy office chair, filled with pride over doing it myself. I'll admit it wasn't a tremendous deal. I wasn't performing brain surgery. For me, it felt like a hurdle I had climbed over.

I sat there admiring the typical Connecticut view of masses and masses of trees out of my window and wondered why Bruce was always the one who dominated this office when I was the one who worked from home. We'd deemed his work more important because it was our only source of income for many years. Back then, the kids were young, and it made sense for my desk to be closer to where they played, but it had been a long time since they needed my constant supervision. When I got my part-time editing job, I didn't earn as much as Bruce, and when he worked from home sometimes, he needed a quieter area—whereas I'd learnt to block out distractions.

It didn't matter now. The office and the view were mine to enjoy until we sold the house. I sat there a while, noting the leaves were changing. I vowed to enjoy one last 'Fall' in New England. Perhaps I'd even take some drives further north when the colours were at their best and most vibrant. I could do what I wanted, but I needed some breaks with all this work planned.

First things first, I had to clear out a lot of junk, and Teena and Abby would visit soon.

***

I'm not sure Teena understood what she was letting herself in for when she agreed to help me, so I insisted on paying her, and she insisted on giving me a friend's rate. Abby Allerton, a children's author, couldn't make it on the first day but would be with us for dinner, overnight and the following day. I had plenty of wine chilling in the fridge with a huge salad, a spit-roasted chicken and garlic bread. Needless to say, there was a decadent dessert tucked in there, too.

Teena and I started in the basement, going through boxes of old school forms, reports and childish art that had taken a turn adorning my refrigerator door. I narrowed the pile down to a handful of each kid's art that I would keep, and the rest went into three boxes, one with each kid's name. I messaged them to find out if they wanted to go through them or if I should ditch them, and in the meantime, I kept filling them up.

Teena reviewed my task list, which was now much neater on my iPad, with checkboxes and everything. I'm such a grownup sometimes. "Do you think you have everything on here?"

"I don't know. I bet I'm missing some things." I pulled a face that was a mixture of sad and frustrated—I hoped.

She grinned and rolled her eyes. "Perhaps there's a website about it or a Facebook group you can join where everyone tells you what you need and recommends places for shipping and stuff."

"That's a good idea." I grabbed my phone, eager to take a seat on the giant foam beanbag Bruce had bought when the kids were young. All three of my lovelies could probably still sit comfortably on it. They had loved watching it expand after we ripped open the sausage-shaped bag it had arrived in. I wouldn't have room for it in a UK house. It would be a definite sell if neither Bruce nor the kids wanted it.

"Yes, here it is," I explained from my seat cocoon. "Ex-Pats Returning to the UK—that's me." I hit the join button, then attempted to wriggle my butt off the foam monstrosity.

Teena offered me a hand up.

"Thanks. Fifty and fat—I'm probably going to be on the shelf for a while, if not for the rest of my life," I complained.

"And fabulous. Don't forget fabulous. You're a catch for anyone and never forget it. Plus, who's to say you aren't the one perusing the shelves, not just sitting on one?"

How great it is to have such a supportive friend.

"Fifty, Fat and Fabulous," I declared. Perhaps if I said it often enough, I could even believe it.

I took a photo of the giant beanbag and sent it to Bruce for a thumbs-up or thumbs-down. We'd worked out this system, so we didn't have to talk to each other.

Teena had opened a box of Christmas garlands I decorated our bannister rails with each holiday season. She spread them out on the ping-pong table—table tennis table, I corrected myself. I had to get back into the UK lingo.

"Keep or sell?" she asked. They were substantial artificial lengths of fir tree sprigs and pine cones decorated with tiny LED lights.

"Sell if Bruce or the kids don't want them." We plugged them in, and the lights twinkled. I took some photos, sending one to Bruce, but I soon got a thumbs-down response.

I sent the image to my chat with the kids, and the usual fight started between Holly and Beth. I let them sort it out. My money was on Holly as her house was much bigger, and I think Beth's husband, Al, would put his foot down. For them, it wasn't just a case of room to display them, but storage for the other eleven months of the year.

I gave Teena a wistful look.

"What are you looking all sappy about?" she was always practical, and there was no bite to her words as she grinned.

"Just remembering how small my UK furniture was when we first moved into this house. I had a tiny terraced house in the UK when we met. It's all gone now and replaced with all this huge furniture that I can't take with me."

"Are you sure you want to ship what you've planned to? They sell beds and sofas in the UK, don't they?" she teased.

"I love my mattress, and that's coming with me. The bed frame underneath is fine. It's just the huge surround that won't fit. Then I'm taking Beth's old bedroom furniture, as it'll fit in the spare room, and if I'm shipping all that, I might as well take the sofa bed. You never know—maybe you'll visit me sometime?"

"I would love to. That enormous sofa in the lounge, though?"

"It's only two years old. We got it just before the pandemic. As it is, Bruce will probably keep the table and chairs for when he buys something bigger than the apartment he's in now."

"Do you think he'll remarry?"

"Probably. Bruce needs someone to look after him." I was pleased to note my criticism of him, not myself. He stuck me in the mother role. I tried to wriggle out of it, but it's hard to do and raise three kids.

"What about you?"

I snorted. "Unlikely." I spread my arms in a look-at-me gesture.

"Fabulous, don't forget," she chided.

"Well, I'm not feeling the need or desire to be with anyone right now. If that changes, maybe, but I think my standards are higher."

"That's fair."

"Honestly, I think I need to work out what I am. Who I am. There are parts of me I haven't even considered before. Not sure I'm making sense."

"I get it. Let's talk about it with Abby tonight. Any decision on these?" She brought my attention back to the garlands.

I checked my phone. "Holly."

We repacked them and wrote Holly on the box, putting it underneath her open one, collecting smaller bits and pieces.

***

When Abby arrived, Teena and I were ready for wine and dinner. Prep was a simple matter, but the wine opening came first. We sat at the enormous dining table at one end, enjoying the food and each other's company. Abby detailed how well her latest children's book was selling and ran an idea past us for the next one she planned. Her excitement triggered a long-dead memory of stories I would make up to help myself get to sleep in my tween years—when did I stop doing that?

Teena smiled before making an announcement, "I'm extending my decluttering business to become a personal coach. Helping sort someone's house and mind, I'm providing the complete package."

"That's a fabulous idea." I reached over and hugged her. "I know you haven't been happy in your job. Will you wait to see how it goes before giving that up?"

"Nope, I handed in my notice yesterday. Phil earns enough for me to try it and see if I can earn at least as much as I do now. We've agreed to give me a year."

"I'll promote you on all my social media, Teena," Abby offered.

"With your followers, I have a great chance of success. Thanks."

"You know it might be an idea—" Abby said, but Teena raised her hand.

"I thought about that, but no," she said.

"What?" I demanded. They were speaking in code, and I didn't have the cypher.

"It doesn't matter," Abby said.

"I'm not in the same league, but I'll promote you too," I said.

"You won't be able to promote me when you return to the UK. I can't come over there to declutter someone's house," she complained.

"I still have plenty of Facebook friends that live here from the kids' friends' moms and school contacts," I pointed out. "I'm happy to keep posting."

"Best friends ever." She sighed, and Abby agreed.

"Besties over the Pond," I declared. We clinked our glasses to make it official.

***

"You have an amazing book collection," Abby observed as we cleared the table.

"Thanks. I'll probably just save my favourites. Many are signed, and lots are Bruce's. I'll have to see if he wants them. I could do the colour thing once we weed out his. It would make these shelves pop." On one side of our dining room, we had box-type shelves, and I could put some ornaments and knick-knacks on alternate shelves with books.

Eager to get stuck in, Abby soon pulled books off the shelves despite the wine we'd consumed.

"I can send Bruce photos of his books to see if he wants them," I offered.

"No." Teena stopped me from making too much work for myself. "We'll box up his, and he can sort them himself."

"What was I thinking? Thank goodness you're here to stop my habit of mothering him."

We boxed up the few I wanted to keep—ones I'd edited that had done well and some absolute favourites from book shows. Then Abby and Teena picked out a few they wanted to read—everything else we sorted by colour. By the time we made it to bed, we were giggling from the alcohol and exhausted from our labours. Thankfully, they agreed to draw the line at pulling their mattresses into my bedroom to complete the feeling of a teenage sleepover.

In bed that night, I put a bit of a drunken post up on that Ex-Pats Facebook group.

"I can't believe I'm single again after thirty years with the same man—married for twenty-eight of them—now we're getting divorced. I've decided to head back home to the UK—Norfolk. I'd love any advice you can throw my way."

Then I rolled over and groaned at my head spinning. I was going to regret this in the morning. I grinned, though. It had been a great day with Teena, then evening with the addition of Abby, aside from the sorting help. I felt full of my best buddies' love and support—there's nothing like it.

***

I woke up to over a hundred comments of encouragement and things to add to my list. Abby was cheerfully reading through them while I nursed my hangover headache. Teena had my iPad and noted items I didn't have listed as Abby called them out. A loud ding made me wince.

Did I drink that much more wine than either of them?

"Oh, a message from a new contact. I bet that's someone from this group." Abby tapped the notification and read it with a snort.

"What?" I groaned in pain at my voice reverberating inside my head. The Tylenol and coffee hadn't kicked in yet.

She read it out for me, *"Hi, Joanna. I'm Paul. I'm also getting divorced and moving home to the UK. Perhaps we could support each other through the process? I love your profile pic of your kids. You must have been young when you married."*

"I did marry young," I protested. "Probably a creep or a bot just messaging like that."

Abby moved to delete the message, but Teena halted her.

"What's he like? Any clues from his profile?"

"Hmmm, he's a firefighter."

"Seriously?" Hangover forgotten, I snatched my phone back from Abby. She laughed at my sudden interest. "Retired firefighter," I corrected her, slightly less enthusiastically. I scrolled down his feed, which, to be honest, was a bit too public than was wise. Then I found a post I was interested in, clicked on the link, and my eyes bugged out.

"What?" Teena snatched the phone from me, checked the link, and accessed the website on my iPad. We crowded around the bigger screen.

He was based in Vancouver, Canada, and had posted a link to a 2020 calendar. Six-packs, biceps, delts, and pecs filled every month as we swiped through the calendar, mouths agape.

"He said he's October in the post he put up," I offered, and we found Paul's Halloween photo.

Unlike the young, supple muscles of the previous nine months, Paul's muscles were bunched and veined; his unshaven chest sported a good amount of hair that I loved. His thick hair had a red tinge, and a tartan kilt was his only clothing—assuming he upheld the old tradition of wearing nothing underneath it. Halloween decorations hung behind him, and a jack-o'-lantern on the wooden bench he leaned upon flickered its creepy grin towards him. Much like our own smiles, I suspected. The only other thing on the worktable was his upside-down black firefighter's helmet with the most adorable black kitten. Its paws rested on the brim, its bright green eyes regarding us as steadily as Paul's similarly coloured eyes did. We all sighed.

Who needed coffee and Tylenol?

Teena had picked up my phone now. *It's a good job I have no secrets from my besties.* "He only just joined that Ex-Pats group. I think he's legit. Why not chat with him? He's over the other side of Canada, and assuming he's from Scotland, she pointed at his kilt, he won't be moving close to you if he turns out to be an ass."

"Teena makes a good argument," Abby agreed. "Go for it. You need to practise talking to men."

"I talk to plenty of men," I argued.

"None that you find attractive and are single," Teena pointed out.

"Here goes then," I offered, then typed.

'Hi, Paul. Thanks for reaching out; that was brave. I guess you had plenty of bravery as a firefighter. I'm an editor. My biggest risk is a paper cut or spilling coffee on my keyboard. Ha-ha. I would love to share the progress of our moves on this chat. How long is your list? My iPad has two screens worth of checkboxes for me to tick. Where are you moving to? Jo.'

The three of us watched the phone for a minute, finishing our breakfast, before Abby declared we needed to get moving. "I'm only here for the day. Let's finish this basement."

Her enthusiasm was optimistic, given the number of boxes down there still to sort. We'd each made a start on our second box when my phone beeped. If it was Paul, given the three-hour time difference, he was an early riser.

'Oh, oh-oh,' we all managed, and I glanced at each of my friends before swiping the screen and bringing up the Messenger app.

I read Paul's reply, "Okay, here's what he says, '*Great to hear from you, Jo. I love your sense of humour.* My firefighting days are over, and I'll begin a training job in Edinburgh upon my return to the UK. *My mum lives just outside the centre, so I'll be close to her. We're both happy about that. How about you? I assume you can do editing anywhere? Here's an image of my list. It doesn't sound as long as yours, so hopefully, you'll let me know what I'm missing. Right, I must get to my run; that's why I got up so early. Hopefully, there will be no bears today and definitely none when I'm back home. Happy about that.*' He sounds very outdoorsy." I pulled a face. The outdoors and I don't mix well.

"You don't get abs like his sitting around," Teena pointed out.

"You're just practising and getting some help. Don't forget, Jo," Abby confirmed.

True, I didn't need to marry the guy. While Teena checked his list that I'd Air Dropped to my iPad, I thumbed in a reply and compared it to mine. "I've added things from his list that you didn't have in blue. There were only a couple. I've put red dots next to things he doesn't have, but some might not be relevant, so it's up to you what you share."

She handed me the list, and I typed a few to him. There might be others, but I don't know if he's still in the house he shared with his wife. Maybe we'd chat later or another day.

Partway through her second box, Abby pulled out two ragged notebooks. "What are these?" she asked, opening the first one.

I dived for them, recognising them instantly, though it had been decades since I'd seen them or even thought of them. "Nothing." I dragged them out of her hands, apologising instantly for being rough.

"Are they your diaries?" Teena teased.

"No. Not really." I hesitated about sharing something so personal with these women, but if not them, who? "They're my stories."

"You write?" Abby was astonished, but not incredulous. "I always thought you would be an excellent writer, given your aptitude for editing."

"I wouldn't exactly call it that," I defended. Actually, I couldn't remember any of the stories in the books. I just didn't want to be embarrassed.

"Can I read one?" Abby asked gently.

"I don't know. I don't think so."

"Okay, no pressure. I know how difficult it can be. When did you write them?"

"Before I met Bruce, I wanted to be an author. I forgot."

"You forgot your dream?" Teena sounded kind but incredulous, and again, I felt somewhat defensive.

"No. Well, kind of. I used to make up stories to get to sleep at night. I guess I grew out of it."

"Did you?" Teena asked. "I bet you could start again if you wanted to." She really would be great as a personal coach.

"It's silly. I'm too old to start that now."

"Are you saying I shouldn't start my new business? I'm only six months younger than you."

"No, of course not." I smiled at her, caught out in my objections.

"Kathy Reichs was forty-nine when her first 'Bones' book was published," Abby pointed out. "Sue Grafton was forty-two when 'A is for Alibi' came out."

"Unfair," I laughed. Abby had deliberately picked two amazing authors whose books I'd read more than once. "That's four women I admire who have paved the way for me, including you two." Teena gave me a little bow.

I set the books aside to look at another time and cringe at my efforts alone.

We didn't hear further from Paul, and my trash and recycling bins were full by the end of the day. I had a huge box to shred a little each day and another half the size to scan into my computer before shredding. Boxes lined the wall near the basement door to the garage with things in them that Bruce or the kids wanted for themselves. I would get them to collect their choices regularly, except Ethan. He'd promised to see me off on my plane, if not before, so he'd get his box then.

By the time Teena and Abby were gathering their belongings to leave, we were all exhausted. The closer the time got to say goodbye, the more I had a sinking feeling in my gut.

As they headed to their cars, I practically wailed to them, "Am I doing the right thing?" and realised where Beth got her dramatic gene.

Teena and Abby rushed back and smothered me in a group hug.

"Yes, of course," they chorused.

"If you don't do this now, you'll regret it," Teena reasoned.

"I don't want to see you go three thousand miles away," Abby confirmed, "but you've always spoken of England as being home. Here, it's your family that's home."

"Friends and family," I managed through my tears.

"We will always be here, and we will always chat. You aren't escaping us." Abby tightened her grip.

"We'll always be besties," Teena gave me one more squeeze and ducked out of the group. "I need to beat the traffic and will get this lot on Facebook ASAP." She gestured to her car, which contained all the stuff she would sell for me. We'd wait until after the house sold to worry about what furniture. I let them go on their way. Hopefully, we would see each other again before I left, but as they were close to an hour away in opposite directions, I wasn't sure it would be the three of us again.

I walked back through my house, and memories that came to me in each room played out in my mind. With a sigh, I returned to the kitchen and threw together a meal of leftovers from the past two days, including a third of a chocolate mousse cake. I flicked on my phone screen to play some music and lighten the silence that pressed in on me.

A white number two in a red circle hung over the top right corner of the messenger app icon. Was it Paul? With a forkful of chocolatey goodness in midair, I tapped it open.

GOING HOME

If you're really missing
The green, green grass of home
You can return to England
Back to a town past known

You're going to need to clear out stuff
Maybe a house to sell
Perhaps ship some belongings home
And sort out pets as well

Check you have your passport
Fill in the customs forms
Make sure to correct your slang
To the current UK norms

You're going to need a lot of help
Before your journey's through
So, make sure you join a Facebook group
That helps ex-pats like you.

When you're home and settled in

Never more to roam
It's your turn to give advice
To help an ex-pat home

THREE

T he chocolate mousse melted in my mouth as I devoured his latest message.

"Cheers for helping me with those additions to my list. I hope mine were helpful," Paul had written. "My soon-to-be ex-wife is keeping the house, so I don't have to sell that, but she's buying me out, and we can't agree on a price. I need to sort through my belongings, but I'll probably take suitcases home and start again with the furniture. How about you?"

I swallowed the mouthful of delicious goo as I typed my reply.

"It seems like I'm the one doing all the work here. My soon-to-be ex doesn't want to live in the house and has moved out already. I'm left clearing everything we've hoarded over the last too many years. A few friends came to help the last two days, which was fun, but it's so quiet here now."

His reply came quickly, so I guess we were chatting now.

Paul:

> I understand that. I've moved out into a one-bed place that creaks at night. I'm getting used to the noises.

Joanna:

> I keep expecting Bruce to walk in like always after work, or I hear a noise and think it's him.

Paul:

> I want to manage one day without thinking about her.

47

Joanna:

I don't know if that will ever happen because I think about my kids every day, even though they live their own lives now. Do you have kids?

Paul:

No, she didn't want them. One thing we argued about. Many of my firefighter lads had kids, and we would have barbeques and other events outside of work, so I got to interact with them and channel my inner child. I got called 'Uncle Paul' a lot.

Joanna:

Cute. Are you hoping you'll meet someone who will have kids then?

Paul:

To meet someone I get along with would be good. If she already has kids or is young enough to have kids, that's just a bonus. At my age, I'll not be picky. How about you?

Joanna:

Too old for more kids myself. My kids refuse to talk grandkids, though they're all in relationships. I think I would be picky, though I'm unsure how, so maybe I need some time to figure that out. My sibs have grandchildren, so I'll be an excellent great auntie instead.

Paul:

Sounds perfect. No siblings here. You're making me feel a bit lonely.

Joanna:

Nah, you'll make plenty of bro pals once you get into the training. Instant family. Any old friends you'll be looking up (or ex-girlfriends)?

Paul:

Yep, I can't let myself get down. I'll be back in my home country and look up some old friends for beers. Go to some Gers games.

Joanna:

I'm guessing that's Rangers?

Paul:

Aye. What about you—Norwich City fan?

Joanna:

I don't follow much sport these days, though I've enjoyed a few Yankees games. Of course, my heart is with Norwich #OTBC, but I don't 'follow' if that makes sense.

Paul:

Perfect sense apart from #OTBC. LOL

Joanna:

'On the Ball City'. It's part of the oldest football chant in history, or so the Norwich fans claim. But back to the big move. Today, my friends helped me sort loads of papers and such. So, I have two enormous boxes full of scanning and shredding. My trash is full. How about you?

Paul:

I have a full day at the house tomorrow. Wish me luck.

Good luck and goodnight. Let me know how it goes.

Night, lass.

I closed the app and grinned. *Paul called me lass.* I poured the last of the wine from the night before into my glass and carried it with the forgotten dessert through to my office. With some mood music in the background, I made a dent in the boxes Teena and Abby left me, vowing to be disciplined, doing some each day, and getting rid of it all as soon as possible.

Full of chocolate mousse and elated by the progress I'd made over the last few days and my chat with Paul, I eyed the two notebooks Abby had discovered that sat where I left them earlier on top of my row of reference books.

I considered, *No time like the present*, but to what aim? I wasn't sure at this point. When editing, I often marvelled at the ideas the writers had put into words—where do they come from? Was it innate or as simple as nurturing your mind into making up stories, like I did as a child?

I opened the first book. The date was September 1984. With my birthday in December, I was close to fourteen. 'The Indian Prince' was the title of my first story. My best friend and sometime crush in high school was Nish Jaitly. We're still friends on Facebook, and he's still extremely attractive.

I turned on my desk fan to dispel the effects of a hot flush and began reading. I cringed, sinking further into the chair as I read the swirly lettering I'd favoured back then. Nowadays, my writing is a scrawl, but mostly, I typed everything.

"Stupid idea," I muttered aloud. What was I thinking? How could I switch my career and write an actual book that actual people would pay actual money to read? Then Abby's words came back to me from when she stood at this office door and observed me place these notebooks on my desk.

"When you read them, Jo, don't think like an adult. Remember the child you were back then and nurture that child to keep trying and keep writing. Just as you would've if it had been Beth showing you a story she wrote back when she was fourteen."

I sat up straight and then turned the page, considering what a blessing it was to have friends and read the following story with fresh eyes.

By the time I went to bed, I'd read both notebooks twice, and my head was spilling over with stories, memories and ideas. I dreamt more vividly than I had in decades and often woke scribbling thoughts down on my iPad, squinting at the bright screen and hoping I could remember the relevance of my words in the morning—assuming I'd be able to read them.

***

The following day, my thoughts began with plans to restart my writing, though realistically, I had too much going on to think about what I wanted to write. Sensibly, I should concentrate on my move and my divorce. We had a mediation appointment that afternoon.

I allowed myself an hour to write a plan that involved flexing my writing brain by joining a writing group, entering competitions to write one hundred-word drabbles, and jotting down ideas. Flicking through my old notebooks again, I realised the first page was a little stuck to the cover—probably one of the stickers I used to like to adorn my work with had folded over. When I separated the two pages, I was startled by what my younger self had written there.

'Joanna James' Journal'

I had forgotten entirely the pseudonym I used to write under. If I recalled correctly, I even insisted my family refer to me as Joanna James often. I suppose I just liked the alliteration. My conversation with my mum came back to me when she asked if I would revert to my maiden name—gosh, I hate that term! No, I decided right then and there. For once, I will choose my own name. Not my dad's name, not my soon-to-be-ex husband's name, but the one I chose for myself long ago—Joanna James.

I would start right away, introducing myself to anyone I met as such. Meanwhile, I looked up how to change my name legally here. I would worry about the UK when I made it over there. Probate court, here I come, I thought as I printed off the forms I found online. I followed that with a trip to a vast Staples store and purchased two more lined notebooks to write in and a fancy pen, so I didn't always have to use my laptop or iPad.

Unable to concentrate on my job leading up to our mediation, I started planning a trip through Connecticut and Massachusetts to view all the best locations for the leaf changes. Finally, I would end up in Boston to see Ethan and Matt before returning home. Holly had promised to check in on the house every few days and not allow her father to go in. I would let the contractor have a key and go on my trip while they came in to refurbish the kitchen and repaint everywhere. That would be my opportunity to write more and perhaps gain some inspiration. Bruce had taken all the pictures and TVs that he wanted off the walls so the contractor could make all the holes good and paint them over. I ordered the quartz countertops on the credit card Bruce promised to pay, and I agreed to pay the contractor.

We decided on a judicial mediation to avoid the expense of a court case. The date that came through was a few days before my birthday in December. We'd agreed on everything except alimony, so I hoped that one day would see us all set. The open house for the sale of our property would be the next month after the holidays. Given the buoyant property market, I was hopeful for an asking price offer at a minimum. That would give us the time to compile and sign the separation agreement to get the paperwork done for the house sale contracts. Once that was all signed and a moving date agreed upon, I could start booking my flight and some accommodation, then secure a shipping company for my furniture.

***

If you imagine taking a holiday to view the spectacular colours of New England in the Fall—Autumn as I'm going back to the UK—you would probably think of a hiking holiday, walking up the tallest mountain in Massachusetts to see millions of trees in a multitude of colours ranging from browns, through reds, pinks, oranges and yellows spread out below you. That isn't my idea of fun. Neither is camping, trekking, bugs, nor toileting in the woods. Bugs love me, but I don't return their affection. I have a particular aversion to ticks. I've done enough tick checks and removals on my children, their pets and even Bruce to have had enough of them, so don't preach to me about the great outdoors. You love it, good for you. You go out there and enjoy. Just leave me alone with a book and a glass of Chardonnay. That's as much of a challenge as I need these days.

I planned to drive, stop and take photos at convenient and picturesque moments, sing along to my Spotify playlists and give an occasional 'hell, yes!' when listening to the various political or feminist podcasts I enjoyed. I set off through northwest Connecticut's picturesque county of Litchfield—my first stop near the border of Connecticut and Massachusetts was a cute hotel with a small restaurant. Not very brave the first night, I ordered room service. Perhaps I'd eat alone in a restaurant sometime and people-watch. I set up my laptop and glanced through my photos from the day on my iPad, typing out some descriptive paragraphs for each one, including the few selfies I talked myself into taking. I needed to work on a positive body image.

On the second day, the views became more spectacular the further north I travelled. At one point, it rained over a small town nestled in a valley, but up where I was, the sun was shining. I took a photo to describe the phenomenon later. At the next stop, I braved the small hotel restaurant, keeping one of my new notebooks by my plate as I jotted down the various people I saw—two men by the bar arguing over sports on the TV, a couple in a shadowy nook doing what couples do, the server arching her back to stretch out the kinks.

An older woman eating alone and gazing out the window struck me the most. I'd caught up with the rain, and the droplets ran down the window, obscuring her view. I wondered about her story, what she saw out there, or if she just looked at her reflection, wondering where the years had gone. I opened my notebook and started writing about her.

"I saw you scribbling away and came over to see what you were writing. Are you a spy?"

I jolted at the bony finger appearing over my shoulder to tap my notebook. I flipped it over and watched as the woman I'd been observing came around my table.

"Just a writer—well, trying to—I'm an editor."

"So you've made them all look good and thought you'd try for yourself? Do you mind—?" She gestured to the seat opposite me.

"Please. My name is Joanna James. Jo." I offered, happy I'd remembered to use my pseudonym. She certainly intrigued me. "I wanted to write when I was young."

"I'm Dorothy Baker. What stopped you from writing back then?"

"Marriage, children, so on and so on."

"Excuses, nevertheless, you've lived a bit. It looks good on you."

"Hardly," I gestured down my body.

"Not there. In your eyes. And you're not from around here, either."

"Not originally, but if we're getting personal, would you like a nightcap?" We ordered drinks. "How about you? I can't tell from your accent."

"Oh, I lost that as a child, but Ireland."

"Have you been back?"

"Many times, but something keeps pulling me back here."

"I'm going back to England to live. I feel guilty, though."

"Because of your children? I assume they're all adults."

"Yes, and happily married. Well, not my son, yet, but he's in a good relationship."

"Then there's no need for guilt, is there?"

"I suppose not."

"Their father?"

"We're getting divorced."

"Your choice or his."

"His—" I hesitated. "Actually, mine, if I'm honest. Things weren't good, and I wasn't happy. I asked if he would help me make us happy again, and he refused."

She nodded sagely. "And the writing?"

"I'm trying to restart the passion, I guess. I couldn't restart the passion of my marriage without Bruce, but I can do this on my own."

"Good. We women need passion in our lives in one form or another."

"I'm just worried I left it too late."

She gestured to my notebook. "May I?"

I handed it to her and sat back, sipping my wine as I tried desperately to appear composed, as if this happened to me every day.

Dorothy took her time, perusing each page carefully, seemingly respectful of my private world. I squirmed in my seat and resisted the urge to snatch the notebook back. If I wanted people to read my writing, I had to stop thinking of it as 'my private world', but why let this stranger read it when I stopped one of my best friends?

When she closed the notebook, Dorothy looked up at me. "I can confirm that you haven't left it too late."

"Thank you. I don't mean to be rude, but how can you be so sure?"

"I'm a voracious reader, and I would spend good money to read anything by you. Now, I'm not a publisher, editor, literary agent or other kind of expert, but I think the reader's opinion is most important, don't you?"

"Absolutely."

Before returning my notebook, she pulled a pen from her handbag and wrote inside. "I've included my address, email, and phone number. If you want a keen eye on your work, anytime, you let me know."

"I definitely will."

We spent another hour chatting, with me engrossed in Dorothy's life story. Well, part of it, at least. She was ninety-one and seemed to have lived several lifetimes. When she declared she needed her beauty sleep, I let her go and went to my room with a story burning in my mind.

It was a short story of an older woman the protagonist met on a trip through Massachusetts. After a delightful evening of setting the world to rights, they went their separate ways but exchanged phone numbers. When the protagonist called two weeks later, she found out the older woman had been ill and bedridden for two months. She had died the night they met. The woman she spoke to on the phone was a lifelong friend of the woman who died. The protagonist returned to the hotel and met the woman from the phone call. She could see the ghost again, and talk to her, but her friend couldn't. She passed on the message that the ghost would wait for her friend there because she loved her but had never said it. Her friend declared her love, too, and vowed to meet her at the hotel when her time came. It had quite an emotional ending.

I sent it to Dorothy with a bit of trepidation, and then, after a good night's sleep, I headed off on the next leg of my journey. Dorothy was going in the opposite direction, to Connecticut, to see her family. When I received no response the next night, I reasoned she was busy with her family and no doubt exhausted, but I worried she was offended because I had effectively killed her off.

Halfway through my last leg to Boston, I stopped at a diner for lunch and checked my email on my phone. I had a reply from Dorothy.

"My dear Jo. What a wonderful story. My heart is light reading it, and I flatter myself that I inspired your ghost character. Unspoken love is so heartfelt, but sad, too. When you have put your life back together, I hope you open yourself up to whatever love might come your way. He (or she) will need to be very deserving to earn love from a creative mind and heart like yours. I'm so glad to have met you and hope to call you my friend in the not-too-distant future. A woman can never have too many friends."

***

Encouraged by Dorothy's words about my creativity, I started thinking about a romance novel. As I drove, I put various scenarios to the test of a possible romance. Perhaps writing about a romance might open me up to love, as she suggested, though I doubted I had finished putting my life back together. I thought of a tall, strong Canadian firefighter with a tender heart that somebody had broken. He meets with a young woman escaping an abusive partner. Hmmm, I would have to think more about this.

Stopping at my last scenic viewpoint, I took pictures and sent them to Paul. Let's see what he has to say today. We had chatted again since that first time, and I gave him a few more pointers. I was surprised he had offered no help to me. The last time we messaged, he had just asked me a specific question about shipping and the customs Transfer of Residence form the group we were both in discussed often. He had decided to ship over some furniture and other belongings, after all. I trolled some of those posts to find the answer for him, and it occurred to me I had swapped a husband who needed my help with this guy. I looked forward to Paul completing his move, so helping him with it would end, and we could carry on a friendship.

My phone pinged as I checked into my hotel. After unpacking, I would call Ethan and see if he and Matt were still up for meeting me for dinner. I had two nights here and wanted to make the most of them. Leaving my suitcase in the middle of my room, I sat on the bed and checked my messages.

Paul:

> Beautiful scenery. I hope your enjoying your trip. No pics of you, though. Did you take a selfie?

I had taken a selfie. I even used a selfie stick to get more of the picturesque view. It meant I also had more of me in the photo, including my big boobs and one of my tummy rolls. I wasn't sure I wanted to share that with a muscled, kilted firefighter—yes, I always imagined him wearing that kilt from the calendar photo. I'd quickly shared my selfie with my kids on our WhatsApp chat, but they love me regardless of my appearance. I gritted my teeth over the typo and answered.

Joanna:

You first.

There was no quick reply, so I got to my feet and unpacked my suitcase. Then I grabbed a shower. My phone pinged as I wrapped my hair in a towel and sat on the loo lid to look at the message from Paul. He'd attached a photo of himself with a backdrop of woods and mountains. Unlike the Paul I had seen before, he had grown a pandemic beard. He'd gained a good bit of weight, too, and there wasn't a kilt or a kitten in sight. It was a little disappointing at first, but my brain soon kicked in and pointed out how much he had been through since the beginning of twenty-twenty, just like me. A person's appearance doesn't define them. I know that first-hand.

Joanna:

Beautiful view, and that's one hell of a beard. Looking good. How far did you hike that day?

Paul:

Thank you. That was a ten-mile hike. I'm working on getting some weight off to outrun the bears again.

Joanna:

I'm sure you'll get there.

Paul:

Your turn.

I took the plunge and send him my selfie even though I was pulling a funny face. After hitting send, I distracted my mind from his response by getting ready to go out with the boys. I was excited to see them both and brought Ethan's box of things. My phone pinged with a notification, which wasn't what I expected.

Paul McKinnon has blocked you.

So much for a Scottish romance.

OUTER APPEARANCE

His hair is thick—none out of place
His teeth a perfect line
His lips kissable, plump, firm
His eyes, like pools, are fine

His skin so smooth, unblemished
His muscles bulge and flex
Stomach slim and ridged
Moving up to perfect pecs

I look away—unworthy
My older body wrinkled
Rounded belly, breasts sagging
A face devoid of dimples

Then I recall how I have lived
My body's given life
I've survived difficulties
Loneliness and strife

To others on my path

I have given help and hope
And reached behind me to
Pull people up life's slope

I must acknowledge I am more
Than the outside of me
And though godlike he may look
—so is he

FOUR

Holly and Ethan insisted on accompanying me to the airport. Then they insisted they would park, help me with my enormous suitcases, and get them checked in. Although, as a family, we visited the UK every few years, and I was the one who managed three little kids and five bags, they treated me like I'd never seen the inside of an airport before. Okay, back then, Bruce did most of the lugging of bags, but I did the planning, the potty breaks, and the meal plans. On the flights, I would sit at one end of a group of four seats with the three kids, then Bruce across the aisle from Holly. He was never the one sitting with the kids; he always put on his headphones and watched movies, eating his food while it was still hot. No such luck for me.

I let Ethan and Holly help me now, knowing that was what they needed, and thought of poor Beth stuck at the hospital covering for a sick doctor friend she was interning with. Perhaps that was just as well for the both of us—I might never have left.

Despite having a first-class ticket and therefore being able to skip waiting in the security line, I let them walk beside me, giving me instructions, asking for texts and calls as soon as I had switched my SIM card and was able to. With only a dozen people left ahead of me, I insisted they step back and let me get on with it. Giving them both a last hug and trying to hold my tears in check—for their sake—as I had done for every scraped knee, every wasp sting and every broken heart.

What am I doing? I considered with one last mini panic attack. Then I reached for my resolve and Teena's wise words, 'You'll regret it if you don't at least try it.'

"I love you all. Take care of each other."

"We love you, Mom."

Oh, that wondrous, three-letter palindrome that holds within it far more than any three-letter word ever should—the most profound love, the enormous sacrifice, the worst pain and fear, and yet the highest heights of joy and pride.

"Next," called the TSA agent, waiting patiently for me. I turned my back, unloaded my devices onto the conveyor belt, slipped off my shoes, added them, and passed through the scanner.

I repacked my phone, tablet, kindle and laptop back into my carry-on, slipped on my shoes again and hurried away with a last wave so I could stop wondering if I was making a mistake. The last hugs and tears all around had weakened my resolve. I reminded myself that my kids were well-situated in life and even love. Their father was about if they needed help, and I could always hop on a plane.

It was my duty and pleasure to spend some time with Mum. Dad had died long ago, so Mum was fiercely independent, but that couldn't last forever, and I was well-placed to help.

I had been a surprise for my parents after a childless decade. My two sisters were married with grown-up kids of their own and some grandchildren. My brother was still unmarried, and since Ethan had come out to me, I speculated about my brother's sexuality.

Aside from all of those very valid and important reasons to move back home to the UK, I had to admit that the biggest for me was simply that I missed my home—rainy days, walks on a cold beach or the pier, and the impossibly big Norfolk skies.

I walked through the general shopping and duty-free area of the airport. My flight already had a gate assigned, so I headed that way, taking advantage of those people conveyor belts. Upon boarding, I was grateful to be spared the judgmental and disappointed looks of those adjacent to me in an economy row as I headed to the front of the plane.

***

"Fifty, fat and fabulous," I recited under my breath, sitting in my comfortable first-class seat.

I'd left my laptop and Kindle in my carry-on and stored them in the cubby by my seat. I set my phone and iPad on the top of the console with my earbud container. I had a new book file on my iPad and intended to get well into editing it on this flight. I planned to start my new 'super remote' job at thirty-five thousand feet.

As the plane turned onto the runway and the engines roared with the beating of my heart, I took a deep breath to regain control. I closed my eyes, and then the tears fell silently with all my emotions about leaving and the thought of going home to live after all this time. I sniffed and imagined how my life would be. It was no longer a case of making the right decision; now was the time to make the decision I had made right—my new chapter. The plane evened off, and the seatbelt light dinging brought me back to my present situation.

My eyelids opened to the concerned face of an attractive man as he crouched by the side of my seat.

"Are you okay?"

I didn't know him, but he seemed familiar. Concern showed in his blue-green eyes, and he'd brushed his sandy-blond hair back, but a cowlick defied the styling and fell forward.

I swiped at my cheeks. "Fine. Sorry. I'm moving back home and am emotional."

"No worries. I didn't mean to intrude. Just wanted to check on you." He smiled, concern still showing, as he retreated to his seat across the aisle and slightly in front of me. His shoulders were broad, and his waist narrow.

"Thank you. I'm okay—really," I spoke to his fine ass before he sat down, and a view of his profile jolted the recognition into a name—Sam Harmer.

It dawned on me why he was so familiar. I had seen several of his movies and remembered him as bare-chested and very muscled. He had even been in a miniseries based on a book I edited. The actor I had imagined when reading it was very different, but Sam fit the role superbly and made it his own.

I couldn't help gushing out, "You're Sam Harmer, right? I loved you in Redway Acres."

"Thanks."

His voice was tight, and he looked a little crestfallen. I imagined he was thinking, *Yet another fan and I'll get no peace for this entire flight.*

I needed to make myself seem less creepy. "Oh, I meant you brought so much more to the role than I pictured when I edited the book. I'm Joanna James. Jo."

At this, Sam perked up, and we talked a little longer about books we had read and others I'd edited. He was flying back to the UK to film a new movie and then on a tour of Europe to fulfil his obligation to complete various press junkets before his latest release.

Then he shocked me by asking, "Have you ever thought of writing?"

My hesitation brought out his laugh. Honestly, it's inhuman for such a good-looking man also to have a glorious laugh. He clicked his fingers twice, then beckoned me to give him something. *Cheeky little f—!*

"What?" I gave him an innocent look like I had no idea of his meaning, and that laugh came easily again.

"Come on, Jo. Give me what I want." His voice was as smooth as golden syrup.

My insides liquified. Sam Harmer was flirting with me. *We're flirting—right?*

"What would that be?" I couldn't help but smile. Damn, the man was nearly twenty years younger than me.

"You've written something. Let me see it. Please, Jo. I'll tell you honestly what I think, and I'm a fast reader."

I've no idea why Dorothy should pop into my head at that moment, but I'm guessing it was because she would tell me to expose this part of me to this man—oh, yeah, my mind was elsewhere.

I had a copy of the latest draft of what I called 'Firefighter' on my Kindle, so I fished it out of my bag, opened the relevant book, and handed it over. Don't worry, my firefighter wasn't Scottish but Irish—they wear kilts too, you know.

"I hope you appreciate how difficult it is for me to let anyone read this. I've never let anyone else see it."

"A virgin, eh?"

"Oh, stop it." I put on my best mothering voice, but it only garnered me a smirk that could melt the knickers off you as he turned to face forward and concentrated on my book.

A flight attendant came over to find out his meal selection and chatted with him for a minute. After that, he put his headphones on and a movie on the screen before him. I was amazed. Was my book so bad that he was bored after five minutes? They returned with his drink shortly after, and the interaction was much shorter. He turned back to look at me.

"It's on mute," he whispered.

I realised he'd put it on to avoid too many interruptions and gave him a thumbs up. With his concentration elsewhere, I continued to study him for a moment more as I thought of the man behind the movie star.

Like any fan, I knew his rise-to-stardom story—raised by a single mum. He grew up without all the trappings celebrity now afforded him now. He loved the performing arts, but his school couldn't afford drama lessons. The most they managed, with a young Sam pushing the hardest, was a drama club occasionally putting on a school play. His music and art teachers supported the group of rag-tag kids who turned up, but the money they made from ticket sales went to those subjects and not back into the drama club.

When he was old enough, Sam worked at McDonald's evenings and week-ends—pulling out his books during any lulls to get the A-level grades he needed to get into university and study performing arts. Someone on the board of people choosing the applicants saw something in him, no matter that he didn't have a drama qualification. His mum's breast cancer diagnosis and inability to work full time to help pay his fees changed everything. Sam bet on himself, took out student loans to cover the costs, and continued working when he could.

He was very popular with his classmates, and there was great anticipation for his graduation speech. Unfortunately, his mum died two weeks before, and he attended her funeral instead. Years later, with several successful movie and TV roles behind him, Sam returned to give the commencement speech, in which he referenced the address he would have made had he been at his own graduation. There wasn't a dry eye in the house after it, and it was one of the most-watched YouTube videos.

Our food arrived, and as I ate, I wondered if his movie-watching had changed since becoming an actor, even though I knew this one was on mute. Did he dissect others' performances, thinking about how he would have done it differently—better? That's how I felt when reading for pleasure. I couldn't help myself and always spotted a typo.

I finished my meal and concentrated on editing for a while. Sam stood, stretched, and dug his pillow and blanket out of his cubby. I ventured, "Sweet dreams." Then, I packed away my iPad and settled down as they dimmed the cabin lights.

I smiled at his sleepy, "You, too. I'll read more after a nap. I promise."

***

I've never slept well on a plane before. On one transatlantic flight, Bruce had an empty seat next to him, and I asked him to take Ethan or Beth, so I only had two kids to manage in the middle. He insisted he needed to sleep if he was going to be driving on the left when we landed. Even my pointing out that I was more capable, given I had learnt to drive on the left and had done it for several years before I joined him in the States, didn't sway him. So, while he stretched out on two seats by himself, I tried to get three grumpy kids to sleep while crunched up in my tiny seat.

Consequently, I was surprised at how soundly I slept this time and, therefore, annoyed when I woke, inevitably desperate for a pee halfway through a deep sleep.

Manoeuvring my seat back into a reasonably upright position, I wriggled into the aisle and headed to the toilet, hoping I'd get there in time. I shrank from the bright light of the tiny room as I locked the concertina door. This was one of those times I felt my size—my hips nearly touched a wall while I sat to do my business, and the sink was so tiny. I knew from experience that if I leaned forward to peer into the mirror, my top would come into contact with the wet top edge that jutted out. I took a couple of deep breaths to dissipate my mild claustrophobic tendencies.

Satisfied that my clothes were straight and had no wet splodges on them, I considered grabbing a paper towel and wiping down the little shelf from which the sink protruded. But I resisted. *I didn't make that mess, so why do I feel the compulsion to clean it?*

I opened the door. Sam was standing right outside, leaning against the wall.

"Hi, Jo." He smiled—his hair mussed, his hands in his pockets causing his biceps to bulge at the cuffs of his t-shirt.

I smiled back. "Hi."

His head gestured to the bathroom. "Wanna see if we can both fit in there?" He raised his eyebrows, and the heat of a blush rose in my cheeks as my mouth performed its best guppy-fish impression. I imagined my jeans yanked off and onto the dirty floor, my bum resting on that wet little shelf I now regretted not wiping down and my view over his shoulder of the loo with no water in it.

Grabbing hold of that firm ass or snaking my hands up inside his t-shirt over those fabulous muscles might have been worth it, but the thought of his view of my butt in the mirror and his hands around my spare tyres had me shaking my head.

"You're too young for me."

"Hardly, and I like older women. They know what they want."

Cheesy.

"Well then. Thank you, but it's been a while for me, and frankly, a quickie in an aeroplane loo won't cut it. That's what I want."

He leaned in and whispered, "Then what a shame we're not staying in the same hotel."

He kissed my cheek—his closeness so intoxicating the noise that escaped my lips was a cross between a squeak and a whimper.

Squimper?

A kernel of regret rested in my chest as he moved past me and into the bathroom.

Reluctantly stirring from my dream, I opened my eyes to Sam's gaze upon me from across the aisle.

"Sweet dreams?" he asked, his eyes sparkling.

How is it possible for someone to be so gorgeous after six hours overnight on a plane?

"Something like that," I mumbled as I grabbed my bag and hurried to the toilets. Had I been squimpering in my sleep?

When I exited the bathroom, I was only a little disappointed he wasn't outside the door. I had, after all, wiped down that little shelf.

***

When the plane came to a halt, and we were gathering our belongings to disembark, Sam handed my Kindle back to me. "I've written a note at the end for you, but I'll just say, if you finish it, I'm going to need to practice my Irish accent because I see that as a movie for sure, and I want to play Kieran."

My mouth opened and shut a few times while he laughed at me.

"Oh, and my number is in there, too. So, you can let me know how it's going. I want to read the finished product."

"Seriously?"

"Seriously. Look, I'm going to have to dash. People will be waiting for me, but it was nice meeting you."

"Thank you. I'll let you know."

He bussed my cheek, then tore off ahead of the crowd, jostling to exit the plane and be on their way to holidays, returning from holidays or meeting up with family members.

I moved to follow at my own pace, then remembered that Sam said he'd left a note. I plopped back in my seat, bemused, and grabbed my Kindle to check what he'd written.

"Jo, this is great. I always judge a book or a script by whether I can imagine the characters as real people. You have filled this couple with life. I felt Kieran's every emotion. You truly have a talent. Keep at it and keep in touch." He'd left his number after that.

"Excuse me, madam." I glanced up at the flight attendant, who had been chatting with Sam earlier. "Unless you want to fly back to New York, you had better exit the plane, and well done."

"What? Oh, thank you. Sorry, I was a little—"

"Star-struck? I can't blame you. I wouldn't wash my cheek again if Sam Harmer kissed it."

"What?" I was repeating myself. I needed to gather my thoughts. I rubbed my cheek where he'd kissed. "No. He likes my book."

But I was talking to thin air. I imagined she had whisked off to do whatever she needed before getting a good rest.

"Sam Harmer likes my book."

Repeating it to myself didn't make it seem any more true.

THE FIRST ONE

Teenage fumbling
Teenage mumbling
Fiddling, flicking
Touching, licking

He'd been the first
To do all things
Not the worst
Not just a fling

The first should be
The someone who
Enjoys your body
And you do, too

Every minute, every day
You below, you above
In absolutely every way
To explore and to love

It could've been a love forever

With fun and sex and such a catch

But teenage life just didn't weather

The first one as a lifetime match

FIVE

I gazed in disbelief at the guy behind the car hire counter.

"You can't be serious. No automatic cars available at all?" I was kicking myself for not clarifying what I needed on the booking form. Bruce usually booked our rental cars. *Rookie move, Joanna!* I'd called late yesterday when I remembered that an automatic car wasn't standard in the UK, as it is in the US, and they'd said they'd see what they could do. When Bruce and I first moved stateside, I thought that if I ever moved back to live, I would go back to driving a manual. Now that it had been so long, and frankly, it was far easier to drive an automatic, why would I switch?

"I apologise. I had hoped to get you one, but the manual is cheaper, so that's good, right?"

Sure, I thought. *Let's hope it has plenty of insurance, as it's been over twenty years since I drove manual.*

"But if you're okay with it, you'll be fine, and—"

"Yeah, I know. It's cheaper."

I was exhausted. My short, disturbing sleep on the plane had helped little. The buoyancy of Sam's comments on my book had temporarily dissipated after I tackled the Heathrow crowds and manhandled my suitcases in and out of a transport bus without help from the driver. *Boy, I missed the service people at JFK who were happy to help you. Of course, you tipped them, but it was so worth it.*

Now, I faced several hours of manual driving from Heathrow. I supposed keeping my mind on remembering to change gears would keep me awake. I roughly knew the roads I needed, M25, M11, and A11, but junction lanes had changed since we made this trip long ago. I had to negotiate getting off for service stations and then back on again. My phone no longer worked with the wrong SIM card, so I had gone old school and printed off directions. Thank you, Google. My sister, Susan, had purchased a UK SIM for me and would drop it off with groceries at the flat before I arrived. I wouldn't see her until the next day, as she couldn't wait for me today.

By the time I reached the outskirts of Norwich centre, I was rather pleased with myself. My mind had quickly gotten back into the groove, and aside from banging my right hand on the door a few times, instead of reaching for the gearstick on the left, and grinding the gears a bit, I'd succeeded. I'd stalled several times at the first service station, but kept to the left side of the road. *Suck on that Mister 'I'm-Bruce-The-Man-I-Must-Drive-Everywhere'.*

For those who have never had the pleasure of visiting, Norwich is a beautiful city full of old buildings and history. A twelfth-century cathedral's spire was the most dominant in the skyline, but they constructed a second cathedral in the late nineteenth-early twentieth centuries. The Norman-built castle, which now boasts a museum, was a gaol until the late nineteenth century. There are many old churches in the region and many more pubs—read into that what you will. To keep the castle grounds unspoiled, a mall stretches underneath it, and entrances pop up in several spots in the city. But the most fun shopping was under the multicoloured striped stalls of Norwich's year-round market. Whenever I imagined it, I thought I could still smell it—hot chip grease and overripe fruit.

I was due to meet someone at the Airbnb I'd rented out for a few months. After a day of resting, I already had an appointment booked to view a house I had my eye on. But, before that, I needed to move more money from the US. I was still working on my relocation list.

My mother and siblings had all offered to let me stay with them, but I needed space to move around at my pace. A day or even a week might have been fine, but months on end? I didn't want to risk alienating the people I had returned to the UK to be with.

I turned off the major city street into a cul-de-sac. The dead-end finished with a gated garage, the key to which was with the person cleaning the property. Hoping where I stopped, the car wasn't blocking anyone, I considered the building as I waited. I was only a few minutes early. The grey stone and concrete apartment block—block of flats, I corrected myself, towered above. Panic accosted me. *What on earth have I done?*

Despite the cool weather, I cracked my car window an inch and took calming breaths. Unfortunately, it didn't aid me much, and I felt the beginnings of a hot flush. The person meeting me was taking ages, which wasn't helping my anxiety. *What if they've taken my deposit but don't have a flat available?*

I was looking for the address of the rental company when a knock on the passenger-side window startled me back to my current situation—shock temporarily overcame the panic.

"Hello," a woman said as I wound down that window and quickly put a hand on my papers that blew around on the seat. "Take this card and leave this permit on the dash. Tap the card on the keypad there and park in space number twenty-four."

"Thanks," I managed.

"I'll meet you there. Help you with your bags."

"That's very kind of you." I almost burst into tears. *Time for a good cry when you're on your own,* I admonished and pulled away from the curb towards the garage.

It was a relief to get out of the car and not have to think about driving correctly. I busied myself, wrestling my enormous suitcases out of the vehicle. I had squeezed one into the car's boot; the other was on the back seat. I fixed my carry-on bag on the top of its matching case and extended the handle.

"Oh, great. You're ready. I can wheel one for you if you'd like." The woman had caught up with me again.

"Thank you. How is the apartment—flat? Is it as nice as the online photos?" I held my breath.

"Oh yes, it's lovely, and I just finished cleaning it for you. You'll love it, and you're right near the shops in the city and the pubs, but hopefully, they won't be too noisy."

I hadn't considered that and internally groaned as we manoeuvred my suitcases into the tiny lift. "I'm sure it'll be fine," I said, more to convince myself than my companion. As the flat's door opened, I cleared my mind and the first glimpse of my home for the next few months pleasantly surprised me.

A long corridor with hardwood flooring and storage cupboards opened out into a square foyer off which two bedrooms and a bathroom were visible.

"Your washing machine is in here," the young woman said, pointing to a large cupboard. "And your kitchen and living-dining area are through here."

We abandoned the suitcases in the foyer and walked through to a large open kitchen with the living and dining opposite it. Everything was clean, and the whole place was light and airy. Patio doors opened onto a tiny balcony overlooking a large courtyard. It was only big enough for a chair or two and a small side table. Given the many apartments surrounding it, I doubted sitting out there would be very peaceful, but it would be fun for people-watching. For now, it was still too cold.

I half-listened to the cleaner's instructions—everything was in a folder I would peruse at my leisure after a good night's sleep. Once alone, I took a long shower, put on my most comfy pyjamas, and fixed myself a light meal—thank you, Susan. I would see her tomorrow when she came to visit. While I ate, I sorted the new SIM in my phone and tested it out, group texting my kids first.

Joanna:

I made it.

Nothing but tumbleweeds. I was about to give up, dig out the rest of my devices, and set up all my cables with converter plugs when my loves joined the conversation.

Beth:

> Mom, I miss you already.

She followed that up with a lot of heart emojis.

Joanna:

> I miss you too.

Beth:

> What's the apartment like? Flat, I meant flat. LOL

Joanna:

> LOL It's nice. Hang on, and I'll take some pics.

Beth:

> How was your flight?

Holly:

> Mom, I just got out of a meeting. How are you? Can't wait to see the pics.

Joanna:

> All questions answered in a moment. You won't believe who I met on the flight.

Ethan:

> Who did you meet, Mom? Only you could make friends the minute you left the country.

Joanna:

> Well, I wouldn't call him a friend.

Beth:

HIM??

Holly:

If not a friend, then what?

Ethan:

I've just messaged Matt, and he thinks you joined the mile-high club. Ha-ha.

Beth:

NO! {hear no evil emojis}

I ignored their messages for a while as I took photos of the rooms in the flat. Their messages changed to comments about the flat and a couple of the views I sent them—one had the top of the cathedral spire in it. Then, they got down to business.

Holly:

So the flat is good. How are you?

Joanna:

Knackered. I slept a little, but the drive-up was hard. They didn't have an automatic for me.

Beth:

You drove stick? OMG, Mom.

Ethan:

Cool. Glad you didn't crash.

Joanna:

Me too.

Holly:

And—who did you meet?

Joanna:

You can't tell anyone except your partners, and they can't tell anyone else.

Beth:

OMG, who was it, The President?

Holly:

He has his own plane, silly. Mom didn't fly on Air Force One.

Joanna:

Sam Harmer.

Holly:

Who?

Ethan:

OMG, as Beth would say. THE Sam Harmer, movie star and all-around decent guy—muscles on his muscles and as hot as all hell. {strong arm and fire emojis}

Beth:

Mom, you didn't—you know—with Sam Harmer, did you? {shocked emojis}

Joanna:

No, I didn't. He was a bit flirty but not serious. Obvs. We talked books, and he persuaded me to let him read my book.

Holly:

Mom, you aren't supposed to let anyone read the books you're editing.

Joanna:

I mean the book I wrote. Well, am writing. I haven't finished it yet.

Ethan:

What? This is bigger news than Sam Harmer, and I can't even start on how big that news is. Matt's already said he'll never talk to you again if you don't introduce us.

Beth:

I didn't know you could write, Mom. Not a whole book, I mean.

Joanna:

Just good for notes to school and shopping lists, eh?

I added a winky face to that one because I didn't want her to think I was upset.

Holly:

Why didn't you tell us, Mom?

Joanna:

I didn't know if it would be any good.

Beth:

Are you any good?

Ethan:

Of course she is, butthead.

Joanna:

Ethan James Newberry!

Ethan:

Getting told off by your mom from 3K miles away. {eye-roll emojis}

Joanna:

I like the support, though, E.

Beth:

I mean, did Sam Harmer like it?

Joanna:

Yes, he did. He said it could be a movie, and he wanted to gen up on his Irish accent to play the lead.

Beth:

{Squee GIF}

Holly:

I'm going to need a dress for the red carpet.

Ethan:

Hold your horses, glamor girl. Movies don't get made because the movie star wants them done. Execs have to decide.

Beth:

Er—Deadpool, butthead?

Ethan:

Mom, Beth said a bad word.

Joanna:

Suck it up, butthead. Just kidding. I love you all. Ethan is right, though.

Ethan:

> Three words that are music to my ears (aside from Matt saying ILY)

Holly:

> TMI, E.

Joanna:

> It isn't a screenplay, anyway; it's a book. Even if a publisher wanted it and it got made into a screenplay, then a movie, that would be a long way down the road. I was happy he thought it was that good when I hadn't even finished it.

Beth:

> You could write the screenplay.

Joanna:

> It's enough to be writing a book, for now. At this very moment, I'm tired. I want to finish setting up my desk and connect to the Wi-Fi. I'll message again tomorrow. Love you all very much, and don't forget that me meeting Sam Harmer is a SECRET. He won't talk to me again if it gets out, and then Matt'll never meet him.

***

The flat was quiet while I set up my PC and connected to the Wi-Fi. The Twitter app beeped with a notification. A blast from the past had liked one of my tweets. Graham had been the first guy I went all the way with, and definitely not a disappointment.

After the initial split with my ex-husband, I searched for several exes on social media to see where they were, who they married, and, with a bit of shame, what they looked like now. I imagined they must look at my profile pic, if they even bothered to search for me, and thank the lord they dodged a bullet. Then I shook that thought away, acknowledging the decades of social thought conditioning that made me feel that way when looking in the mirror or even at other people's photos. If I was ever going to have sex with someone again, I needed to view myself differently.

Scrolling through Graham's Twitter feed, I couldn't see any mention of a wife, significant other or children, so I liked a few of his tweets, pleased to note he'd retweeted some political posts that matched my views and that we followed some of the same celebrities and commentators.

After I edited all my profiles to show my move back to the UK, my phone beeped with a message via Twitter. Graham had 'slid into my DMs', as the kids like to say. I chuckled at being so old, saying shit like that.

Graham:

Hey, Jo. I see you're back in the UK. Norwich?

I gazed at the message, wondering if I was hallucinating in a jetlag-induced state of sleep deprivation. Should I answer? What harm would it do? Being tired made me more emotional, which isn't an excellent decision-making combination. However, I had been the one who broke us up decades before, so his making the first move here was a concession on his part. I couldn't remember why I'd split us apart, except my mum hadn't liked him much.

Joanna:

Hey, back. Yes, in Norwich to stay after twenty-plus years. I want to spend quality time with my mum and sibs. Where are you?

Graham:

> I moved to Manchester for work in my twenties. Been here ever since. My dad's still around, but Mum died during the pandemic.

I remembered Graham's mum was a heavy smoker. So if she'd caught COVID before vaccinations were available, it wasn't surprising she died. Still sad, though.

Joanna:

> I'm so sorry, Graham.

Graham:

> The toughest part about living away was that I couldn't get back to Norwich to help.

Joanna:

> I feared for my mum. Thank goodness my siblings are still here. I thought I'd never see her or them again. Do you live in Manchester with your family?

Graham:

> No family up here. I never got married in the end. Got close a couple of times. I guess work has kept me busy.

I yawned, and frankly, after all these years, if we were going to catch up, it would take some time—more than I had the energy for right now.

Joanna:

> Can we chat another time? Jetlag is beating my ass right now. So I'm going to get some shut-eye.

Graham:

> Of course, I didn't realise you were back TODAY. Welcome home. Ass? You sound so American.

I smiled at his last comment and crawled into bed. It wasn't as comfortable as mine, making its way across the Atlantic. I wondered where it was and snorted a laugh at my bed's legs, paddling furiously through the waves and sharks.

I drifted off to disjointed dreams of the escapades Graham and I used to have—including one on a bed in the middle of an ocean surrounded by sharks. With every thrust, the mattress sunk further into the waves and closer to the hungry shark's mouths. Waking intermittently, I nipped to the loo and checked my phone whilst there, rereading our conversation before digging out the first-class gift bag I'd brought with me and grabbing the eye mask. These early sunrises and thin curtains were going to do me in. Then, I headed back to dreams of times when I had been seventeen. So young and so very sexual. How lucky I had been to have such a great first partner.

***

At ten in the morning, five a.m. back on the US East Coast where I had lived for so long, I woke with the face mask askew, wondering where the heck I was. My first thought was of the messages I'd shared with Graham, followed by a roll of my eyes at a man being on my mind so soon after my return. As I showered, I considered he might be good to start my reawakening to relationship possibilities when he was the first to introduce me to many pleasures.

Stupid. Graham will never message you again when he sees how fat you are. Remember Paul. The mirror on the back of the bathroom door mocked me critically as I dried off and applied some moisturiser everywhere I could reach, which wasn't everywhere. I needed to change the record of my inner voice. "Paul was an asshole," I declared to the mirror and marched out of the bathroom to dress.

Frankly, it wouldn't be that bad if I never had a relationship again, would it? Hadn't I felt lonelier in a relationship than out of one? More so, as there seemed so little possibility of improvement.

Is everyone's life like this? Or is it just me?

With renewed determination, I decided it was time to get on with my new life—no need to focus on another man. I would live the way I wanted for a while and see what happened. My sister was coming over to help me empty those enormous suitcases. It was time to investigate this flat more, figure out how all the appliances worked, and unpack my vibrators before Susan arrived. What would my sister say about those if she found them? Maybe she had her own? I hoped that for her.

Shortly after Susan arrived, and following the bear hug she gave me, she had us motoring around that little flat in a flurry of activity. A wash load of clothes I'd worn at the hotel I stayed at for the two nights before our house sale completion was set to run. Then we figured out the clotheshorse, a combination of rails and arches, ready for the wet clothing—no dryer. What would my kids say? We found suitable locations in the flat for the remaining contents of my two suitcases. She tested out the bed in the spare room to see if she'd like to stay over, and we talked about going to a show at the theatre together or having some wine and saving her the drive home from the city afterwards.

It wasn't until we carried two shopping bags each back from the nearby shop and stocked my cupboards with various necessities, some of which weren't strictly necessary, that I persuaded her to stop and have a cup of coffee with me out on the balcony. It was cool, but we'd worked up a sweat with the shopping, so we cooled off nicely.

We regarded each other over the rims of our coffee mugs; she was the sibling I resembled most, and it was so warming to look into her kind and familiar eyes.

"It's so good to have you back at last, Joey."

"It's so good to be back. Love you loads, Sis."

"Me too."

Feeling a little more at home and less tired the second night, I got into bed and opened the bedside drawer where I'd hidden those vibes from Susan's prying eyes. I pulled out my Kindle and opened up a sexy book where I had bookmarked a couple of, let's call them stimulating, scenes I 'enjoyed'. That was weird—I noticed a highlight on one that I hadn't put there. I clicked it, and the note came up, causing an involuntary yelp.

"Oh, you naughty thing. THIS is what you bookmarked? Having read it, I'll enjoy wondering—Sam." I flushed from top to bottom, and I'm not telling you what I imagined after that.

Susan had a barbeque in her back garden that weekend to celebrate my buying a car that would be ready the following week. Though cheaper for a manual, the hire price was still too expensive to maintain for long. I was determined to buy a hybrid, though unsure how I would charge it up at the flat. Near to the airport was a Toyota garage. I decided, as that was the first I saw when I arrived, I'd try there and found myself a nice little hybrid Yaris. Bonus: it was automatic, and the electrical side charged up as you drove it around—how cool was that?

With everyone assembled, I could break the news that the people in the house I'd seen shortly after my arrival had accepted my offer. They were buying a new house, so I was at the end of the chain. Although I had to pay twenty thousand over the asking price, it was in an excellent location and size for the furniture I was bringing over.

Meeting my nieces and nephews again and their spouses was fun. I tried to keep all their names straight. Anne's children had a child each, and her daughter had another on the way. Susan's eldest daughter had two children, one just a babe-in-arms and so cute. Her son's wife was pregnant, and her youngest daughter's wedding would be the following spring. Great-Aunt Joey was a novelty and, therefore, very popular. I'd brought over some American candy and sportswear for them all, including Twinkies that everyone tried—to varying degrees of success or disgust.

After collecting my second sausage in a bun—no one can beat a British sausage—I collapsed in a garden chair next to Elliott, who watched all the kids with amusement but little interaction.

"Hey, bro," I offered by way of greeting. "Did you miss me?" It was the first time we'd seen each other since my last visit to the UK before the pandemic, and aside from a tight hug when he first arrived, we hadn't had time to interact. Given the age difference of fifteen years, I couldn't say we were close, but I had a big spot in my heart for him.

"Have you been away?" he teased.

"For too long, it would seem."

"I've missed you, baby girl."

"Awe, Daddy used to call me that."

"I remember. Well, you're still the baby of the family."

"Hardly." I gestured to the young 'uns running around on the grass. We were so lucky to have a warm April day.

"Perhaps while you're staying in the city, we could visit a few places of interest together? You know how much I love a church or museum."

"I'm in, providing we include stopping for coffee and a scone, lunch, then afternoon tea."

Anne joined us in time to catch my last words and plopped down next to Elliott. "Joey, you and I need to get walking. You can't eat all those treats and not walk it off."

"I'll be walking it off around the museums," I complained.

"There are a lot of trails around Norwich that we can explore, and some hikes in Norfolk I'm sure you've never seen. You've done too much driving in the USA." She had a point. I mean, there were plenty of places to walk, but it wasn't an option I enjoyed. Perhaps I would if I had her company.

"Well, take it easy on me," I complained. "At least Norfolk is reasonably flat."

"We'll start with St. James' Hill. The view is worth the short walk up there."

I groaned, then got up to get myself a slice of chocolatey dessert. I figured I would need the sugar energy.

***

That night, Graham was online when I settled down in my pyjamas to my last cup of tea and tried to tackle writing more of my 'Firefighter' story. After Sam's lovely message, I hadn't come up with a single word. It all seemed too important now that he'd mentioned how good it was and wanted it to be a movie—added to that was the stress of getting everything lined up for the move. *Writer's block is real!* Now, I had a house offer accepted and a potential move date at the end of June when my contract ran out on this flat; it all seemed to slot into place.

Graham:

> Hey, Jo. You about?

Joanna:

> Yes. How are you?

Graham:

> Going well. You?

Joanna:

> Feeling good. I got a new (to me) car and put an offer on a house.

Graham:

> That's great. Wow, you're off and running.

Joanna:

> A bit tired. Family barbeque today.

Graham:

At Susan's? Those were always fun. Did she make her triple chocolate cake?

Joanna:

Yes, I brought a huge slice back after eating a big piece there.

Graham:

Looks good on you. I loved that pic of you with the leaves all changing behind you. Where was that?

Joanna:

Massachusetts on the way to Boston. My son and his boyfriend live in Boston.

Graham:

Brilliant! You know, I was thinking about you the other day and remembered how you always said you would become an author. Did you ever write a book?

Joanna:

Funny you should remember that. I'm attempting to write one now, but I seem to have writer's block. Who knew that was a real thing?

Graham:

Yeah? Share the outline with me. I read nonfiction, but happy to see if I can help jolt some ideas for you.

I ran through the plot and explained what I was missing. Graham shot through some ideas, some fun and some ridiculous. It felt good to laugh.

Joanna:

Thanks, you've been so helpful.

Graham:

Really? I gave you something useful?

Joanna:

No, but you made me think of a different idea.

Graham:

I'll send you my bank details for my royalties. {laughing emojis}

Joanna:

Good try, but thank you. 'Night. I'm going to get this idea down.

Graham:

'Night, Jo.

***

The flat made it so easy to walk into the city and meet Susan for some shopping. I was pleased to note that the market smelled the same as it always did. Elliott and I got into a routine of meeting once a week to visit sites of historical interest, including the castle, its museum and the battlements, which afforded a fabulous view of the city, the cathedral and coffee room, the site of the old library and the new one.

Our first trip was a walk along the river Wensum, starting at Prince of Wales Road. Sitting at one of the outside tables of the Compleat Angler pub, where the steps down to the riverside path began, was a stout man of similar age to my brother. Elliott stopped at the table.

"Joey, this is my—friend Alastair."

A brief flicker of what I thought might be disappointment clouded the other man's eyes for a moment before he stood and held his hand out to me.

"Joanna, it's such a pleasure to meet you. Elliott has told me a lot about you and your recent move back home. He's so pleased you're in Norfolk again."

I shook his hand firmly. It was soft and warm but dry, and he gently squeezed me before letting go. "I'm so pleased to meet you, Alastair. I know nothing about you, so I will ask many questions, assuming you're coming with us on our walk?"

"With your permission." He was gentlemanly and old-fashioned in his voice and manner, but not condescending or priggish.

"Oh yes, you must come," I declared, and once we were on the lower path by the riverside, I took his arm.

"Elliott is very proud of you for making this move alone." He glanced back at my brother. Though the path was wide enough for three abreast, Elliott walked a pace behind us. Taller than either of us, he could view the river between our heads, and we spoke loudly enough to include him should he wish to join in.

"Baby steps, a good friend in the USA told me. Once I'd broken it down, each task wasn't so hard. Each day, I pushed everything a little further down the road. Still doing it now, in truth."

"You have a house offer accepted, I understand."

"Yes. Twenty-K over price, but that's the current market. But I don't want to talk about me. I want to know about Alastair. How long have you known my brother?"

"We met twenty years ago on a tour of Chatsworth House in Derbyshire. Do you know it?"

"Isn't it the location where Jane Austen based Pemberley?"

"Quite so," he sounded so properly English as a Pride and Prejudice character that I laughed, and Elliott snorted. "I supposed you would know, being a literature lover."

"Did you both live in Norwich back then?"

"I lived in York, but we started a friendship, and when I retired, I moved here. We enjoy visiting all these historical places together. Setting off on our adventures from the same locale seemed easier."

"What a fabulous story."

We'd reached Pulls Ferry, and Elliott reeled off several facts about it, including the ghost who purportedly lived in the house. I looked up at the windows, half expecting to see an apparition standing at one of them. Then, we walked towards the cathedral, following the lane away from the river, which used to be a canal for ferrying the stone to build the cathedral over nine hundred years ago.

As we approached the cathedral, we stopped at the resting place of Edith Cavell.

"The Germans executed her in World War I for aiding British soldiers in escaping occupied Belgium," Elliott informed us. I knew this already and was sure Alastair did, too, but neither of us pointed it out as we nodded solemnly.

"Did you know," Alastair said to me, "that the King had to grant an exception to an order in council from 1854 to allow her reburial here?"

"I didn't know that. She was an exceptional woman and from this area."

"And," Elliott added, not to be outdone, "she treated all wounded soldiers alike. Not just the allies. You would have thought that fact might have spared her, but not so."

"We can all learn from her example," I offered with a glance either side of me at the two men I believed to be completely in love with each other. I could easily imagine them informing each other of these minor facts as they strolled around a National Trust house, famous gardens or other places of historic interest. I linked my arm in each of theirs and led them away from the grave. "Come on, Elliott promised tea and cakes."

We rounded the corner to a vast tree with a super canopy providing a cooling shade on this bright, sunny day. Its first two boughs reached up as if welcoming an embrace as we walked beneath it.

"The hugging tree!" I exclaimed, and with a laugh, pulled Elliott over to embrace the tree with me as we had done as kids. "Alastair, would you take a photo?"

He laughed, a high, giddy giggle, and I looked over to Elliott, whose arms were hugging the tree with me, one overlapping mine. Elliott's laughing face turned from mine to Alastair's as he took the photo, and a look of pure and happy love crossed his face. An expression that I wish Bruce had aimed my way just once. I smiled, too, and Alastair took the photo.

"What's this all about?" he asked as he held up his phone.

"Just a family tradition," I explained. "I'm not sure where it started. Probably to appease me on a long walk because I was so much younger than everyone else and had much shorter legs."

Leaving Elliott, I ran over to see the photo, begging Alastair to share it with me, and took his phone to put my number in while I pushed him over to the tree. "You must try it, Alastair. Hugging trees is therapeutic for you and the tree, too."

Eagerly, he ran over to join Elliot, and I snapped a photo of them laughing at each other with Alastair's phone. It was such a joy to see. I'll argue with anyone who would say otherwise when I tell them hugging a tree is good for you.

We made our way to the Rectory Bakery and Café, apparently based on the site of the original monks' dining room, according to Alastair, and I had no reason to disbelieve him. It tickled me to think women now ate and drank on a site that historically would've been entirely for men.

I was finishing my last bite of a fabulous Eccles cake when Elliott excused himself to use the facilities. Alastair watched him go, then turned to notice me scrutinising him.

"You know, don't you," he stated.

I picked my words carefully. "I know nothing until Elliott chooses to tell me."

"I don't know if he will ever be ready to do that. Meanwhile, I get excluded from your family events like the barbeque the other day, because no one knows me."

"Well, I know you now, so I'll invite you to my housewarming party, and after that, everyone will invite you to everything because we'll all know you then."

"You are very kind."

"Bruce never looked at me like you two look at each other. You can't deny love.

When Elliott returned, I announced I had adopted Alastair as my friend and invited him to my housewarming party. Elliott looked at me and mouthed, *Thank you*.

***

After dinner with Elliott and Alastair that evening, I returned to the flat a little merry to see that Graham was online. In a buoyant mood after a great day out, I messaged him.

Joanna:
> What are you up to?

The photo he sent shocked me into laughter.

"So this is a dick pic?" I asked aloud to no one, then clicked away from it. My first taste of twenty-first-century dating, I supposed, and moved to put the kettle on, but I couldn't forget what he'd sent me. My eyes must have been deceiving me, I reasoned. No one had ever sent me one before.

Opening the photo again, I stared at it, scrutinising it from all angles. Did I recognise it? I couldn't say for sure; it had been over thirty years ago, but it had that red-chestnut tinge to the pubic hair, with a scattering of grey just like the hair on his head on his profile picture.

Finally, I dared a reply—

Joanna:
> How much have you had to drink? LOL

Graham:
> A bit. Want to join me?

Joanna:
> In the drink, or—?

Graham:

Either. Both.

Joanna:

I've never—

I supposed he would be the first one with whom I'd have this experience, too.

LANDLORD

A landlord from old Market Deeping

Was incredibly fond of just peeping

Up a ladder he crept

To watch while she slept

Its collapse left him injured and weeping

(Limerick contribution from Jane Jago)

SIX

I had three months pre-booked in the city centre flat. It seemed like a lot, but I soon discovered that while selling a house in a buoyant market was fun, buying was less so. Another buyer had come along and gazumped me.

Living in the USA, I'd forgotten about this phenomenon because it didn't happen there. In the US, the buyer and seller sign a contract after an offer's acceptance. Here in the UK, someone else had come in with another ten thousand over my offer, and that was that.

A visit to my mum soon had my spirits up again. I'd been to view a house with the tiniest of bedrooms and had no hope of my bed, currently paddling in the Atlantic Ocean, fitting in. I already missed my comfortable mattress, and that brand didn't sell in the UK.

"I predict the next house you see will be perfect for you," Mum sagely commented.

"From your mouth—, Mum."

She was standing in the bathroom doorway while I valiantly wiped at least a year of dust and cobwebs from behind the toilet.

"You could get a cleaner, you know, Mum."

"I can do it," she said.

"But *I'm* doing it." My knees screamed in protest, and I rested my arm on the side of the bathtub to hoist myself back up.

"You need to lose some weight, Joey," she commented.

"Seriously, Mom?"

"Oh, that sounded American. Am I in trouble for caring now?"

"Just for stating the obvious. What's for lunch?" I changed the subject.

"Pizza and I bought a couple of fresh cream puffs from Toni's tearoom."

"Of course you did," I muttered. Not that I was going to turn down cream puffs—*Yummy.*

***

I called my big sister Anne. She used to be a realtor, sorry estate agent, and the price for her advice was a walk up the highest hill of the wooded area of Mousehold—St. James' Hill. Her house was a stone's throw from there, so the plan was I would park at hers and we would walk.

Anne suggested the safest option would be a new house. Once I'd reserved one, it would be mine. I just had to wait for the development company to build it. Two days later, she and I were looking at the plans for a three-bed semi-detached house—no garage, but a driveway and a little shed. The rooms were good-sized and double-fronted, so the kitchen/dining room was on one side and the lounge on the other, with the entrance hall in the middle. I could make the second bedroom a guest room and the third an office with a sofa bed if needed.

We put on hard hats and high-vis jackets and checked it out on the building site with the salesperson. They were working on the ground floor level, and a green area would be in front of the house, on the other side of the road. It would mean kids playing out there in pleasant weather, but I didn't mind that. I took plenty of photos to show Holly, Beth and Ethan later. Then, I put a reserve on that plot and crossed my fingers. It would be ready by the time my agreement on the flat ran out. It was smaller than I'd planned, being a semi with no garage, but spending less on a house now would leave more money in my retirement pot. As it was new, there would be other expenses on top that are usually included in an existing house, like flooring, wardrobes (because this house didn't have closets as they do in the USA) and an outside tap.

With that completed, I drove back to Anne's, and we headed off on our 'little walk', as she wanted to call it. It felt like an uphill marathon to me.

"You know, Anne, there's a reason I drove through the Berkshires and didn't hike," I panted, and we weren't even halfway up.

"Nonsense," she insisted, striding off through the long grass, following a path I could barely see.

I'm all for a nice relaxing walk, but this felt like torture. However, when I reached the top, the bright sky and strong breeze were my reward, and the view of Norwich City spread out before us—the big cathedral's shining spire most prominent, the squat castle and green dome-topped city hall easy to spot. The monument with the map helped us spot everything we weren't sure of from that distance.

I turned to Anne. "Thanks, sis."

"For what?" she asked with a confused expression that made me smile, given what a confident person she was.

"Helping me out today, your advice, and putting up with my complaints so we could enjoy this view."

"Happy to."

"Selfie time," I yelled and pulled out my selfie stick to get a good one with plenty of the view behind us.

'I reserved a new-build house today.' I typed as a caption with the photo to my sibs' chat.

***

Holly was the one who surprised me the most when I got on the video call with the three loves of my life later. "Dad should give you more money to buy a bigger house, and then you could have had us all stay with you when we visit. I'll mention it to him when I see him next," she complained. Holly was Bruce's greatest defender, but I guess she had her heart set on the six of them descending upon me someday.

"You don't need to talk to your father. I'm responsible for myself now, and this house will be a perfect size for me. In the unlikely event of all of you visiting in the same week, I'll pay for an Airbnb near the beach for us all."

"Will you be okay though, Mom? Are you sure?" Beth worried.

"I'm sure. I'm a grown woman, you know. I raised the three of you and looked after that big house."

"I miss the house," Ethan chimed in. "I hope the people who moved in aren't changing too much. That's all I can say."

I laughed. "You moved way off to Boston, Ethan. You can't be that worried."

Once we moved past that hurdle, I sat back and listened to their chatter. I missed them all, but they were busy with their lives, which was how it should be.

***

I've learnt you must count your blessings when they happen—even green traffic lights when you're in a hurry—so when shit hits the fan, you have good things to weigh against it. The news a week later wasn't good—it would take another month beyond the end of my flat rental before my house would be ready.

My first idea was to stay in the flat and extend the rental. No luck—someone else booked it. It was probably just as well as it forced my hand. It had been hot for a few days in June, and the air didn't circulate well in the flat. Boy, I missed my air conditioning. Instead, I started looking at beach places. It would be cooler on the coast in July. Unfortunately, holiday goers had booked many for some or all of the weeks. Norfolk is a popular destination, and I couldn't dispute that. Finally, I found something suitable—a converted stable behind a large old house about a mile from a beach. Perfect for my simple needs of beach walks, editing and self-sufficiency. More importantly, it was available.

I chatted with the owner through the Airbnb website and was comfortable renting from her. The stable was out of the way, but Colleen lived in the larger house with her husband—if I needed anything. Susan planned to stay over a few times around her part-time job. With her visits, walks on the beach and fish and chips calling my name, I decided it would be the perfect location to get well into my new editing job—the next in the series of Redway Acres, which was about a stable. I wondered if they would make another miniseries about this book. If so, would Sam Harmer take on the same role? I couldn't help but smile and knew I would picture him while I edited the book.

I messaged Sam about it and my writing efforts.

Joanna:

> Hi, Sam. It's Jo from the plane back in March. You probably don't remember, but you read my book. Anyway, I'm editing the next Redway Acres book and will think of you. I'm not doing so well with my effort. I need a good ending.

Sam:

> Of course, I remember you, Jo. Can't chat right now, but soon. Perhaps I can help with an ending? I'll let you know.

I packed up one suitcase with my winter/spring gear and a few other bits and pieces I wouldn't need at the barn and left it with my mum. That left my other suitcase, the two tower-fans I'd bought, and a few other appliances I'd had to replace as the UK plugs differed from US ones—three pins instead of two and something to do with voltage. Soon, I'd packed my little car full.

As I headed out towards the coast, the Norfolk fields spread out in front of me, and the high sky dominated the view with tall, fluffy white clouds breaking up the blue. There was nothing like it, in my opinion. I drove through the seaside village with the beaches on one side and holiday homes with a sprinkling of shops on the other—groceries, seaside essentials with a rack of postcards outside, a mini arcade and, of course, the obligatory fish and chips. My mouth watered.

Turning away from the breezy sand and sea, I drove down a narrow lane of hedgerows before coming upon the manor house and took the driveway around the back of it. There, I found the entrance and small parking space for the barn conversion. Retrieving the key from the pass-coded safety box, I unlocked and checked out my new abode. It was the perfect combination of quaint and modern. The owners had carefully incorporated the original features of the stable into the décor—beams, ring-ties and jutting rafters. All the fixtures were modern and clean. What more could I want?

***

I spent the first two weeks blissfully walking to the beach every day, paddling in the sea and exfoliating the dry skin on my feet in the warm sand. After lunch, I worked at the rickety table on the little brick patio, with my washing drying on the line. If it got too hot, I sat inside with the fans switched to high. My hot flushes were killing me on those hot days—thank goodness for my Embr Wave watch.

The Redway Acres author seemed to have considered my previous edits with this new book, which I appreciated. It allowed me to dig deeper into the editing process. When I got my new house, I decided this series would take pride of place on my bookshelves and wondered how many books the author planned.

Susan visited and stayed overnight as promised, which were the only days I deviated from my usual routine. We started with a quick shopping trip for all our needs over the two days, which might have included a bottle of wine—or two. When we returned, I heard a loud buzzing as I opened the door.

I had noticed a few flies around the place and utilised my handy flyswatter, which was a fantastic one and included a little dustpan and a pair of tweezers for picking up dead insects. However, the sight of one of the high skylight windows set my heart racing. Flies swarming almost blacked it out, trying to get out. I'm not a good insect person. Thankfully, Susan is, and being a practical person, she grabbed the pole to open that window and quickly hooked it through the latch. The flies zoomed out of the opening, and the almost deafening noise abated. It took maybe thirty seconds more for my heart to resume its regular rate.

We guessed there was a dead something in a cavity around the house somewhere. I hated to think of all those flies as maggots not long ago, munching away on a corpse hidden in a place I was living.

That evening, we demolished a bottle of crisp white wine with fish and chips, which helped me forget the swarm of the flies. Then I shocked Susan with a childhood revelation.

"Do you remember your Famous Five collection of books?"

Oh, my word, I loved those books. What a shame they haven't stood the test of time. Anne hated that the books always praised her namesake for preparing picnics, predicting she'd make a good housewife when she grew up."

"Mum told me not to touch those books because they were yours. They were up on a bookshelf around the corner from the lounge seating area. I used to sneak downstairs at night when you were all watching TV and grab one or two to read in bed." The wine made me giggly.

"That's not so bad. Mum always said you were reading at a younger age than any of us."

"I ate them."

"What?"

"I was annoyed not to be allowed to touch your books, so I would tear off a corner of some pages and eat them. They were parts of your books you could never have back. I thought it was hilarious."

Susan's expression was priceless, and I started rolling around on the sofa in hysterical giggles and holding my stomach.

"You—ate—my—books?" She was incredulous and started picking up every cushion she could lay her hands on to throw at me. "I can't believe you ate them."

"Didn't you ever notice?"

"No, not that I remember. You little minx." With that, she added herself to the cushions on top of me and said, "Revenge is a dish best served cold."

"I can't breathe." I was still giggling, though.

"Oh, I'll give you can't breathe." Then she farted on me.

"OMG, that is so rank, Susan."

We dissolved into a laughing fit before I escaped my mountain of cushions to tackle her into a hug.

"It's so good to have you back home, Joey," she said into my neck as we squeezed each other.

**

The Sunday after my second week, my email pinged with a message on the Airbnb site. Colleen was letting me know she was heading off to a week-long conference. If needed, her husband, Dave, would be there. I wasn't worried because I'd seen nothing of either of them during my two weeks so far.

Two mornings later, I woke, not with the sun streaming through the skylight as usual, but with a man's grinning face. He gave a cheery wave with a squeegee and disappeared. I hurriedly dressed in the privacy of the windowless bathroom and headed outside. The man leaned his ladder up against the fence opposite the door lengthwise to store it, but I'd never noticed it there before.

"Hi," I ventured.

"Oh, hello. I'm Colleen's husband, Dave." He moved to shake my hand, but I didn't respond.

"I would rather you didn't leave that there, Dave," I said.

"Well, I didn't finish all the windows, so I thought I'd return tomorrow."

"I would prefer you leave the windows and do them at the end of the month when I leave."

"They can get pretty dirty."

"I thought Colleen mentioned you use a professional window cleaner with one of those long poles, so he doesn't need a ladder?" I thought I'd cornered him with this comment.

"But when the birds shit on them, it's best to get it off as soon as possible, or the sun bakes it on."

"I didn't see you here these past two weeks doing this."

Dave did, at least, have the decency to look sheepish. "Colleen and I don't agree with me doing it."

I bet she doesn't, I thought. "She probably worries about you falling," I offered instead. "Here's a compromise. I'll check the windows a couple of times a day, and if I notice any bird shit, I'll let you know."

Reluctantly, Dave agreed and headed off. I cleared my throat and looked pointedly at the ladder when he turned. Dave picked it up. What else could he do? I'd cornered him nicely and gave myself a pat on the back. As he walked away, I imagined those flies swarming around his head.

Some bird poop appeared one day, but thankfully, the window cleaner visited that afternoon and took care of it—phew!

***

The late July days were hot-hot-hot, and I missed my air-conditioning terribly. A paddle in the sea was welcome whenever I could get over there. My routine became chores in the morning while it was cooler, though I still ended up a dripping mess of sweat. Leaving my washing out on the line, I would head for a late morning paddle while the tide was out. Once I'd washed off the sand on my return, I sat down for more editing. My only deviation included visits from my siblings or a trip to the city to see Mum or shop.

With a week of my stay remaining and photos of my new house from the salesperson now showing painted rooms and bathroom fixtures, I picked a cloudier day to take a deck chair to the beach and push it into the sand a short distance from the waves. The sea lapped lazily over my toes, my feet sinking into the sand. I brought a book from Colleen's collection to read purely for pleasure—my favourite Agatha Christie murder mystery—and waited for the sea to creep towards me.

My eyes fluttered, and I felt myself drifting off to the sounds of children squealing, seagulls squawking, the waves, and the breeze. I'd shifted my chair back and reckoned I had twenty minutes before the sea got as high as the chair's seat, or it fell back under the wet sand. I hoped no one would film that and put it online for shits and giggles. Cautiously, I set the timer on my watch. The peace seeped into me. I was the most relaxed I'd felt in years.

The water was halfway up my shins when my watch buzzed on my wrist—time to get back to the barn, wash off my sun lotion and start work. When I arrived back, the gate was open, though I had been sure I'd closed it before I left. I'm meticulous about security in other people's houses. Cautiously, with my phone out, ready to call the police if needed, I padded to the back, where the clothesline held my morning wash load. Peering around the corner, I spotted Dave with his hands over the chest area of one of my t-shirts. He was cupping and squeezing to his heart's content, and I shuddered as if his hands were over the tee I wore right now. I felt a little vomit up in my throat and almost retched aloud when he moved to grab the crotch of my sensible white knickers. Then, to my absolute horror, he sniffed right in the gusset. With a vow in my mind that I would throw that pair away when I had a chance, but not in his trash, I took a photo for evidence and cleared my throat.

His flushed face turned to me. "I thought it was going to rain, so I came over to get in your washing. I was checking it was dry."

"By sniffing it?"

"I—"

"Save it, buddy. I'm not interested in excuses, and I'm leaving."

Thankfully, he made himself scarce rather than belligerent, so I packed everything haphazardly into my car, grabbing a bag to shove my clothes off the line into. I sat in the car, momentarily relishing the air conditioning after the confrontation and my rush around gathering everything together. I took a healing breath and put on some Annie Lennox—for who couldn't feel strong listening to her powerful voice? I drove to the safest place I could think of, grateful I still had that choice—Mum's house.

So much for my earlier peace of mind.

"Oh, Joey. What a creepy bastard," in her usual succinct form, my mother sympathised as she loaded my first wash into her machine. "We'll wash everything twice."

My thoughts exactly, as I planned an M&S shopping trip for new knickers.

***

As horrible as that experience had been, being at my mother's was fun. If there was one thing Mum excelled at, it was a crisis. I washed everything I'd taken to the holiday place. Who knew if he had a spare key and went through my things? Then my worst thought was, *what if he went through my vibrators?* It isn't like I had an entire collection, but you have to try things out to see what you like best—right? I bagged them up to throw in my trash when I had my own place and promised myself a 'first house purchase' of a new one. It seemed apt.

Later that night, I messaged Colleen and attached the photo of her husband.

"I've moved out for fear of my safety. Please arrange a refund for the last week."

She apologised, of course, and I felt for her. She was a decent woman married to a jerk—been there, done that. Then, she asked me not to leave a bad review.

"I can't do that, and I'll be making a complaint to Airbnb and any website I find your property for rent. You have to realise he won't stop, and you can't always be there to rein him in. What if his behaviour escalates, and he hurts a woman or a young girl? How will you feel then?"

I waited for her response, but none came. What did was a refund of all my money, which was unexpected, and I held my breath, wondering if she expected me to leave it at that. The next day, I couldn't find the place on any holiday websites I checked, but I still reported it to Airbnb. Hopefully, if she tried to put it back up, that would be enough to stop her. I hoped she'd moved him out there and filed for divorce.

Thankful for a couple of warm, dry days, I got all my washing clean, dry and packed back in my suitcase in time for my move and squeezed in some time for underwear shopping. There would be a week between getting the keys and my furniture arriving. Mum tried to persuade me to stay with her, but I was too eager to settle in and have my own space. I'd found a table and chairs on Facebook Marketplace for a reasonable price—the enormous set Bruce and I had bought a few years back wouldn't have fitted in my kitchen-diner, let alone allow me to walk around it. It was a beautiful set—chunky and distressed wood, which I loved. He'd put it in storage until he bought a house. I'd been tempted to draw a dick and balls on the underside of the table, but my half-joking mention of it horrified the kids. Probably at the thought that I would know what it all looked like. Despite Matt roaring with laughter while trying to encourage me, even offering to come over from Boston to help me, I refrained, but only because I thought Holly would blab.

Elliott had a single mattress he would run over to my house when I had the keys, and I borrowed linens from Mum. Finally, I would get a package for my Wi-Fi delivered on my move-in day. All I had to do was plug it in and log in for internet access. I hoped so because that first night, I planned a late-night call, for me at least, to my three kids so we could all celebrate. I had champers ready to cool in the fridge.

I was all set.

HANDY PERSON

Put up shelves
Fit them together
Fix to the walls
Make them last forever

Adjust the cabinets
Attach a mirror to a wall
Arrange the pictures
Don't let them fall

Lift heavy furniture
Stick down a carpet
Screw in some coat hooks
Make filler hard set

Sand down rough walls
Nail down wood
Paint and finish
Until it's all good

If you can't do this yourself

And you need someone who can

The only person you can call

Is a handy handyman

(Or woman)

SEVEN

I was huffing and puffing as I carried a glass of champagne in one hand and my iPad in the other around my new house that first night, showing the kids every room on the video chat. They used the identical engraved champagne glasses I bought for their housewarming gifts. They had all bought me the same set for my housewarming gift, so I carried the glass carefully.

"That's going to be my room when I visit," Beth squealed at the empty second bedroom. She never could hold her alcohol, bless her sweet heart and liver.

"It's anyone's room when they visit, Beth," Holly corrected, forever the oldest sibling.

"It's my bedroom furniture going in there, though." Beth pouted.

I smiled. I was happy they supported me and said they would come over, even if their busy lives didn't allow it. Hopefully, they'll find the time soon. I showed them the back garden from the window even though it was ten p.m.

"I can't believe how light it still is out there, Jo," Matt chimed in from over Ethan's shoulder. "Look at those tiny gardens all backing onto each other."

"Sunrise at four-thirty a.m.," I complained, "and I've got no blinds until Monday morning. The guy took pity on me and fitted me in early. I'm thankful I kept my eye mask from the flight over. At least no houses overlook my bedroom yet. They'll probably build those houses next year."

"We're in an apartment, Matt. We don't have a garden at all." Ethan pointed out. "When do you get your shipment, Mom?" He was managing again.

"Next Thursday. Not too long to wait now."

"I wish we could be there to help you unpack."

"I'm looking forward to it. I'll take my time and put what I want where I want it. When I packed everything, I rushed. It'll be good to remember everything I have. When I got the welcome tour today, the site manager said they would remove any empty boxes as needed. So that's helpful."

"What do you need to do before the delivery, Mom?" Beth was the practical one.

"Set up all my accounts with the utilities, buy a TV and a TV license and keep the turf watered out the back and the plants out the front. They left me a hose and a sprinkler. I'm going to need a lawnmower and a clothesline."

"Put the clothes in the dryer, Mom. You can afford the electricity," Holly is a busy woman who loves her laundry room because it's large and set out so efficiently—and larger than my new third bedroom.

"There isn't a dryer, Love." The looks of horror on the three faces in front of me would be comical if a twinge of guilt didn't sit behind it. I had brought them up so privileged. "Don't worry, I've learnt my lesson about hanging my underwear out there."

Beth said, "I bet you'll be like someone in one of those romance movies. You return home and reconnect with a past love you let slip away."

I blushed. I hadn't told any of them about Graham, and we hadn't messaged as much lately. Well, not since—definitely no need to mention that.

Matt reappeared at Ethan's shoulder. "Oh yes, Jo. Wait and see who moves in next door. Perhaps it's a grieving widower or a wronged divorcee. He'll have a cute kid, and you'll fall in love with both."

"You all go back to your romances. I need some sleep. I'll update you all soon. Keep WhatsApping. I miss you all so much."

Before heading to my lonely mattress, I said a mildly drunk and teary goodbye. I couldn't wait for my bed to arrive. Divorcees and widowers? I rolled my eyes, then rolled over to sleep.

***

Having my furniture a few days later was a relief, especially my bed. After a few nights back on that beauty, my hip stopped barking. Well, it would have if it hadn't been for unpacking and folding flat enormous boxes. I questioned my going to the expense of shipping so much over, especially when some pieces didn't fit, and I had to sell them—thank you, Facebook and the local community page. I had thought I'd be getting a bigger house, of course. However, my bed was worth it, and I didn't have to go to the expense of buying new, except for the electronics. I took my time, finding the perfect spot for everything after the delivery guys had put the furniture where I wanted it and reassembled everything.

You'd be wrong if you think everything will be move-in ready when you get a newly built home. I considered this as I dug through my suitcase once again. My furniture shipment had arrived, but I needed new wardrobes as I had built-in closets in the USA. The ones the builders would have put in were too basic. Where better to turn than IKEA? I measured, then scoured the site and added more and more to my basket online. With no local shop, I had to trust the photos and place the order. Thankfully, when it arrived, the delivery men popped each box into the bedroom it needed to go in. I filled their to-go coffee cups and gave them a bag of different chip varieties, remembering to say crisps and some chocolate. They were happy, but frankly, it was worth it for me, as I never would have managed if they had left all the boxes and bags in the hallway.

With hammer and screwdriver in hand, I wrestled a bedside cabinet box onto my bed and methodically worked at putting it together—I checked the contents twice, huffed and puffed, screwed until my wrist was killing me and hammered the tiny nails in the back, getting them mostly in straight. I want to say it took me an hour, but a work conference call pulled me away from my task before I'd even turned a single screw. Then Susan turned up for lunch, which was a pleasant distraction, but I didn't want her offering to help me with it. The first cabinet, at least, I wanted to tackle by myself.

Finally, a worker from the building site came to my door without a prior appointment. He held up the document from my snagging inspector. Who knew there was such a thing? Luckily, one of my neighbours in a community Facebook group did. The inspector had spent a day going around my house before my furniture arrived, taking photos of issues and detailing them in his report. Builders aren't fans of snag inspectors, especially ones as thorough as mine. The site manager had gone through the house with me, trying to malign all the points my inspector had made, but I was ready with all the arguments the guy had outlined.

"They asked me to deal with some of these, and I've got a spare couple of hours, so I thought I could do them now."

My mistake was letting him in. He tried to argue every little point in the same way his manager had done, but I just gave him my best Paddington hard stare—these days, this was a reference both US and UK people understood.

He headed into my lounge, where somebody patched the ceiling so severely they couldn't have possibly hoped I would miss it.

"Oh yeah, there was a leak in the plumbing upstairs they had to access from underneath. I patched it after they fixed the issue." Why did he sound proud of it?

"You know, I've just remembered that my mum is expecting me over at hers right now," I said. "So you had better come back another time."

"No problem. I see you've had all these IKEA wardrobes delivered. If you need some help, call me. I can do DIY stuff like that for you at a reasonable rate. Let me leave you my number."

I made a performance out of not really taking down his number in my phone as I chivvied him out of the door. Then I called the site manager.

"Hi, it's Joanna James. Okay, first, don't send the man who made a pig's ear out of my house in the first place to fix the problems he left. Second, please ask anyone you send to arrange an appointment with me. Just because I'm home doesn't mean I'm available for anyone to swan in. I know you're used to the houses you build being available to you at any time you want, but once someone buys one, your crew needs to appreciate that it's now someone's home."

He agreed and said someone else would be in touch.

By bedtime, I was happy to put things safely on top of my cabinet, but I had no time, strength, or energy left to finish the two drawers.

There was nothing else for it, I contemplated as I reached for my glass of water on my half-built nightstand. I needed to get a man in—though I'd be happier with a woman.

***

I can't say I wanted someone in my house, specifically my bedroom. Some men liked to walk around a single woman's house as if they owned it. Given half a chance, they would mark their territory by pissing in every loo and leaving the seat up.

Back in the USA, there was one guy from the boiler service company I used who I firmly refused to have in my house ever again. The first time he turned up, the bell rang, and I went to answer the door only to find no one there. I glanced to the side, and he had gone to the end of my wraparound porch. He stood there, arms outstretched on the railing, surveying my garden as if it were his domain. I should have just closed the door and hid.

"Hello," I called from the doorway, and he sauntered over without a care. "What were you doing over there?"

"Enjoying the view."

"It isn't yours to enjoy."

He just shrugged and sauntered a bit more as he went inside, looking around as he made his way to the basement door I indicated.

"Would you like me to call my husband from upstairs? He works nights, but I'm sure he would happily talk to you." I asked, well aware that Bruce was at work. They were like magic words.

"No, that's fine, ma'am, if you're happy to tell me the problem." He suddenly quickened his pace and set to his work.

Now in the UK, I searched Facebook for a local handy-person, figuring I would have them come over for a quote and see what I thought of them. I found a woman, and she was a wisecracker. She said she'd be happy doing my work provided I supplied her with plenty of coffee, and her rates were reasonable. I liked her immediately. Though she passed herself off as having low intelligence, she wasn't, and her humour had a clever use of words, even occasionally dirty, but not offensive. To top it off, if she needed to use the loo, she always put the seat and the lid down, which was my preference.

Within a week, Nicky had the wardrobes up for all three bedrooms, cabinets in all three bathrooms, some heavier picture frames up where the sticky hangers I'd bought wouldn't cut it, and some coat hooks for good measure. It was a fun time seeing it all go up and the boxes disappear from my house—Nicky loaded them into her truck and disposed of them for me. I heated the kettle regularly, and had someone to talk to at home, which was fun.

I took photos of everything and took my iPad to Mum's, showing her the progress.

"A handyman would be a good man to have a relationship with," Mum suggested. "How old is he?"

"Don't even go there, Mum. *She's* the same age as Anne's Tim," I told her. I thought about how old I was when my first nephew was born. "That fact makes me feel like her—"

"Mum," she provided with a smirk.

"No! Honestly, Mum. You forget how much older than me Anne is. I was going to say, big sister."

I was delighted to give Nicky a recommendation on the community's Facebook group. I think she got a bit more business that way.

ROMANCE MOVIE

In a romance movie
When you return to home-town
There's a gorgeous guy
With a smile and no frown
Who's miraculously single
Widowed or divorced
Not looking for true love
But you arrive, and he's forced
To reconsider all his choices
And ask you on a date
You reconnect with your best bud
Who'll help you dress—not be late
The date is a disaster
Though you're a super match
It all works out in the end
And he's the perfect catch
But in real life, you end up friends
And honestly, that's real groovy
Rather than try to fit your life
Around a romance movie.

EIGHT

One afternoon, I struggled with the hose from my outside tap out the back to the front garden. Thankfully, they had left behind a very long one I'd used with the sprinkler head for the turf, moving it every thirty minutes. The sun would be on that later, but I had to wait to water the front plants baking in the morning sun. I pulled and panted, unravelling the hose as I went. I wondered what on earth I looked like to my neighbours? Thankfully, none of those within view of my house had moved in yet. The joined side of me was a family moving from abroad, but they had yet to arrive. The builders still worked on the next two houses beyond mine, and they confirmed their owners would move there in a couple of weeks.

I started watering near the joined property line at the far end and worked the hose back around. I had nearly finished when a car pulled up outside the detached house next door. An older couple got out and started walking around it, peering in the windows. The woman caught me watching and gave a friendly wave.

"Hi," I offered.

"Hello. Do you live here?"

"Yes, I just moved in. Are you and your husband moving in here?" *So much for widowers and divorcees,* I thought. *Wait until I tell those meddling kids.*

"Oh, no. Our son is going to live here. He recently got divorced. You'll love his daughter. Emily is such a cutie."

"I'm sure you must love her. How old is she?" I swear I could hear my kids laughing all the way across the Atlantic.

"Nine and doing so well, given how tough it is. His son from his first marriage is at university."

"My kids are all grown up now, but they still feel it, don't they? I left them in the USA, where I've lived for the past twenty-plus years, to move back near my mum."

A conversation followed about kids, divorce and the USA whilst my stomach churned with missing my babies. They were a lovely couple who seemed happy to get to know their son's new neighbour. Later, I spoke on the phone to my mum about them.

"Well, there you go then," Mum said, somewhat cryptically. Water was spraying in the background. She was watering her plants at Horseshoe Hamlets, the property Dad left her, which she had been managing ever since. Last I saw it, it was just the old horse racetrack and a horseshoe of stables. I would have to make it over there to see how it looked. Those old stables had probably fallen down by now.

My eyes were rolling. "Where do I go?"

"You know what I mean. He's divorced and right next door. It was meant to be."

"I haven't even met him yet, Mum, and maybe he's twice divorced for a reason. Did you think about that?"

"That means nothing these days," she said sagely. "Does he have all his own teeth?"

"That's a low bar. I think I'll stay single. It seems like a lot of trouble to me."

***

When I'd unpacked all my boxes from the USA, I'd left a few boxes of memorabilia, paperwork and Christmas decorations to unpack later. Now, it was later, and I couldn't put the task off anymore as the boxes were annoying me. I couldn't hoard anymore, as I no longer had a nice, big basement to store it. A folder inside contained several of the kids' drawings I'd kept when Teena and I went through them. Some were over twenty years old and had adorned my refrigerator at one time or another. Holly, Beth and Ethan were the names in kids' handwriting at the corners of those pictures.

In a fit of reminiscing, I imagined each sweet face as they proudly showed me their work. I remembered the magnets I'd used to hold them in pride of place—large letters that they used to spell out their names. Bruce would always spell 'boobs', 'poop' or some such nonsense. The memory overwhelmed me, reflecting on a time full of future and possibilities.

When there was a knock at the door, I swiped my tears and moved to see who it was—a large man, smartly dressed. His smile faded at the sight of my no doubt splotchy face.

"Are you okay?"

"Sorry, just some memories knocking me sideways. What can I do for you?"

"I'm Denis-one N. My mum was a Blondie fan, but I pronounce it as if it has two or people look at me weirdly. You met my parents the other day, I think? I've just had a tour of my house, and Mum told me to introduce myself." He gestured to the detached property next to mine.

"Joanna. Hi. Do you do everything your parents tell you to do?" My mind was busy calculating his age based on the late seventies release of the Blondie song.

"Always have, probably always will."

"Always? Why do I doubt that?"

"In the things that matter, at least." He had a charming grin.

"Come in, have a cup of tea or something." *What was something?*

"I don't have time today." He looked genuinely regretful, which was nice.

"Good luck with the move. Is it next week?"

"Yes, Thursday."

"Let me know if you need anything. Even if it's just a cuppa."

"Will do."

I watched him walk away because—why not? Well, the tears had stopped, at least. I put the pictures back in with the Christmas stuff and found a space in the upstairs closet. There was plenty of time for reminiscing then, and I had more future and possibilities to pursue.

***

I'd watered my new lawn so well that several weeks later, I purchased a new battery-operated lawnmower. One warm day, I decided to assemble it and cut the grass. I'd done the new turf test of pulling on the grass to see if the roots had taken hold below the level of the original turf carpet. Amazingly, given the hard-packed earth underneath, the roots had found their way.

I unpacked the mower, checked that I had all the requisite parts according to the instructions, and sat down with a cup of tea to find out what to do next. At this point, I must say that the instructions' author must have assumed another man would assemble the mower, thus making it likely that no one would read them. Already frustrated, I headed back out, determined not to be foiled.

As I battled the piece of machinery, I thought about why women are so single-minded to do a job deemed 'traditionally male', yet men aren't so keen when it's the other way around. My conclusion is that men see 'traditionally female' work as demeaning. You can tell by the language used by men—

'He's under the thumb.'

'Put your apron on.'

'Look at what the old ball-and-chain has him doing.'

And women tend to praise men who do these things—

'All this, and he cooks too.'

'He's so good with the baby and even changes the odd diaper.' (Though I bet it wasn't a poopy one.)

'If he goes down on you, he's a keeper.'

I snorted to myself at the thought of that last one. I mean, every man wants the same, right? It seems only fair they should reciprocate.

For women, at least for me, doing what's deemed a 'man's job' gives me a sense of pride. Putting this lawnmower together was me pitting my wits against the dreadful instructions and coming out on top. I achieved this, but not without a significant amount of swearing. At the point where I swore as I tried to push on the supposedly snap-on wheels, I heard a snort from Denis' side of my fence.

"You can shut up," I shouted back reasonably amiably.

"Would you like some help?" he offered.

"I just can't get these wheels on."

"I can pop over if it's okay that I bring Emily with me."

"Your daughter? Sure, come on over. If she'd like one, I have some ice pops or ice creams in the freezer."

"Can't I have one?" he said in a sulky voice, and I heard a sweet giggle, which must have been Emily.

"If Emily says you can," I offered.

Running feet faded from his garden, then got louder near my gate before they barrelled in.

"Hey, nice to meet you, Emily." I gestured into my kitchen. "Go check out the freezer and see what you like—top drawer." She ran in, and I turned to her dad, who smiled.

"Hi, Jo."

"Hi." I handed him the wheel reluctantly. "I wanted to do it myself."

"Does it just snap on?" he asked.

"Seems to, according to these sh—rubbish instructions. A man wrote them. Sorry about the earlier swearing."

"Don't worry, she's heard worse, but that's my fault." He glanced briefly at the instructions I'd shoved at him, then positioned the wheel. "Put your hands here and here."

He positioned my hands opposite each other, reached around me, and put his hands on either side of mine.

"What are you doing?" I yelped.

"Push on three—three."

We pushed, and the wheel snapped in place. Then we turned the lawnmower over and did the other one while Emily sat on one of my patio chairs and watched. She cheered.

"Are you going to eat that or let it melt?" I teased.

"I wanted to make sure a lolly was okay cos you only said ice cream or ice pop."

"American English, sorry. Yes, a lolly is fine."

Denis turned the lawnmower onto its wheels and attached the basket on the back. "Why don't you have one while I cut this for you?"

"Why don't you get something while I mow *my* grass?" I countered.

Denis put his hands up in submission and moved to sit with Emily. Aware of an audience, I struggled to get the mower going and then made a reasonably straight line. The grass was long, so it wasn't the best cut it could be, but it felt good.

"Can I try?" Emily asked while chewing on her lolly stick, and I emptied the grass cuttings into a bag I could take to Mum's garden bin later. She was going to love this story.

"Up to your dad."

I remembered how all our kids loved helping Bruce mow our vast lawn area, especially Ethan, when Bruce finally got a ride-on mower.

"Okay, but I'll help," he insisted.

"I can do it, Dad," she moaned.

"It's hard to start, Emily," I offered. "Once you get going, I bet you can do it."

Denis had to help her push to get going, and at the turn, he gave her the basket of cuttings while I held open the bag for her. After that, in true male form, he took over and even re-mowed the parts we had done to our loud objections.

"It was long and just needed another go over."

While I disconnected the battery and turned the lawnmower over to brush it clean, Denis went around the lawn edges, pulling up some weeds. I didn't discourage him. I smiled at the thought of him tending my other 'garden' at some point, which sent some warmth swirling in my lower quarters. To distract myself, I asked Emily to get our ice creams out of the freezer, and she ran in. Denis looked over his shoulder from his crouching position and shot me a smile.

"She's great," I confirmed.

"No idea how I had anything to do with it, but yeah, she is."

***

Proudly, I mowed the grass myself a couple of weeks later, though pulling up the nettles and thistles was harder on my knees. I rewarded myself with a slice of cake and a cup of herbal tea. I recently found a great brand that delivered and tried to keep my caffeine intake down. The treat wouldn't help my knees, though.

Denis and I had exchanged numbers the last time, and before long, we were bringing in each other's parcels. One particularly windy day, I chased his empty food bin down the road before it got squished. Our texting became friendly exchanges about our lives. I got the lowdown on his marriages, and he supported my worries about leaving my kids in the USA. It was great to get a dad's perspective that was not their dad.

One Friday afternoon in early December, my phone beeped.

Denis:

> Hi, I'm in London and missed my train. I won't be able to pick Emily up from football practice. I can arrange for her friend's mum to take her to my house, and I wondered if you could look after her. Yours or mine, it's up to you. She has a key. If not, I'll ask her mum, but I don't want to get it in the neck, and Emily wants to be at mine tonight.

Joanna:

> Of course. I'll see what she wants to do. Will she have eaten?

Denis:

> No, but I'll pay for whatever you want–for take away or delivery.

Joanna:

> Maybe we'll cook. I'll give her the choice, no worries. Should I get her to call you when she's here?

Denis:

> That would be great.

Joanna:

> No problem.

After calling her dad, Emily chose sausages and chips at mine over any takeaway food. I think she just wanted to try my air fryer out for herself. I said she could, provided we steamed some veggies, too.

"I've got zucchini, cauliflower, broccoli and brussel sprouts."

"No sprouts!"

"Okay, no problem. Everything else?"

"What's zucchini?"

"Courgette. Sorry, I went a bit American on you there."

"Yeah, that's fine."

We then went through a few American English versus English words, which had us both in hysterics, especially when I told her what Americans call a bumbag.

"My dad has a bumbag but calls it a waist wallet. I'll call it a fannypack next time he wears it. But what do they call a—you know—a fanny?"

"A vagina. Americans are forthright." I wasn't embarrassed, but Emily sure was. I raised two daughters and didn't care too much about it. Being the medic, Beth would have chastised me and said that, technically, it was a vulva, but I'm not getting explicit about it to someone else's kid and getting into trouble. Even though I think all women should learn not to be embarrassed about their bodies. Men like to talk about their dicks at every opportunity, after all.

While we waited for dinner to cook, she asked me what I did for a living.

"I'm an editor."

"Like a newspaper?"

"Like books. A newspaper editor is very different. I can work from home, which is cool for me."

"What do you do to the books?"

"I suggest changes to the author that might make the book read better, and I spot errors."

"Like grammar?"

"Yes. Here, why don't you write a paragraph on your dad? Things you like about him. I'll write a paragraph on what I like about you, and we'll compare them." I got out a couple of pens and a notepad. She seemed keen to try it, which encouraged me to believe I wasn't entirely too nerdy for this young person.

I wrote, 'Emily sometimes lives next door to me with her dad. She loves playing soccer, and I hear she scores more goals than anyone on her team. She's curious, funny and has the brightest smile ever. Emily is friendly, and I enjoyed looking after her today. I hope she considers me a friend, as that is how I think of her.'

When she had finished her paragraph, we switched, and I watched as she read mine and blushed, but she also flashed that lovely smile. Her effort was good for nine, as far as I could remember from my children at that age, but she had some repetition of 'my dad' and a long run-on sentence in the middle. I wouldn't edit it, though. All that would do was knock her down.

I gave it back to her.

"I'm going to dish up dinner. Do you want to give yours another try now you've read mine?"

Emily nodded, so I got up and left her to it while I served our meal—no sprouts for her.

When I sat down to eat with her, she returned the two pages. Her second attempt was so much better. Then, I almost burst into tears when I looked at my page. She'd written, 'I'm glad we are friends.' Unable to speak, I wrote, 'Me too', underneath it and handed it back to her to keep. She had crossed out soccer and put football, though, so I kept my composure. We grinned at each other and tucked into our sausages and chips.

"Wash or dry," I asked, holding rubber gloves and a tea towel.

"Dry."

There wasn't a lot because I would run the dishwasher later, but some prep things and the pans from the air fryer.

"Do you have a boyfriend right now?" Emily asked me.

I gave her a crooked smile. "No. Why?"

She shrugged. "I wondered how long it takes people who get divorced to meet someone they like."

"I guess it depends. Some people don't enjoy being alone and will be very active in trying to meet someone. I prefer to take my time. Get my mind in the right place and get to know someone. I'd rather take my time to find that special person before I get too involved. Neither way is wrong."

"Is there someone you like?" She was fishing, but whether under her own steam or Denis had put her up to it, I didn't know.

"Oh, is there a boy you know who likes me?" I put on a girly voice and clutched pretend pearls.

"I think my dad does."

"And he's pretty special, right?"

She gave me a sheepish grin.

I ripped off the rubber gloves and swiped at the fairy liquid bubbles on my t-shirt—time to change the subject.

"What do you want to do now?"

"What were you going to do?"

"I have Christmas cards to write, but we could watch TV while I do them, or do you have to write some?"

"I'd like to do some for my mum, dad and grandparents."

"Come on then. I have some spare ones for you to use. My sister crafts cards and sells them via her website. You can pick out some fun ones. I bought a stack off her."

"What will you use?"

"I have plenty, and I'll buy some more if I need to. When you give them to your family, show them the back. See, the website is on there."

When I spotted her yawning, I suggested we go over to her dad's house so she could go to bed. I took my laptop with me to edit until Denis got home. How strange it felt to keep an ear out for a child again and wait for her father to come home. It was nearly eleven by the time he made it. The poor man looked so tired I beat a hasty exit and left them to it.

***

The day after my birthday, I was putting up a series of photos on my lounge wall when my new doorbell made my watch tingle on my arm. I'd treated myself to a set of twelve photo frames for professional photos of waves and other sea original prints I bought from the photographer's website.

I answered the door with a photo frame under one arm while I tried to peel one of those sticky hanging strips off my finger. Denis looked well turned out, though casual, and the blue polo shirt brought out the blue in his eyes so well that my tummy did a little skippity-skip. I was hot, sweaty with my hair escaping its tie, and I'm sure the lounge trousers I wore had a couple of holes up the arse seam. I hoped they were low enough to be between my legs and out of sight.

"Hi," he said before lunging forward to grab the frame slipping from my elbow's grasp.

"Oh!" was all I managed as Denis nearly bumped me. He was pretty spry for a man not much younger than me with a little tummy on him, and his cool hand circled my wrist to steady me.

"Can I help?" He indicated the picture frame as he turned it over to view the photo. "Nice. You didn't take this, did you?"

I laughed. "No way. The guy who does these is an Australian surfer and gets right in the water. I don't quite see me doing that."

He laughed, too. "Let me help you." Competently, he removed the sticky strip from my finger. "You know you're supposed to stick these together, not to your fingers."

"I managed one already." I gestured to the lounge indignantly, and he looked over my head through the door. "The doorbell surprised me, is all."

"I've got a bit of time to help with a couple of these if you want an assistant." He slipped off his sneakers as he spoke and followed me into the room. I gave a surreptitious sniff, but his feet didn't smell bad, and he had his own teeth—*Jackpot, Mum.*

With a quizzical look at my smirk, he took over. He picked up the pack of strips and started applying them to the frame he'd rescued. I wanted to do it myself, but enjoyed how his big hands moved as he carefully lined up the strips. Before removing the backing paper, he asked, "Where do you want it?"

I waved vaguely towards the first frame.

"Why didn't you pull out the sofa?"

"Because I'm not as tall as you, and the sofa is heavy."

"I don't want to climb over your furniture. Let's pull this out."

"Wait. If you do that, I'll have difficulty putting it back when I've finished."

He glanced at me and then at the sofa. "I can pop in later. Actually, I came over to see if you wanted to come out for a meal with me and Emily tonight. She keeps pestering me to ask you."

"She wants me to come out?" I couldn't help but smile. She really was the sweetest kid, with a massive grin that you can't help but smile back at.

"We both do, of course. Okay, her pestering has given me an excuse to ask you. Just casual. Fun. No expectations."

"Sure. For Emily. I'm glad it's casual cos I don't do dress-up."

"I figured that. Right, let's move this sofa then."

When he had moved behind it to position the second frame, he held it level with the first one so they were side by side. What was he thinking? Two rows of six evenly spaced apart or three rows of four? I was tempted to let him go ahead and rearrange them in the scattered pattern I wanted later, but then he'd see it when he came in to move the sofa back. Plus, I was done doing things like a man wanted to and saying nothing.

"I was thinking—I was hoping to—What I'm going to do is this." I held up my page with the scattered arrangement I'd drawn out.

"Really? That hurts my head."

"It's going to look great."

"Okay, what number is this?"

I'd numbered the frames on my drawing. I think he liked that part.

"Two, of course." I grinned, and he just laughed at himself, a deep rumbling in his chest that I knew I would feel vibrating right through my bones if he did it when holding me tight.

After he left, I finished the job at hand and then decided I'd better have a shower. I didn't dress up or do my makeup, but the minimum I could do was shower, blow dry my hair and put on clean clothes. When they rang the bell to pick me up, Denis bustled in to move the sofa.

"I can't even look at those photos all higgle-de-piggle-de."

I encouraged Emily to come in to show her the wall while we watched Denis reposition the sofa.

"I love it," she declared, which was enough for me to give Denis a victorious smirk.

***

The evening was fun, just the three of us. I told Emily stories about New York City and Niagara Falls and promised to show her photos. She showed me pictures on her phone of her football team that she told me off for calling soccer. Some words just stuck after such a long time away. Beth was a soccer player in her youth. I think she still has a game now and again.

Denis asked me to come in for coffee when we got back, but I didn't want to impose on his time with Emily.

"I'm going to bed anyway," she said with her bright smile.

"Then I don't want to disturb that." Neither of them could budge me. Instead, I offered an opportunity. "Perhaps another time?"

When I got inside my house, I locked the door, put the kettle on and went upstairs to tie up my hair and put on my pyjamas. As I descended the stairs, my doorbell buzzed on my wrist again. It tingled right up my arm. Damn, it was Denis, and I'd already taken off my bra. I opened the door with my arm under my boobs.

"Denis, is something wrong?"

"Yes. I didn't get to kiss you goodnight. Can I?"

Nothing is sexier than when a man asks permission. I gave a little nod, and while no squimper escaped my throat, it was kind of close. I expected cupping my face and a light brush of lips, but instead, he stepped right into my personal space, pushed me back against the outside of the open door, and devoured my mouth. It was no big mouth and invasive tongue—I've had that happen before, and yuck.

His lips were soft and sensual, his tongue warm and a little chocolatey from our dessert. I could only enjoy and wrap my arms around his neck to keep upright. Unfortunately, that meant my ladies were loose and free for him to run his hands up my sides to cup over my silky pyjama top. I was embarrassed because my boobs had sagged in recent years, and as I thought to pull away, he groaned, his erection pushing up against my tummy. Well, I thought, perhaps I shouldn't worry about it if he's getting that much enjoyment from a kiss and a grope. My hands went to his hair, and I pulled him further into the kiss.

"You aren't wearing a bra," he said when he finally released my lips. His arms snaked behind me, pulling me away from the support of the door. I leaned against him, and the chuckle that erupted from him shook right through me in a wave of pleasure I had thought I might never feel again—that body closeness, the heat and the comfort.

"That was—" I hesitated, feeling emotional from the connection.

"—a perfect end to the night. I had a lovely time, Jo."

"Me too. Thank you, that was some kiss."

"Nice to know I still have moves."

"Back at ya. Goodnight."

"Sweet dreams."

Oh, yeah.

***

I rode the high of that kiss with Denis for a few nights. I'd seen him driving past in his car with Emily, and they exchanged a friendly wave with me. If he was that good at kissing, how good would he be at everything else? I chastised myself at the thought. One kiss wasn't a promise of sex from either of us. I had no idea how slow he might want to take things after his divorce, nor, when it came down to it, how slow I might want to take it.

It was approaching Christmas Day when I saw Emily heading into their house one day and gave her a 'Happy Christmas.' She said the same and dashed into the house. I still loved that grin.

Somebody had parked their car outside their house all the night before, and I wondered if it was that of a girlfriend. A man who kissed the way Denis did wouldn't be single for long. Perhaps he had wanted me to message him, whereas I was waiting for him to make the next move. Oh well, I assessed my feelings on it. Being neighbours, it might have made things awkward if we had sex and then nothing progressed beyond that. Aside from the thrill of kissing him, I felt friendly towards him rather than romantic. It might have gone further if nurtured, but we'd both have to be willing.

Christmas Eve, I got up the nerve to message him.

Joanna:

Merry Christmas. Hope you have a fun day tomorrow.

Denis:

You too. Should be a good one.

Joanna:

Will you get to see Emily? Wish her the best from me.

Denis:

I will do. I'm having Christmas dinner with her and her mum. I probably should've told you, but we're giving it another go.

Joanna:

It would have been nice of you to say before now, but I get it. I wish you the best of luck.

Denis:

> Thanks. We'll see how it goes. I'll let you know if it doesn't work out.

I interpreted that as me being a consolation prize if he didn't get what he really wanted. *Er, no thanks.*

Joanna:

> Either way, I'm happy to be your neighbour and friend.

Denis:

> Ouch.

I didn't know what to reply, except 'What did you expect?' That sounded more bitter than how I felt. I just wanted to set out the reality for him. I think he got it when he said—

Denis:

> Fair enough.

Joanna:

> I thought so. Seriously, though, pal, have a great day tomorrow, and when you get a chance, tell Emily she's welcome over here anytime. I'll pop her card through your letterbox tomorrow. Merry Christmas.

Was that a double fuck you? I said she was welcome, but didn't say he was. I don't know, but I'd got her an iTunes gift card, and the kid needed to know nothing her parents did was to do with anything she did. I told my kids that, and they're adults.

Denis:

> You're a good friend. Thanks.

You've got no idea, mate.

FRIENDS

Friends are to have fun with
Friends don't let you down
Friends talk when you are happy
Friends will hug when you frown

They will listen when you need to vent
And defend you right or wrong
Their eyes well up if you are sad
Or they'll join you in a song

Friends keep you going step by step
Through the mire so deep
When you make it to the other side
Those are the friends you keep

When you blame yourself at lowest point
When tears fall unchecked, unbidden
Friends tell you true where it should lie
Those friends never stay hidden

If inspiration strikes

Friends encourage or will join you
Create, motivate and innovate
To strive for something new

The dust settles the view you see
The spoils are yours to share
True friends are still at your side
Your future bright and clear.

NINE

January was rather cold and icy to bother with much. I mooched around my house, trying to motivate myself to tackle some paperwork, get my finances in order and be ready to file my taxes. It wouldn't be cheap, but getting an accountant to do them was worth it. I would have to pay taxes to US and UK governments, but at least I could offset one against the other. It just depended on what each of them charged.

Denis was back with his wife. I'd see them drive past and always wave and smile. Emily looked so happy, and I couldn't wish her anything different. As good as Denis' kiss was, there was no guarantee things would have progressed much further with us. But he had awakened something in me with that kiss, and I resented him for it a little.

My kids video called me looking so hangdog that I was sure someone was dying. *Is it me?* Turns out it was my ego. Bruce was living with someone new, adding to my misery. That wasn't the worst of it. The worst was that when he moved out of the house so I could sell it, he moved out to live with her. He said it was the apartment of a friend from work but didn't say she was the friend and was still in the apartment. When I was trying to save our marriage, was he sending dick pics to her? Why didn't I see it? Maybe I didn't want to.

"Sorry, Mom," Holly sounded contrite. No doubt because she always defended her father. He's her father, though, so that's fair enough.

"Hey, it's not for any of you to be sorry, but thanks. I'm going to have to process this. It makes me glad that I confronted your dad before I knew, but he didn't have the balls to come out with it."

"Mom." Beth shuddered as she said it. "I don't want to think about Dad's balls."

"He doesn't have any, Beth. That's what Mom's saying," Ethan pointed out.

I tuned them out while they argued about their father's balls, or lack thereof. It was all very humorous, but I was trying to analyse my feelings.

"You okay, Mom?"

"Sure, just thinking, if people fall out of love with someone, why can't they just say that? I'd respect that more than having an affair."

Matt, who'd appeared on Ethan's screen during the ball-talk, said, "Some people like the thrill of an affair, Jo. Or for some, it's finding out if they like this other person enough to leave their spouse."

"But how can they love their spouse, or even the other person, if they cheat on them? At least I don't have to get tested. It'd been years since your dad bothered with that kind of intimacy. I guess he went elsewhere for it, but it wasn't like he couldn't have had it at home."

"OMG, TMI! *TMI!*" That was Beth again.

"What's her name?"

"Sandi, with an 'i' apparently," Holly offered. "I'm not inviting her round for Thanksgiving."

"Don't be silly. She'll be your stepmother if he marries her. You might like her," I suggested. With me not in the country, it was easier to say that. Had I still been there, I'm not sure I could've been so generous. "Anyway, you've got to feel for her. Anyone who cheats with a married spouse has to know that he'd be capable of doing the same to them, given time. I'm sure that doesn't feel good."

"Hey, Mom," Ethan spoke with genuine sincerity in his eyes. "Are you going to be okay? I was hoping to visit in the summer. Matt and I plan to tour some of the UK, maybe go to Ed-in-borrow. We can come sooner if you need us, or I can at least." Matt, still hovering at his shoulder, kissed Ethan's neck.

I smiled. My kids knew how to say Edinburgh correctly; he was trying to cheer me up in his way. "I'm good. Or I will be, at least. I'll get on a call with Teena and Abby and vent to my gal pals."

"You need some besties over there. Have you looked up any old school friends yet?" Holly suggested.

She was right. I had to get out more here. I needed to get out of my funk.

***

A few days later, Teena, Abby and I coordinated a call. I'd already filled them in on what had happened with Denis and the news about Bruce.

"Get yourself a lovely new notebook or fancy journal," Teena advised. "You know how much you love new stationery. Then write about it. Not necessarily for a book or anything, but for yourself. It will help you work it all through in your mind."

"That's a great idea, Teena," Abby agreed. "You never know, Jo. You might end up writing a book about all this."

"Yeah." I was still mopey. Sulks are very addictive and challenging to shake sometimes. "Jo and her Disasters with Men. I must be allergic to them."

"You just need to find the right one," Teena offered.

"Jo's Search for a Hypoallergenic Man?" I suggested with a laugh.

"Or maybe you'll end up quite happy to be alone," Abby said. "As much as I love George, there are days—"

"One hundred percent," Teena said.

"I think being single might be the best thing for me. But for right now, it sucks."

"Allow yourself some time to grieve these recent developments," Teena said. "But don't let it drag on too long. Bruce has had enough of your life. You don't owe him any more time because of his assholery."

I snorted. Teena had a way with her expressions.

"Exercise is a good idea. What do you like doing? Yoga? Hiking?" Abby's comment made me groan.

"I suppose swimming, but I'm not even sure if my swimsuit fits me anymore."

"Treat yourself to a new one."

"Teena, you don't have the idea of treats right. They're supposed to be cakes, chocolate or wine—or all three."

"A treat is whatever you need that is good for you at that time. It doesn't have to be food or alcohol."

"I know you're right, but I'm not ready yet. The notebook idea is good, though." I never could resist a bit of stationery.

After catching up with their lives, I hung up from my dear friends and made myself a cup of tea. I'll admit I got a piece of chocolate cake from the fridge and put it on a plate. Armed with my version of treats, I went to my computer to peruse journals.

***

I allowed myself a week of moping. Okay, I'll admit, it was more like two. Then I located the nearest leisure centre with a pool, stuffed workout gear, and a swimsuit in a bag with some towels and headed out. Getting some exercise should give me a good feeling, right? Endorphins—or are they called endolphins if you get them when in the pool? After paying my dues and booking a session with some young, very fit (in the healthy sense—if you please) instructor to learn how to use the weights and machines, I squeezed my reluctant flesh into the bright red swimsuit and made it out to the pool.

It was frustrating to wait to use the exercise machines because I exercised a lot when I was younger. I guess the machines have changed over the decades, and I should be patient.

I checked out the lane markers—slow lane was the one for me. I started with a breaststroke. Who was I kidding? I could only do breaststroke. Someone in the moderate-speed lane was lapping me. For every one of my lengths, she did two. When I stopped at the shallow end to get a good look at her, I was sure I was correct as to who she was. I wasn't keen on making a fool of myself if I was wrong, but I was at least ninety-five percent certain. She stopped beside me, and I ventured, "Didn't you used to be Ivy Porter?" I giggled because it was a take on a line from my favourite movie, Shirley Valentine. I really want to see the play one day.

She looked over. "Joanna, is that you?"

"Yes, in the flesh, literally." I wrestled a side boob more modestly into my swimsuit. "How are you? When was the last time we saw each other?"

"School. I don't want to think about how many decades that is. I've just finished if you want to catch up." She gestured to the tables behind the glass windows that lined the pool.

"Sure." Any excuse to get out of swimming more lengths. Plus, I had met no old friends since I'd been back. As the kids said, it was about time. We agreed to meet by those tables, and I considered what wonders the vending machines might hold.

I gathered my bag from my locker and went down the rows of tiny changing cubicles. I'd rather shower at home in the comfort of my walk-in shower. At the end was a perpendicular row of family cubicles against the wall. I snuck into one to peel myself out of my wet swimsuit, dry and dress myself without knocking my elbows against the side walls as I would in a regular-sized one. When I exited, I avoided the accusing gaze of a woman with her toddler. There was another cubicle available, so what was her problem?

Ivy sat at a table, brushing her long-wet hair out. I'd tied mine back in a ponytail, my face already flushed from the humidity in the pool area and changing rooms. She had a recyclable bottle of water in front of her, and I eyed the chocolate protein bars in the vending machine behind her—I'd do without. It wasn't like I'd swum enough lengths to work it off.

"Hey, there you are. I don't have long because I must get back to my dog grooming business. I give myself Monday mornings off these days and make the most of them."

"Dog grooming, that's fabulous."

"Do you have a dog?"

She looked hopeful, and I hated to disabuse her, but I wasn't about to buy a dog just to cover up a lie. "No. I just got divorced, and thankfully, I don't have to care for anyone but myself now."

"Good plan. I got divorced, too. Took care of the house and raised the kids, then he went off and had an affair. I got the house and the dog, but I needed a vocation. My place is in Horseshoe Hamlets."

"What? My mum's Horseshoe Hamlets?"

"One and the same. Mrs Sherwood didn't tell you?"

"No, she didn't, the secretive little minx. I know she keeps some plants behind the old stables, but I haven't had time to check it out."

"Some plants? You could say that. Do you remember Harriet Sadler?"

"Yes. Is Harriet still into books?"

"You could say that, too. Harriet runs 'The Reading Stable'. It's the bookshop that started it all at the Hamlets. She contacted your mum about doing the place up when the pandemic hit. She knew a father-and-son contractor business that needed some work. They stayed there while they worked to keep up with regulations. She would pay them in lieu of her first year's rent on the shop, and once it was complete, she roped Toni Banner in to run a tearoom there. Toni got into cooking when she married an Italian chef. Her name is Tortini, now."

"Toni Tortini? And your dog grooming business is there?"

"Yep, going around the horseshoe, there's Harriet's place, my dog grooming, Daisy Timmons' craft shop, The Pottery Place, a candle shop and Toni's Tearoom."

"That's amazing. I'll go over when we leave here and check it out. I think Mum is there this morning."

"Your mother is inspirational. She's helped us so much—all women with different stories."

"All tales as old as time? But not the ones they make princess stories about."

"Exactly."

"What does Harriet do these days? Is she married?"

"Never married. Harriet goes on 'European Adventures' as she calls them. She runs The Reading Stable at the Horseshoe. She has various groups running from there and tries to educate as many kids as possible in literature through various clubs. We should get together so Harriet can tell you all about it. Book Club is on a Thursday, but perhaps we need somewhere just to chat."

"How about my place? I moved back here last year from the USA after my divorce. We could compare notes. I'll invite Toni, Daisy, and Harriet when I pop in this morning. You're all high achievers with your businesses. I'm feeling a little inadequate."

"None of us got to live in America, though. Do you work? Daisy constantly talks about retiring and just doing her crafts that someone else can sell in the shop, but she loves the face-to-face with the customers. I think she'd miss it."

"I'm a book editor. What's the current Book Club read?"

"We just started the Redway Acres series. Do you know it? They made a miniseries out of the first book."

I couldn't help the smug grin. "I edited it, and I met Sam Harmer on the plane ride here last year."

"Well, forget all our businesses. *That's* really amazing. I'll get us all on a WhatsApp chat, and we'll sort a date to come over to you. I've got to dash."

"So great to see you, Ivy."

***

"Mum," I called as I trudged around the back of the newly updated stable buildings, now Horseshoe Hamlets' shops. I stopped short at the sight. My mum was elbow-deep in rows of tiny earth pots in trays on a large trestle table. As I approached, I noticed her pop a few beans into one, press the earth gently over them, and then move to the next.

"Oh, Joey, you're here. Great, you can help me plant these seeds." She pointed to a bag labelled parsnips (shudder) and the trays opposite, which were already filled with pots of soil.

Obediently, I began planting and glanced around me. Rows and rows of raised plant beds lined the ground that had once been a field for parking for anyone attending the racetrack. Grass walkways ran in a grid around them. Behind my mum, two large greenhouses held multiple shelves with rows of the same trays already planted. A young man appeared from one of them.

"These are the other broad beans, Sean," Mum said and thanked him as he removed the tray from the table. She pulled out another and began arranging pots in it.

I finally found my voice. "Mum, what's going on here?"

"We're planting for the spring and summer, Joey. We have to put them in the greenhouse so they survive. Sean pops over to water them. He lives about a mile away, but he uses the delivery tricycle. I don't mind."

"Delivery tricycle?" I felt like someone yanked me out of time and dropped me into an alternate universe. She gestured to the side of one greenhouse where the vehicle rested with a huge trailer, presumably for deliveries. "No, I meant all of this. The shops and everything. Why didn't you tell me?"

"Oh, Joey. You had so much on your plate that I didn't want to worry you with any of it. Then, it seemed like a big thing to tell you all at once. I'm sorry. I hope you weren't too shocked. Wait until you see this place in full bloom."

"Here, I thought I had to come home to look after you, and you have built this entire community. I'm so proud of you, Mum."

"We're proud of each other then."

We carried on planting tray after tray for the rest of the morning, with Sean organising them all in the greenhouses. After which, we washed up and went to get lunch in Toni's Tearoom. As we sat there, each of my old school friends popped in, and we chatted for a while before arranging a date for them all to come to mine for a ladies' evening.

My endorphins were high that afternoon, but I don't think the exercise contributed to them.

***

I'm going to find a cleaner for my little home. Admittedly, I should do it myself, but I'd been working flat out, and when I'm not editing, I've been at the leisure centre. I can't say I feel much better for it yet, as everything aches, but my knees don't hurt as much.

With my girlfriends visiting me this coming weekend, I figured I should make the place reasonably clean for them, and I spent a good portion of the day before scrubbing, dusting and sneezing—so much dust—the downside of living on a building site.

Everyone brought one dish for us to eat, and we had covered savoury and sweet. I promised to provide the wine, not that we'd drink much because my friends would all be driving, and a constant supply of tea or coffee. By the time the evening arrived, I was a bag of nerves. From what Ivy said, they all seemed to be successful businesswomen. I didn't think they'd look down on me, but I felt inadequate anyway.

I needn't have worried. It turns out that my friends were all very interested in hearing about life in the USA. Honestly, it wasn't much different from life here. We just got to vacation more easily to Boston, Niagara Falls, Cape Cod, skiing in Vermont, plays and sight-seeing in New York City, museums in Washington D.C. and the obligatory trips to Disney World in Florida. None of which I enjoyed much because it was still my job to look after the kids, decide what and where we ate, pack and unpack and repack bags and wash clothes. At least at home, I could do all those things more easily. I'd be happy never to get on a plane again, except if the kids needed me, but hopefully, they'll visit here.

Bruce loved to say, 'Let's fly by the seat of our pants and just eat when we find a place.' The trouble with that was three kids would never go for that. They wanted to eat when they were ready, would only eat certain things and never the same thing at the same time. If sushi were the only thing available when they were ready to eat, it wouldn't fly. They would be miserable until we could find a Burger King. Ethan denies that now. He thinks he invented sushi, the way he talks about it.

I regaled the ladies with the story of Bruce saying, 'I don't know'. Before long, as I mentioned each part, they were chorusing, 'I don't know' along with me. I have to admit that it felt great. But it wasn't all about me. Ivy told her divorce story. Daisy arranged the beautiful bouquet they had brought me—apparently, Daisy sold them as part of her craft shop. The other day, I'd seen inside it, like a treasure trove. I could spend a week there trying to find all the different riches. I wondered if she sold cards and how she would feel about having a local cardmaker's merchandise to sell in her shop. She said she'd call Susan about it.

Toni had baked her famous chocolate cake—so moist with chocolate ganache filling, fresh whipped cream, and chocolate shavings on top. If I had a shop next to her teashop, I would double in size in a month. Then Harriet got going about her bookshop, The Reading Stable. I could tell it was her passion.

Unlike Daisy's craft unit, The Reading Stable was all shades of purple with black trim. It had a black, wrought iron sign swinging at one end with book spines cut out and a child at each end of the row of books with open books in their hands. The shop's name hung down from the sign, each word swinging on chain links to connect it to the bottom of the books. It would be a fabulous place to have Halloween events. I asked Harriet, and she tapped her long purple-painted fingernails together with an evil smile.

"Halloween is Harriet's favourite holiday," Daisy exclaimed.

I would have to take plenty of photos for my kids. It was a favourite of theirs, too. One of the few boxes I hadn't unpacked was their collection of Halloween costumes. I couldn't persuade any of them to keep them, and despite Teena's protest, I couldn't bear to part with them. Perhaps I could put them to use this coming Halloween?

Harriet waxed lyrical about the children's corner in her shop with little tables and chairs where after-school and holiday story reading happened. Students from the local college volunteered to read to the little ones for experiences they could then write about in their personal statements for university. Many returned often to see the next generation take it over and impart tips.

"So, what about book club?" I asked her. "When are you reading Redway Acres?"

"Oh, yes. Ivy told me you edited it. Nice work."

"And she met Sam Harmer on her plane back over here."

"I didn't tell you about my dream, though." I imparted my story and had them in hysterics.

"Could you imagine having sex in a plane loo?" Daisy wondered. Clearly not enthused by the idea.

"Well, I imagined it, but thankfully that was all."

When they all left in their various cars, I realised what I'd been missing out on and looked forward to the book club. An idea came to me about a surprise I could hopefully arrange.

***

The night of the book club, I drove over and parked early to browse the shops beforehand. Besides the tearoom, The Reading Stable, the dog groomer, Daisy's crafts, and Mum's gardens, there was a candle shop with candle melts and various holders and a pottery shed with an active wheel. There were some fantastic pieces of animals in that shop. I'd have to come back to see everything.

Last, I browsed The Reading Stable. I bought a few books for my pleasure and was pleased to see many of the books I'd edited on prominent display. In fact, Harriet's displays featured female writers far more than male ones. I loved this because usually, in bookstores or supermarkets, the most prominent shelves of new releases, nonfiction and so on were primarily male writers. Frankly, the men didn't need the extra prominence, in my opinion.

I helped Toni as she brought in a food supply and poured myself a small glass of wine. Some of those sausage rolls and a piece of Victoria sponge would soon soak up the alcohol so I could drive home.

In addition to me and my four friends, over half a dozen other women were in the room. The candle maker, potter, three late-running customers who stayed, and the potter's two adult teen daughters attended, too. I kept checking my phone.

"You got a hot date after this, Jo?" Harriet giggled. She was in her element in her shop, surrounded by books.

"Just waiting for a surprise."

"For tonight?" Her eyes sparkled. I was sure she'd guessed.

"I hope so. I might have a video call for you all, but don't say anything in case it doesn't happen."

"Just let me know when."

Harriet led the group by first getting people's overall opinions and then asking specific questions about the plot and characters. She was very knowledgeable and had some great insights. Then she introduced me as the editor, and I talked about conversations I'd had with the author and offered everyone a signed copy of the newest book. I reached into a box hidden under the food table and passed them out. Promising Harriet she could sell or raffle the rest. The book had only come out last month, and these were hardbacks.

My phone buzzed.

Sam:

How many?

Joanna:

A dozen.

Sam:

Great, start the video call.

I nodded at Harriet, who had been watching me intently. She clapped her hands in delight and helped me prop my iPad against some books facing everyone. I started the call and crossed my fingers. Then his handsome face appeared, and a room full of grown women did a *squee* and a collective *sigh*. I had to hand it to him; the man was a good sport.

He was in the back of a car, perhaps heading out for the night, but he dressed casually.

"Hello, ladies. How is your evening going? How did you like the book?"

Everyone answered at once, and he laughed.

Harriet efficiently took over again, getting them to ask questions one at a time. Before I knew it, he was clambering out of the car but had no intention of cutting short the call. Was he going to a club or a bar? It seemed pretty quiet.

"Hey, everyone. I'm just bringing a friend in to meet you."

The door to the bookshop opened.

"Jo, you in here?" Sam called.

I heard him simultaneously through my iPad and at the front of the shop. I exchanged a surprised look with Harriet before we both did a silent squee.

"Back here, Sam." I rounded a bookcase so he could see me and walked straight into the tall, slim frame of Enrique Perez, who played Capitao Duarte Matias in the miniseries. The man was even more handsome in person than Sam, and I must have blushed from my cleavage up and over my forehead.

"Jo?" I nodded. "Sam said you were cute."

There was a definite squimper.

***

Sam and Enrique read out a couple of scenes for us all, then signed everyone's copy of the second book. They took selfies with everyone before heading out to catch a flight to mainland Europe from Norwich airport. I was concerned they might be late, but I supposed they held a flight for you when you were that famous, or perhaps it was a private flight—I hadn't asked.

"I'd love to connect again, Jo," Sam said.

"Sure, anytime. I'm a hit here now, thanks to you. Though turning up in person was above and beyond."

"One day, I might want to write my memoirs and need an excellent editor."

"I don't think you'll have any trouble finding one."

"I'll need one I can trust."

"Safe travels." I let him go with a shake of my head. The man was in his thirties, but the younger man, who'd lost his mum at such a crucial time, still showed through. I felt very protective of him and needed to call my children later.

160

After everyone else left, Harriet and I helped Toni clear up, and we all took some supplies home with us. I was going to eat well tomorrow. I also had my copy of the second Redway Acres book, signed by the author, with Sam and Enrique's signatures. It was to be the book club's next read, and from my recollection, it had plenty of plot twists to discuss.

THE ONE THAT GOT AWAY

He was the one that got away
But maybe so was she
At school, inseparable every day
At parties, they would smooch and sway

Let's not ruin it, they agreed
Let's be friends forever
Despite their love and teenage need
To always be together

Then they went different ways
Universities and countries
Marriage, jobs and babies
Expanding family trees

But social media wasn't letting
Two hearts stay lost that way
And rectified the separation
From the One That Got Away

TEN

A fter the book club's success with Sam, my friends and I had another gathering, this time at Daisy's. She lived in a modest detached house close to her family's home when she was younger, which I remember visiting. Daisy reflected flair for arts and crafts in her home and garden as much as in her shop. It was busy but not cluttered, colourful but not overpowering, and homely but no less stylish for that. Of her four children, one teenager remained at home, but Daisy's husband, Ted, was taking their son to a football match and then out for burgers. What more could the boy want besides quality time with his father? I felt a pang at recalling Bruce taking Ethan to Yankee games alone after the girls had left home and could no longer go with them.

With the house to ourselves, the five of us poured some wine and nibbled at some snacks while our main course of an authentic Italian lasagna, courtesy of Toni's husband, heated in the oven. It smelled delicious. Our first subject of discussion was the equally delicious Sam Harmer attending Harriet's last book club event. I confirmed I hadn't heard anything more from Sam and wouldn't give any of them his mobile phone number.

I'd put his agent in touch with my boss at Sam's request, but that didn't mean they would agree to terms. They might also prefer an established ghostwriter to an editor or a different publishing company. I didn't mention this to my friends, as I had no idea how serious Sam was about going to bat for me to work on his book.

We were mostly silent as we ate, making noises that, to any non-observer, could've been quite sexual. No wonder Toni was a happy lady these days, with food like this as foreplay. It isn't only a man's heart that can be reached through his stomach. We took our glasses to the lounge and let the main course settle before tackling the tiramisu dessert in Daisy's fridge.

"No, leave everything," Daisy said as I moved to clear my plate from the table. "I always clear up after Ted's poker nights, and he's promised to clear up tonight."

"That's very good. No wonder you two have stuck it out all these years," I commented. "Was there ever anyone else you fancied at school besides Ted?"

Daisy gave a considered look as we all settled in her comfortable lounge seats draped with throws and quilts. "If I'm confessing to a school crush, you all are, too. We'll each tell our story, then write the name and show them at the end." She reached over to the drawer of a bookshelf unit, took out pens and paper to pass around, and began her tale. "There was someone I had fancied for two years of sixth form before he asked me to slow dance at a party. I tried to kiss him but only managed his cheek before he said he knew Ted was head over heels for me, so he couldn't kiss me. I was annoyed at the time. Why ask me to dance if he didn't like me that way? He said he did but couldn't hurt Ted, and I should think about kissing him instead. I cried for two nights, then started noticing Ted more, and there was never anyone else."

"Wow, Daisy, you never even kissed anyone else?" Ivy asked. "I kissed a lot of frogs before the one I thought was my prince, but he turned out to be a dud, too, in the end."

"But you have your prince now," Harriet pointed out.

"Or maybe your white knight?" I said.

"Oh yes, white knight," Ivy mused. "I love that. But here's my school crush story. There was a boy on our street who I walked to school with every day in middle school. He carried my bag for me and held my hand, and I thought he was my boyfriend, though we never said. On the last day of school, before we moved up to High School, he kissed me square on the lips and then ran off. His family went away for the entire summer, and the next year, when we started High School, we were in different classes, and he never spoke to me again. I had a lovely summer, to be honest, and didn't think of him too much, but I fully expected we'd be walking to school together again. He ran off and joined a group of boys instead. I don't think he broke my heart because I didn't cry for two nights, but it was a bit bruised. I would have liked to know why, but what were we then, twelve or thirteen? My boys at that age barely spoke a word to anyone."

We all laughed at that. Everyone but Harriet had kids, and the three of us had boys.

"My turn then," Harriet began. "Not that it's that interesting. I was completely obsessed and in love with the same boy from the beginning of High School to the end, but he never even glanced at me. I think we had every class together. I tried to make him notice me at parties, but he never did. That's the complete story—unrequited love. I didn't date anyone until I got to university, and then there was no stopping me, but I think if he walked back in the door right now, I would be madly in love with him all over again."

"Awe, that's so sweet," Toni said. "I'm pretty sure I know who that was because you stopped talking to me when I dated him. I'd say he's my one, too, because I wanted to be his girlfriend so badly, and when it finally happened, I could hardly believe it. One night, we were in my room getting hot and heavy when my sister barged in. She ran off to tell my mum that she'd seen my boyfriend's bum, and he pulled up his trousers and ran off."

At this, we were all rolling around in hysterics.

Toni continued, "The sad thing was, he called me later and called it all off over the phone. That broke my heart, and I didn't forgive my sister for years. It all worked out, though, cos my hubs is the best."

"For sure," I said. "Talking of food, how about that dessert?"

"We will, but you're not getting out of telling your story, Jo," Daisy warned.

"I promise."

As we got up, I held up three fingers in the Girl Guide salute. When we returned full of cream, fruit, and caramelised sugar, sipping our various hot brews, and settled in our seats, I began my school crush story.

"In our first year of high school, I stood in a crowd around a sand-filled long jump pit on sports day. The boys were competing, and the girls were cheering them on. All I could see of the pit was through the legs of everyone in front of me. A cheer went up, and the various legs blocking my view moved for me to glimpse a pair of strong-muscled legs making their way out of the sand."

Astonished by my tingly tummy at seeing this pair of bodiless legs, I pushed through the throng to find out who they belonged to. A boy close to my height was knocking sand off his black shorts and thighs—those very muscular thighs. I was still staring when he turned around and caught me. He grinned, and heat rose in my cheeks so quickly I was surprised I didn't faint.

"Hey, beetroot face," another guy beside the muscled legs shouted at me.

Mortified, I turned and ran away towards my event—the shot putt. Not that I was great at it, but everyone had to do something, and after the sprint heats the previous weeks, I refused to run. I was pretty fast, but once I got boobs, I knew they jiggled a lot when I ran. No one had heard of sports bras back then, and all the boys had lined up along the last ten metres of the track, jeering and leering at those with the biggest boobs. It was so unfair and embarrassing.

My shot putt effort was passable but unremarkable, so the '*nice try*' surprised me from behind me as I stepped out of the throwing circle. It was the boy with the muscly legs. I couldn't help glancing down at them again; my tummy did another little somersault.

He smiled as I tugged down at the hem of my gym skirt—had it flown up when I did the shot putt and shown off my faded navy knickers?

"Thanks," I mumbled. "Did you win the long jump?"

"Second."

"Well done. I won't be placing here."

"At least you tried."

"I should find my friends."

"Yeah, me too."

"A week later, my guy's best friend asked me out—not the one with the beetroot face jibe. We were only together for two weeks, and he was my first kiss, but now I was firmly in the friends-zone from which we never returned. By the sixth form—"

"Um, years 12 and 13, if you please," Harriet interrupted.

"By the sixth form," I stubbornly repeated with a laugh, "when we had nights out at pubs, parties as people turned eighteen and plenty of dancing, we were friends only. Whenever I wanted him to ask me out, he was firmly set on friends or dating someone else. When he seemed about to ask me, I advocated staying friends.

"We were together at a New Year party when midnight struck, and we kissed. It was a perfect kiss. Our lips moved in sync, our tongues brushed each other, and he pulled me into his arms, where I felt more comfortable than I ever had."

The music started again after Auld Lang Syne.

'In your eyes, I can see my dream's reflection

In your eyes, I found the answers to my questions,' George Benson crooned.

He pulled me to the dance floor. "Let's dance. It's our song."

He held me close, quietly singing the words in my ear.

"This is our song?" Five years later, that tingly tummy still happened when I was close to him.

"Yeah, cos we're friends, right?"

"Yes."

'I can see the reasons why our love's alive,' George sang.

"That's why our love will stay alive and always will," he said.

"So, never anything more?" I ventured, unsure which way I wanted him to decide, but knowing whatever he wanted, I would agree.

"There isn't anything better than friends. Friends will last forever."

"Awe, that's so sweet," Daisy said when I'd finished my story.

"Well, it is, and it isn't," I thought aloud. "We're only Facebook friends these days. We both got married and went our separate ways. Might as well have gotten it on back then and seen where it went."

"So," Ivy started a drumroll on the coffee table, "who are our mystery crushes?"

We all put our pieces of paper on the coffee table. Every single one said, 'Nish Jaitly.'

"I knew it," Toni declared.

"Well, I didn't," I countered, a little put out that the boy I'd always considered mine back then wasn't. "He was quite the tart."

"I guessed about you, Jo," Harriet said. "I was jealous of your friendship with him."

"Didn't get me anywhere, though. And where's Nish now?"

"Italy, with a hot Italian partner. I met up with them on my last trip." Harriet's expression looked a little morose, and I made a mental note to ask her about it one day.

"Exactly. We're all better off as we are," I said, hoping I sounded more confident to my friends than I did myself.

***

When I got home that night, I glanced through some of Nish's Facebook posts from Italy and his comments on mine in the past year since I moved back. This one was in my post about arriving back in Norwich last year.

Nish:

> You made it, darlin'. Well done.

I flicked over to his information.

Nish lives in Rome, Italy.
In a relationship.

I hadn't told the ladies earlier in the evening that we made a marriage pact after that New Year's dance. If neither of us were married by the age of thirty, we would give our relationship a try. We'd lost direct contact by thirty, but I'd heard he was married with two young children. I had my three, with Holly, aged six, and Ethan, just a babe in my arms.

Ten years later, during the early twenty-tens, we reconnected over Facebook.

Nish:

> Well, we didn't need the marriage pact at thirty, but as I'm now divorced, let me know if you're considering leaving Bruce. LOL

Joanna:

> Too busy running around watching dance classes and recitals, buying sports equipment and driving to softball and basketball games.

Nish:

> I'm only joking (half). I know you've got it good over there.

Joanna:

> I feel as if Bruce and I barely have time for ourselves, but when the nest is empty in another ten years, we'll wonder where the time went. How are you coping with everything? You seem to be out of the UK a lot, too.

Nish:

> It's a juggle, and I try to be with the kids as often as possible. Not many years before they're off to uni and won't have time for their old dad.

Joanna:

> I'm sure that isn't true. You're a great dad. I've seen the pics on here. We're dealing with my eldest's first heartbreak at the moment. Holly's throwing herself into her schoolwork, and it's making my brain hurt to watch.

Nish:

> Let's check back in another ten years and see where we are.

Joanna:

> Sure, but you'd better not leave it that long to chat with me. No excuse now, as we're both on Facebook.

We'd chatted, I'd liked and commented on his posts, and he'd done the same. Of course, last year had been ten more, but I hadn't messaged him to check the state of his relationship. Nish looked really happy, and I was delighted for him.

It isn't meant to be Jo. Stop torturing yourself. You're still no surer than you were at eighteen.

I put the long distant memories aside. Hopefully, Nish would visit family here soon, and we could connect again. It would be nice to see him and meet his girlfriend.

OLD SHIP

If you want to repeat
What you've done before
Then get a new ship
Never dream of more

But I'm an old ship
My hull's not sleek
My sails get stuck
And I've sprung a leak

My paintwork's chipped
My engine stalls
Cos I've been through storms
Hurricanes and squalls

But if you look beyond
My list to the right
And weathered outside
Well, you just might

See a gem right here

That will not break
To ride with you
On the journeys we take

A comforting friend
With a familiar feel
To join you in
Command of the wheel

But don't expect me to
Obey your palm
You'll be damn glad
When seas aren't calm

Navigating together
Old me and you
Adventures not dreamt of
With a ship that's new

ELEVEN

I usually swam on a Monday morning to meet up with Ivy and chat briefly afterwards. One particular weekend, my boss threw me a book that needed a lot of work. They'd had to let the editor who was working with this author go, and though they didn't think it was the best fit for the author and editor, could I help and get the work done because the deadline was looming? She agreed to pay me double, and I set to work.

There's a reason I like to pace myself when editing. You need to stay fresh; your eyes need to focus, and there are only so many hours a day your arse will let you sit in one place at your computer. By Sunday evening, I'd nearly finished, but my body ached, my mind was mush, and I needed to rest. Luckily, I had until early afternoon UK time on Monday to finish, given that my boss wasn't in the office until nine a.m. Eastern Time. It meant I missed my swim, though.

I forced myself up and out the door Wednesday morning for a swim session at nine-thirty. I knew I would feel better for it. My red swimsuit fitted a little less snugly these days. I wouldn't win any makeover competitions, but I felt more comfortable in my body and clothes, which was good enough for me. Despite my appointment with one trainer to go over the machines in the gym, I still felt very self-conscious, so I tended to stick with the swimming.

They had allocated half the pool to the over-fifties during this session, leaving the remaining three lanes to younger, faster swimmers. Given the many older people who preferred to swim their lengths close to the long wall, I was happy to swim near the rope in the middle of the pool, next to the faster regular lanes.

I still wasn't quick, but I got out of breath less rapidly and took fewer rests than before. After a few lengths, I got into my stride and started to stretch my body. It felt good.

"You have a good technique," a deep voice beside me said when I was out of my depth.

I was so startled, as I was really in a groove, that I sank underwater and came up spluttering. A firm hand grasped my upper arm and pulled me to the deep end wall.

"I'm okay," I said crossly as I roughly pulled my arm away.

"Sorry," he said, putting his hands up, then sinking under the water.

"Daft git," I snorted as he surfaced.

"Seemed only fair. I really am sorry. I thought you were aware I was there."

"I was in a groove, stretching out some kinks."

"Yeah? I'm not the best swimmer, but I used to come with my wife and stopped while she was sick. I missed it, so I took it up again for myself. I don't usually see you here for this session."

"I missed Monday. Should we—?" I gestured we should swim again, feeling awkward with so much skin exposed on both of us, and we swam the length together. I'd no idea if my pace was the same as his or if he just wanted to swim with me. When we reached the shallow end, I turned and headed back down the lane without stopping. He'd mentioned a wife. I didn't want to give him any ideas.

He swam ahead as we approached the deep end, waiting for me to catch up. He spoke before I could make the turn.

"Have we met here before?" He indicated the deep water, and I laughed. I can't help it; I'm a sucker for a sense of humour. Before I could set off again, he blurted out, "I'm Bill and a widower."

I stopped. "I'm so sorry for your loss. Was it recent?"

"Nearly a year now. Were you going to swim off because I mentioned my wife, and you thought I was hitting on you even though I was married?"

"You are hitting on me, then?" I asked with a smirk, and he bellowed so loudly I glanced around to see if people were watching. No one seemed to pay any attention—they probably had left their hearing aids in their lockers. "I'm Joanna, Jo."

"Sorry if that embarrassed you, Jo. I enjoy a sense of humour. I'll keep my bellowing to a minimum if you'll have a drink with me when you've finished your swim."

"Sure. You mean water or juice or something out there, right?" I pointed to the tables where Ivy and I usually sat on Mondays. "Not double vodkas at the Pig and Whistle."

His grin was infectious. "The first, for a start. I'm going in the hot tub while you finish. No rush."

We swam back to the shallow end, and I watched him climb out of the pool and into the bubbling tub, where he warmly greeted an older couple. He had a pretty trim body, though I placed him a little older than Bruce. Then I started swimming again, but I couldn't concentrate. I wondered if he watched me, but I refused to look over. I did ten more minutes, which I thought was a good amount. Less and he'd think I was rushing out to meet up with him; more and he would think I wasn't that interested.

I dressed quickly and dashed out to the little round tables. Bill had procured two bottles of water for us, and yes, I checked that the top clicked as I undid the bottle. I have two daughters whom I schooled to keep themselves safe. I taught Ethan how to treat a girl, but it turned out I didn't need to—though I'm sure he extended all the consideration he should to Matt and vice versa.

We chatted for a while, and I explained why I was there on a Wednesday instead of Monday. Seeing people wave to him as they left or come over to the table to get an introduction to me from Bill was endearing. He was polite and funny, generous with his time. He had two teenage girls still at home, coping well despite losing their mum. I told him about my children and watched closely when I mentioned Ethan's boyfriend. Bill's expression remained open and interested, for which I was glad.

"What do you do for a living?" I asked him.

"I don't anymore. I left work to care for Carolyn, and now I'm there for the girls. We had a lot of insurance, and our house was mortgage-free. It's just a three-bed place, nothing huge. I used to be a hospital porter. You know, getting people from A to B in the hospital or out to their cars, pushing them in a wheelchair. Lots of other things."

"Oh, that makes total sense. You're so at ease with people." I gestured to another couple leaving the leisure centre who gave a cheery 'See you next week, Bill' and a wave.

"See you, Barb. See you, John."

"I rest my case." I laughed, realising how long it had been since I enjoyed a good laugh with a man.

"So, about that stronger drink? Tonight?"

I had to admire his fast-acting determination. So far, I'd admired several things about him. I needed to think about it a bit longer, though. "Tomorrow night?"

"Do you know The Cottage pub? I could meet you there. I'm assuming you would rather go under your own steam?"

"Thank you, yes, I would. Seven o'clock?"

"I'm looking forward to it already."

***

The Cottage pub and restaurant was more pleasant than the pubs I remembered from my school days—not that we'd ever been here. Those were the days when carding someone to check their age wasn't par for the course—we were all eighteen, I swear, m'lord. It had a homey feel, and many of the regulars looked to be in my age group or older. I wondered if I knew any of them, but I was just looking for school-age faces.

Bill was sitting at the bar and stood up as I came in so I could spot him easily. Very considerate. He wasn't a big, bulky man like Bruce or Denis, but he was comfortable in himself, which showed itself in confidence around his aura. Once I'd got my drink, he suggested we sit at a table. I was grateful for that because I didn't want him to see me struggling up onto a bar stool.

Just one glass of white wine for me, I decided. I'd only managed a few bites of toast before coming out as my nerves got the better of me. Other than the night out with Denis and Emily, which could hardly count as we had a chaperone, this was my first date in decades. My hand shook as I raised my glass to take a big gulp, and then I spluttered valiantly, swallowing while my eyes watered. I put the glass back down carefully.

Bill reached across the table and covered my hand with his. "Nervous?"

I nodded.

"Me too, but all we are tonight is a couple of people having a drink and getting to know each other. No pressure—on either of us."

"That sounds good."

"You look nice tonight, if I may say so."

"Thanks, you too." He had made an effort. His face was clear of stubble, and he had run a buzz cutter over his head, which was mostly bald. He smelled freshly showered and wore an ironed button-down shirt paired with jeans.

"Do you ever wear makeup? Carolyn, my wife, would never go out without her face on. Not even for the groceries."

"Oh, I used to. It's a funny story, actually. Before Bruce and I had kids one Saturday, we got a call from friends to meet them for a few drinks in the city. We'd been slobbing around all day, so I put on smarter clothes and makeup. When I came downstairs ready to go, Bruce looked disappointed. 'You put your mask on,' he said. I wasn't that bad at applying makeup, but I hated doing it, so I turned around to go take it off. He thought I was angry and apologised, but I was thrilled.

I'd only put makeup on for him, and given that he didn't like it, I no longer wore any. Now it's my choice."

"Would you choose it if you were with someone who wanted you to?"

"No. I've realised it's not who I am. Would you?"

"Would I what?"

"You know—" I giggled, "—a bit of foundation, a touch of lippy." I followed it up with a kissing sound.

He laughed with me. "No, but makeup is a woman's thing."

"Not true. What about actors? Some men like to make their eyes pop with some guy-liner."

"I suppose that's true. You're very pretty, and with a bit of makeup, I think you'd be a knockout."

I tried not to be insulted and made my point. "Let's say I was willing to put on makeup, wear shape-forming underwear, and wear heels. Then we go to bed, and it all comes off, so you see fine lines and imperfections on my face, all my lumps and bumps not smoothed out and disfigured feet from the heels. How do you feel when I'm no longer a 'knockout'? How do I feel knowing you preferred me before? My body image will deteriorate if I think I have to look a certain way that I don't look without all the get-up. No, thank you. This is me—take it or leave it. Just don't try to change me. Now that's the freedom a man has."

"Fair enough," he conceded. "You look nice tonight, though."

"Thanks. Sorry to go on about it." I almost went to say more, but I thought it was enough for one night. It had taken me a long time to shake off the social conditioning of society concerning women and body image. Every day of my life, I'd seen examples of it online, on TV, in magazines and on social media, and every day, I had to remind myself that who I am is just fine.

"It's fair. No worries. When did you say your son was coming to visit?"

"This summer. I can't wait to see him, and Matt, of course, but my boy most of all."

"Matthew's his boyfriend."

"Yep."

"How did you feel when he came out to you?"

We talked more about Ethan and their planned tour of the UK. Bill mentioned how great Carolyn would've been if any of their children had come out as gay. I forgave him for repeating her name. It must be a massive transition after being married for so long and so in love and then losing someone. Even after divorcing, I mentioned Bruce's name far too often. I'm glad I'd lost that habit—for the most part.

The door to the pub opened, and in walked Daisy Timmons. My shock must have registered on my face cos Bill turned around.

"Do you know her?"

"Yes, I do, the cheeky so-and-so. She knew we were coming here tonight. I guess she wanted to check you out. Oh, that's her husband. I remember him from school."

Bill winked, then sauntered to the bar beside them and leaned over to Daisy. She laughed and gave me a sheepish look over her shoulder, then came over to our table to see me.

"I like him, Jo," she declared as she sat down.

"Do join us, Daisy," I said sarcastically.

"Bill said we should. Is it okay?"

"Well, if Bill said so," I was less sarcastic, but I thought he could've asked me first. It was nice to see him chatting away with Ted. I remembered Ted as an easy-going chap at school, and Daisy was still besotted with him after thirty-five years. You can't argue with that.

"Look who I found at the bar," Bill announced as he arrived with two drinks. Ted was carrying two, too. Bill bought a white wine for me, but I wasn't drinking it when I was going to be driving home. Why hadn't he asked? I was tempted just to sip it a little rather than embarrass him, but I felt embarrassed instead and wasn't going to get a ticket, or worse, to save his blushes. I waited for a better moment to say something.

"Hi, Ted. It's been a long while since I've seen you. Congratulations on your choice of wife. You're lucky to have her."

"One hundred percent. I'm the lucky one, and I was saying the same to Bill. Good to see you, Jo. How are you finding the UK? Glad you're back?"

"I've been back over a year now. It's like I never left—mostly."

"She still says American words," Daisy provided.

"Guilty." I picked up my purse and leaned over to Bill. "I'm just going to get myself a soft drink. I ate little before leaving, and I'm driving."

He wasn't embarrassed at all, but flew into action. "I didn't think. What do you want? I'll get it and a couple of menus. I could eat."

"Well, if you're eating, we can too. We didn't have anything before coming out," Ted said after I gave Bill my drink choice, and he got up to go with Bill.

"I'm happy to pay," I said, but it fell on ears that wouldn't pay any attention as they were in 'go' mode. I shook my head and looked at Daisy helplessly.

"He's so happy to accommodate you. That's nice."

"I feel—managed."

"He said it's the first date he's been on since his wife died," she offered.

Now, I felt terrible and resolved to be less judgmental.

"Sausage and mash?" Bill bellowed from the bar. The man should have been seven feet tall to suit that voice. "That's what we're all having."

"Sure, thank you," I called back. I'm at least feminine enough not to bellow, and I was grateful Bill had consulted me.

"The sausages are local and delicious," Daisy confirmed.

The men came back to the table, Bill carrying my tall orange juice and lemonade. Americans don't do fizzy lemonade, and I missed that drink when I was there. Daisy was right; the food was tasty, and the company was good. As I had learnt at the pool, Bill was a brilliant conversationalist, and he listened too. At the end of the evening, the three of them walked home as they all lived close by, but in opposite directions. Bill and I stood by my car, watching Daisy and Ted wander off hand in hand.

"What a great couple," Bill said.

"And together for so long," I offered. "Thanks, I had a good time."

"Nice practical ride." He gestured to my hybrid.

"I like it, and it's automatic." I grinned because, during the evening, Bill and Ted argued that a manual car was much better to drive, but I wouldn't budge. I'd distracted them by talking about their 'Excellent Adventures'.

Bill laughed, then leaned forward and kissed me. He definitely stirred something in me, but it wasn't quite like Denis' all-consuming kiss.

"Nice," I said when the kiss finished too soon to get into the passionate zone. Perhaps that was purposeful on Bill's part. If this was his first date, kissing another woman had to feel weird.

"Thanks."

"I should go," I offered.

"Drive safely and text me to let me know you're home, would you?"

"Yes, I will." I was a little disappointed he hadn't wanted another kiss, but I had the feeling he would need to take things slow, and that was fine with me.

HOT FLUSH

A pebble of heat
Within my core
Quick to expand
In molten roar

Fire here
Below my breast
Increases outward
And fills my chest

Flows up my neck
Inflames my face
Each fiery lick
Seems in a race

Like a cartoon
Ears let off steam
Top of my head
Explodes, a dream

I wake up in

A boiling creek
Of sweat and tears
Burning my cheek

I strip and shower
It takes a while
To cool off pressed
Against cold tile

Find a dry spot
In the bed
Flip the pillow
Rest my head

Close eyes and think
This thought is it
That womanhood's
A load of shit!

TWELVE

As anticipated, things between Bill and me progressed slowly. I liked him a lot, and he enjoyed caring for me, which I found endearing and frustrating. He learnt to ask rather than assume, and I learnt to be patient.

We double-dated with Daisy and Ted a few times, and on one occasion, we went out to the Norwich Theatre with all my friends and their partners. Later, during drinks, it was hard to stop Bill from paying for everyone. He was overly generous with me, but I managed to pay for about one in four of our meals. He had no expectations, having paid for our evenings, other than end-of-evening kisses and the occasional ride to his after he'd had a few too many to drive. I wasn't much of a drinker, so I was happy to oblige.

I found it frustrating that he never invited me to come in. I just dropped him off, but he would come to my house for lunch or an evening meal. He would make himself scarce in the garden or reading if I needed to work. I liked to talk about books with him. He had some interesting insights or seemed to appreciate my nose-twitching at a poorly edited book.

We were comfortable—most of the time.

***

One evening, after a meal at my house, which Bill cooked, I popped to the downstairs loo and was horrified when the tissue I used for wiping came away with a heavy splodge of blood. It had been so long since I had a period that I thought I was done with them, but I had wondered if I might have ovulated recently. I felt more sexual, and my mood fluctuated from the high giddiness of joy to a blue disposition that hung over me for a few days. Now I had the evidence, but no sanitary products.

"Fuck!" I shouted, then bit my lip as I realised Bill would have heard me.

My mind started racing in the few seconds it took him to get to the door—I could stick a load of tissues in my knickers and then drive to the local shop. They were bound to have something, but that would mean kicking Bill out or leaving him here on his own while I went. Still, driving might make me bleed more. Perhaps Bill would run me there. I'd have to explain what was going on—*knock, knock.*

"Jo, are you okay?"

"Um, no. I have an unexpected visitor." Would he understand what I meant?

"Okay, you have something in there, or do you need me to get something from upstairs?"

What? Just like that? Isn't he freaked out? Isn't he running for the door?

"Jo?"

"I—no, I have nothing here. It's been ages. Could you drive me to the shop?"

"I'll go. What do you need? Tampons? Towels?"

"Yes. Both."

"Super? Bigger, smaller?"

OMG, this conversation is surreal.

"Super, super plus if they have it and thick towels, with wings if they have them."

"Got it. No problem. I'll be back soon."

I heard his keys rattling, and then the door shut. Sticking a wad of tissue in my underwear, I ventured out. He'd started loading the dishwasher, so I bent over to put some cutlery in the rack, but a gush ran between my legs, through the tissue, my knickers and jeans. Tentatively, I headed for the stairs and made it to the top by squeezing my thighs together to stop anything dripping on the carpet.

I tied up my hair in my ensuite bathroom, removed my top clothing and turned on the shower. Then I stepped in and stripped off my jeans and knickers, letting the cool water wash the blood out of them. I was boiling. I rinsed the blood off me and let the cold spray cool my core. Taking advantage of a calmer moment, I grabbed clean underwear and did the tissue thing again before a knock came on my bedroom door.

"Jo, I'm back."

"Just a minute." My pyjamas were the only things quickly to hand, so I put them on and opened the door. "Thank you. I made a mess." It was all I managed by the way of explanation, taking the 'goodies' out of the bag he held open for me.

"As you've got your pyjamas on, why don't you get into bed?" He offered.

"Stop managing me," I snapped. I knew it was unfair the moment it left my lips, but I couldn't stop it. "Just go."

"I got you a hot water bottle. Let me fill it and bring it up."

It sounded like heaven, but I'd let some of the vitriol out and couldn't stop it from overflowing. "I don't want a hot water bottle. Thanks for these, but I could've got them myself. Just go. That's an easy instruction, isn't it? Go." I felt the hot fluid between my legs again and rushed into the loo, literally leaving him holding the bag, bemused and probably hurt. I don't know for sure as I couldn't look at him.

I dealt with everything I needed to, cradled my aching abdomen and crawled into bed, wishing I'd let him get me the hot water bottle. I glanced at the night-stand next to the bed and noticed my favourite bar of chocolate sitting there. Suddenly energised by how unfair I'd been, I ran to the door. From the top of the stairs, I yelled, "BILL!"

"I'm here," he called, running out of the kitchen and into the hall below.

I took in huge lungs full of air as the sobs assailed me. "You didn't leave."

"I'm your boyfriend, and boyfriends don't leave when their girlfriend needs them," he said as he came up the stairs with a hot water bottle in his hands.

Nothing looked better on the man in that moment than that stupid hot water bottle.

"You—bought—me—chocolate." I managed before he reached the top of the stairs and held out his arms. Then he held me for a long time while I cried. When the tears stopped, I got into bed with that hot water bottle cradled on my poor tummy. "Best boyfriend; worst girlfriend."

"Tampons, chocolate and a hot water bottle don't amount to much compared to what you're coping with, and it's not my first rodeo."

"Can I have a cuddle?" I even put on a pouty face and fluttered my tear-coated eyelashes. It was unbecoming, but when he got in the other side of the bed and wrapped his arms around me, I was so comforted I didn't care.

"This wasn't how I hoped to spoon with you, Jo. But I'll take it for now. Get some sleep."

When I woke, I was alone in bed. After going to the bathroom again, I checked the spare room to see if Bill was there, but no such luck. My spare key was on the mat in front of the letterbox. He had used it to lock up and posted it back through. Not only that, but he had finished filling the dishwasher, and it was happily chugging away. He'd even washed up the pans and other pieces that didn't go in the washer.

I made myself a cup of herbal tea, then took it upstairs. As I sat up in bed drinking it, I considered my behaviour. Bill had managed me, but I could hardly fault him for it. I had needed help, and in my hormonal mood, I'd lashed out. Bruce probably would have liked it better if I'd needed him more, but I just got on with whatever needed doing. I really had to learn to accept help more graciously.

***

About a month before Ethan's visit, Bill sat on my sofa with his newspaper. What was that all about when you could read it far more effortlessly on an iPad?

"Jo."

"Hmm-mm." I was trying to type an outline for a new book. It was a murder mystery I'd dreamt about the night before, and it wasn't going well. I deleted everything I'd written and looked at Bill, who waited patiently.

"Will you introduce me to Ethan and Matthew when they visit?"

"Hang on—" I held up a finger, then typed in a new starting point that had occurred to me, "—done. What? Yes, I thought the four of us would go out for a meal. Before you even suggest it, I'm paying."

"Thank you."

"All of my kids would like to meet you sometime. Perhaps we could get on a video call?"

"I'd like that."

"And perhaps I could meet your daughters?"

"They have been asking."

"Great. How about this weekend? Didn't you want to try out your new grill?"

Bill looked thoughtful as he gazed over at me.

"What?"

"Well, first of all, it's a barbeque, Ms USA. Second, I want to be sure before I introduce them to someone. They're still sensitive, and I want them to know I'm choosing carefully. Not rushing to replace their mum or something."

"That's sweet. What's it going to take for you to be sure?"

"Spend the night here. If you're willing."

"Tonight?" My tummy tingled. It was odd making arrangements to have sex. I thought it would just happen naturally one night after an evening out. This felt slightly erotic—like, this is what I'm going to do to you later.

"Yes."

"Will the girls be okay on their own?"

"They're at their aunt's in Mundesley for half-term this week."

I'd forgotten all about half-term. US schools didn't have a week off in the middle of a semester, but they had about twelve weeks off in the summer.

His quiet contemplation of me confused and excited me in equal measure. When he stood, I noticed a bulge in his jeans that he adjusted a bit before he caught me looking. I licked my lips, hoping he might scoop me up and forget waiting until tonight. Instead, he sauntered over to my office chair and captured me within it by leaning forward and resting his hands on its arms. I had to push back in the chair to look up at him. Instead of kissing my lips, he moved straight down to my neck, kissing and licking his way up to my jaw. Then he kissed me in a way he hadn't before, full of passion and anticipation.

"Now I do need to leave," he said, turning and adjusting himself more out of my view. "I'll go home and pack a bag for tonight."

"Bill, I don't want to be insensitive, but do you think you could refrain from mentioning Carolyn tonight? I won't mention Bruce."

"It's a deal. Pick you up at seven? We're still meeting Daisy and Ted."

"Seven is great."

***

Daisy collared me in the ladies that evening.

"What's going on with you two? You seem really edgy." Her eyes widened when I could only give her a stupid grin. "OMG, you're on a promise, aren't you? Is this the first time?"

I managed a nod.

"Well, it's about time," she insisted.

I rushed to come to Bill's defence. "He needed to be sure, Daisy. That's fair enough, right? After his wife died. He's thinking about the girls, too. They're at their auntie's this week."

"I'll tell Ted we won't be late then."

192

"Don't go making it obvious. I'm nervous enough as it is. It's been a long time for me, as well."

"I'll put Ted on a promise, too. He won't be able to wait to get home." Daisy laughed as if it were some grand conspiracy. "Here, put a bit of lippy on." She offered me hers.

"Eww, no thanks. Germs. Plus, he wants me to wear makeup, but it isn't me, and I'm not going to start something in that department."

"Just in the downstairs department," she giggled like a kid. I rolled my eyes.

Bill leaned in when we rejoined him and Ted. "You were gone a long time. Did you tell her?"

"She guessed. Don't worry and watch."

Daisy put a hand up to Ted's ear and whispered something. His eyes widened, and a big grin spread across his face.

"What was that?" Bill whispered to me.

"She just put him on a promise for when they get home. She said it would mean we wouldn't be home too late."

"She's a good friend."

***

"Come on in," I offered, feeling self-conscious. Bill had been at my place plenty of times but never carrying an overnight bag and that gleam in his eyes. I locked the door behind him. "Do you want a coffee or a nightcap?"

"Jo," he said, setting his bag down at the bottom of the stairs and taking my hands in his. "You're nervous, I'm nervous. Why don't we go to bed and see where things take us?"

I agreed, grabbed a water bottle, offered him one, and slipped off my shoes before climbing the stairs. I was acutely aware of my ass being right at his eye level and tried not to let it wobble or, heaven forbid, a fart sneak out.

"You want to share my bathroom or use the main one?" I asked.

"I'll use this one." He disappeared.

I rushed into my bathroom, grabbing my pyjamas en route and checking the bedroom, which looked fine. Was I supposed to undress? I used the loo, then figured I should wash 'down there'. I hoped he'd, you know, taste. *Oh God, I hope he likes foreplay.* Sex was so much easier in my twenties, the first time Bruce and I had—well. Back then, I just prayed I didn't smell. Now I worried about the smell, stretch marks, haemorrhoids, and how much shaving Bill expected—hopefully, none, as I hadn't felt brave enough to take a razor to my privates and hadn't had time to book a waxing.

After brushing my teeth, I took a deep breath and figured if I didn't do it now, I'd never have sex again. I inched open the door and spotted Bill within the bedroom doorframe. He was wearing boxers and a T-shirt—pyjamas then.

"You can come in. I'll be a minute." I popped back into the bathroom. My pyjamas were a T and shorts, so I figured we'd match.

When I opened the door again, Bill was sitting on the side of my bed an arm's distance away. Saying nothing, he pulled me to him and started kissing me. My desires took over, and I forgot everything but his mouth.

FUCK YOU!

"Write me a poem
About your love
All about me
How we fit like a glove."
I try—fuck you!

"I know you've lost
When you swear
The argument's mine
No more I hear."
I sigh—fuck you!

"I'll fuck you
Till you see the stars
Fuck you to the moon
Break orbit and to Mars."
I lie—fuck you!

"I know what's best
You should lose weight
Stay right at home

But I'll still date."
I cry—fuck you!

"I'll rip your life
If you don't stay
Your heart is mine
Don't walk away."
Goodbye—fuck you!

Now, I live my life
Without you
Don't text or call
You know what I'll do
Reply—fuck you!

THIRTEEN

A s I showered the next morning, I smiled and sang a little song. Bill was a considerate lover, and I had no complaints. He'd gotten out of bed before me to shower, then declared he would make breakfast while I sorted myself out.

I was pulling on my cut-offs and anticipating a leisurely morning while we touched hands, kissed and affectionately enjoyed a morning coffee when my door alarm buzzed on my wrist. Before I could call out to Bill to get the door, whoever it was knocked.

"I'll get it," Bill called, so I picked up my blouse to finish my ensemble.

I froze mid-button when I heard the deep voice. "Hi, I was looking for Joanna Newb— James. Joanna James."

What the actual fuck?

Bill was as friendly as ever. "Yes, she'll be down in a moment. Who are you?"

Bruce? What the f—?

I rushed to the stairs and was halfway down when my brain exploded at his response.

"I'm her husband. Who are you?"

Husband? Oh, no you don't, Bruce.

"I'm—"

"No." I pointed at Bruce as I descended the last few steps. "Ex-husband, and no, just no. You don't walk into my house uninvited like this." I tried to push him outside again, but he's a big guy and didn't budge from my welcome mat. "This is my boyfriend, Bill. Bill, this is my EX-husband, Bruce." I paused as it occurred

197

to me I'd picked two B's, but technically, Bill is a W for William, so that didn't count, right? Damn my brain for distracting me; it gave the men a moment to do their own thing—never a good idea.

Bill stepped aside to allow Bruce into my kitchen. "I'll go and let you two catch up." He skirted me and headed upstairs to get his bag.

"That would be great, Bill. Thanks," Bruce said, all friendly-like.

What are they, best buds all of a sudden?

It was like I didn't exist, but it was my house.

Fucking men!

I had no idea which way to turn. I didn't want Bruce in my house, but I had to stop Bill from leaving.

"Why are you here, Bruce?"

"I'm good, thanks for asking, and the kids are, too. Don't you care about them? Fucking around with your boyfriend."

"The kids are fine. If they weren't, one of them would have called me. I talk with them more often than you do. Where's *your* girlfriend?"

"I wanted to talk."

"Ever heard of WhatsApp? Zoom? Or just a plain old phone call. You didn't have to fly all the way over here."

"Face to face," he said, but I wasn't listening.

Bill had come back down the stairs, and I met him there.

"Call me, Jo. After you've talked." He sounded so reasonable as he reached for the door handle.

"No, wait. Bruce is leaving. I don't want to talk to him. I want you to stay."

He opened the door and headed to his car.

Am I invisible?

I grabbed my keys from the kitchen table, stopping long enough to look at Bruce and his grin. "You're an ass."

How did this morning go from serene to this shitshow?

Outside, Bill put his bag in the trunk—boot—oh, I don't care about words right now. He'd gotten behind the wheel when I moved to stop him from closing the door. He didn't seem angry, but why was he leaving?

"Bill, I have nothing to say to Bruce. It's nothing to do with the kids, so I don't know why he's here. He can leave. I want you to stay."

"He wants you back, Jo. Of course he does. You're a great woman."

"If I'm so great, why are you leaving?"

"Jo, I'd give anything for one more day with my wife. You two had a lot of years together. He's come all this way. You owe it to him to hear him out, at least."

"You aren't listening to me. Bruce didn't die—he cheated on me. I left him, not the other way around, and now we're divorced. I'm happy about that, whether I'm with you or on my own. What he thinks doesn't come into the equation, and I definitely don't owe him a damn thing. I'm still throwing him out of my house, whether you stay or go."

"I know I'm right, Jo. Text me with what you decide."

"Oh my God, will you listen to ME right now, not my ex or your head, which isn't reading my mind. If you go, you're as bad as him trying to dictate what I should do. If you don't listen to me and what I KNOW I want rather than do what HE wants, then we're done. I won't be texting or calling you."

I moved out of the way, hoping that Bill would see sense and come back inside with me. Instead, he closed the car door and drove off. So, that was that.

One down, one to go.

I headed back to my house, opened the front door, and stepped inside.

"Bruce," I called. He peered around the corner, taking a sip from his coffee mug and smiling. "Leave." I gestured outside.

"I just got a coffee." He pointed to the mug.

"I've nothing to say to you except leave, or I'll call the police."

"Don't you want to hear what I have to say?"

I pulled out my phone. "I really don't."

He sounded less sure of himself. "I want you back, Jo. Please let's talk. I want to apologise and take you back to a big house in the USA, not a tiny place like this. You need to be kept in the manner you're accustomed to and be near the kids. They all miss you."

"My kids are fine. They're grown-ups with their own lives and are proud of their mom for finding her way to happiness in her 'tiny place'. You don't make me happy, and I certainly don't want to be kept. I was miserable way before I left you. Leave—last chance."

I typed nine-nine-nine, proud I'd remembered not to dial nine-one-one, then held up the phone to show him and hovered a finger over the green call button.

He threw his coffee into my front garden, handed me the empty mug, and disappeared. I returned to the kitchen and put away the food Bill had prepped for a big breakfast. Hunger was no longer a priority. I poured coffee for myself, took it to the table, and gazed out of the patio doors at the grass rectangle that Denis, Emily, and I had so much fun cutting nearly a year ago.

I won't cry over any of these men. So much for the leisurely morning I'd expected. Then the tears started, and I allowed them to flow, reaching for the nearby box of tissues. I didn't want any of those men, but I felt sad that I hadn't found the partner I'd hoped for so far. I didn't allow myself too much distress. My life plans didn't revolve around having a man, but I had to admit it was nice to feel cared for and, maybe someday, loved.

I could do with chatting to someone about all of this, but who? Any of my family would be biased. My USA friends would still be in bed at this hour, and my UK friends were all happily married, not to mention Daisy, who was entirely enamoured with Bill. I was sadder about her being upset than Bill. Then, I remembered Harriet was the only other single person in our group. I dialled her number.

"The Reading Stable," she rang out so happily, clearly in her element. "Oh, sorry, this is my mobile. Hi, it's Harriet."

"Hey, Harriet, it's Jo."

"What's up, Jo? You sound like you've been crying. I hope it isn't over a man."

"Men, plural." I gave a little giggle at that. Calling her had been the right thing to do.

"Oh, I can help you there. Specific men, or men in general?"

"Specific in the first instance and then general, probably."

"I have a break in an hour if you want to pick up coffees and pastries at Toni's, then pop over. We can sit out back and watch your mum's flowers grow if this rain holds off."

"I'm on my way."

***

Mum wasn't in the greenhouses when I walked around the back of The Reading Stable with a tray of coffees and what was apparently, according to Toni, Harriet's favourite cakes. I sat at the little table and texted Harriet, who popped out just minutes later.

"Oh, yummy. It's a busy week for me with half-term, but it's good for business. A break is just what I need. What's going on?"

I told her the whole sorry tale of Bill and Bruce, and we were laughing by the end.

"Why am I laughing when my life has just gone up in flames?" I asked, while wiping away the good kind of tears.

"Oh, Jo," she chastised gently, "men aren't your life any more than mine. They can be part of it, sometimes. Maybe even always be there or around, but you each need your own lives, interests, desires, goals, achievements."

"You're absolutely right, Harriet. Let's enjoy our coffees without thinking about them."

"Yep, we haven't passed the Bechdel test in this conversation. You messaged that you'd devised an outline for a murder mystery. I'd love to hear it."

"It started as a dream I had—" I began, and we spent the rest of our time before Harriet had to rush back to her own achievement of The Reading Stable, talking about my book.

When I got home, I immediately sat at my computer and started jotting down the ideas we'd come up with. I'd entirely forgotten Bill and Bruce—for now, at least.

***

"Who gave your dad my address?" I demanded of my children when all three faces were on my laptop screen. They were silent. "Holly?" I wasn't truly angry. Thankfully, my chat with Harriet had relieved me of that.

"It wasn't Holly, Mom. It was me." Beth—the least likely of the three. She burst into tears.

"Why?"

"He was contrite, honestly. He said he wanted to apologise and was upset when I told him about Bill."

"Don't be angry with her, Jo." Beth's husband, such a sweet son-in-law, appeared on the screen and cuddled Beth. "She's been working long hours at the ER, and it's been tough."

"You don't need to make excuses for me, Alfonso," she said as she pushed away from him, but not entirely, and he didn't let go. I loved him for that.

"Oh, you're in trouble now, Al," Ethan chimed in. "She used your full name."

"No, shut up, Ethan. I just wanted you to come home, Mom. I thought—okay, I hoped you still loved Dad. He loves you, Mom."

"And where will he live when he returns from the UK?"

"As far as we know, he's still living with Sandi," Holly provided. "I called her yesterday because I couldn't get hold of him. I didn't know he was in the UK. She said he was in Chicago for work and said the signal wasn't good in the place he was at."

"I've a good mind to fill her in," Ethan said through gritted teeth.

"You can't, Love," I soothed them all as best I could. "The only thing you can do is talk to your dad and suggest he should. Beth, if he's still living with her, then coming over here to say he wants me, how can that be love? Look at what you have with Al. Wouldn't you want someone as good for me as he is for you?"

"I do, Mom. I really do."

"What about Bill?" Holly asked.

"That's over and done with," I said sadly, but not as upset as I thought I should be. Bill had been fun and comfortable, but there were signs he could be domineering, and I'm not subservient. "Bill said I should talk to your father and left us to it. He even invited your dad into *my* house while I stood right there saying 'No'. Honestly, it was like I was invisible to them both. Bill said I had to tell him how it went after talking to your dad. I haven't."

"I'm sorry, Mom." Poor Beth, she felt terrible.

"It's okay. Better I find out what he's like now. I'll miss double-dating with Daisy and Ted, though. They were fun. It won't quite be the same with them and just me. I wouldn't be surprised if they still see Bill, as I'm sure he won't be single long. With a bit of luck, he'll have learnt his lesson for his next woman."

"Can you come and visit soon, Mom? I miss you so much." Beth again, and Al was right; she looked tired.

"What about if I come for Thanksgiving in Connecticut and Christmas in Boston? Perhaps each of you could put me up for a few nights? Can you get Thanksgiving off, Beth?" She was the only one whose work didn't close for one of the biggest holidays in the US calendar and one that was all about family.

"Yes, I'm going to book it tomorrow. I won't be on call or anything, I promise."

Roll on November and seeing my family, but first, I had Ethan and Matt's visit to enjoy.

***

It took Bill two days to venture a text.

Bill:

I haven't heard from you, Jo. How did you go with Bruce?

Joanna:

It went exactly as I told you it would. He was gone two minutes after you.

Bill:

How are things with us?

Joanna:

Things with us are exactly as I told you they would be before you ignored my words and sped off.

Bill:

I wanted to know that you would choose me, even if he wanted you back.

Joanna:

I did choose you. You just didn't listen.

Bill:

Can I see you?

Joanna:

Too late, Bill.

He must have mulled it over for a while because it took him an hour to call me when I was into the groove of editing another book Sophie had sent. I let it ring a few times, but ultimately answered it to clear the air.

"Jo, thanks for answering."

"What do you want, Bill?" He'd sounded desperate, so I kept my tone kind.

"I want to give us another try. I promise to listen to you in the future. I just want you to acknowledge that sometimes I have more experience than you and will always have a good reason for how I do things."

What experience had he had that was more than mine? He'd lived nowhere but Norfolk. He meant, 'I'm a man and therefore I know best'. Forget kind. I wanted to run to his house and extract his daughters from his misogynistic control.

"And there it is."

"There what is?"

"The dominant and domineering personality that you did well to hide until that morning—the night before a little, if I'm honest."

"You're wrong. I'm willing to listen and take your opinion into account."

"Can you even hear yourself? First, I gave you my opinion about my relationship with Bruce, and you didn't listen or take it into account. Second, I don't want my opinion to be 'taken into account' in decisions that YOU ultimately make. In any future relationship, I want a partner who will discuss a situation and jointly agree on a decision."

"What if it's something you can't agree on?"

"There's this thing you may not have heard of called 'compromise'."

"Sarcasm doesn't suit you, Jo."

"What doesn't suit me is a manipulative, misogynistic partner."

"I was thinking of you. What if you wanted Bruce back?"

"One thing you'll now learn about me is that when I decide on a man, I don't go back. Goodbye, Bill. Good luck, and for the sake of your daughters, open your mind a bit more." I hung up and blocked his ass.

IMPOSTER
SYNDROME

I can't write
I can't rhyme
Can't hold a tune
Or sing in time
Pretender

I can't hold down
A full-time job
Got one cos
I gave it some gob
Hoodwinker

I can't be worth
What they'll pay
To listen to
What I have to say
Swindler

How can they let
Me own a home
I can't do much
Without my phone
Deluder

Yet I'll try and keep
My dream alive
Not let this syndrome
Drain my drive
Imposter

FOURTEEN

The summer was in full force, and I was melting without air conditioning in the house when Ethan and Matt flew from JFK airport to Edinburgh before coming to Norwich. From Norwich airport, they would fly to London. Then, they planned to spend a few days hiking in Wales before flying to Dublin and back to Boston.

Before they arrived, a video pinged on our group WhatsApp chat with Holly and Beth. In it, Matt stood on a windy hilltop that I recognised as Arthur's Seat. The city of Edinburgh sprawled in the background. Ethan knelt before him, holding a ring box and speaking words of love and forever that flew away in the breeze, so I could barely hear them.

Matt screamed, 'Yes!' so loudly that it was unmistakable, and pulled Ethan to his feet, kissing him passionately while a few people around them cheered and clapped. There were two rings in the box that they put on each other, and the video ended.

Ethan sent photos after that. Selfies with them both holding up their left hands with the rings on and kissing. Then another, with Ethan giving a thumbs up and Matt kissing his cheek. I really love these two. With Ethan's permission, I shared the video and photos on my group chat with Elliott and Alastair. They both sent hearts back.

As promised, I invited Alastair to my housewarming party, introducing him as my friend, whom I had made through Elliott, to the whole family. Consequently, he had been invited to a christening and a wedding, sealing his position as a family member despite no announcement. Elliott just couldn't bring himself to say it. Alastair was happier, but I still noticed a brief shadow of disappointment in his eyes whenever Elliott called him a friend rather than a boyfriend or partner.

I'd arranged with Ethan and Matt to spend a day in Norwich, meeting Elliott and Alastair for a trip around the castle museum. Matt was excited to enter such an old building and listened intently to Alastair sharing how it was built. I lent an ear to their conversation, allowing Elliott and Ethan to get ahead of us.

The night before, I had bent Ethan's ear about talking to Elliott about coming out. "Mom, don't put that on me," he complained. "Uncle Elliott doesn't have to say anything about it. Did you announce to the world that you were hetero?" I knew he had a point, but when I explained my concern for Alastair, Ethan glanced at Matt, who nodded, causing Ethan to promise he would do what he could if he got the chance. Matt was openly gay and in a secret relationship with Ethan before they came out to us as a couple.

We were all hungry by the time we'd finished at the castle, including a trip up to the battlements that Matt was still raving about. The youngsters favoured shopping and grabbing some fast food somewhere, but Elliott asked if I would drive him to Horseshoe Hamlets as today was Mum's day in her gardens and greenhouses there. The three of us agreed to eat at Toni's tearooms, and I would pick Ethan and Matt up later in the afternoon.

***

When we arrived, I dragged Alastair off to meet some of my friends and left him to order a proper afternoon tea from Toni. I headed around the back to see if Elliott was ready to join us, only to see him sitting on a stool in the greenhouse while Mum held him. He was so tall, this would be the only way she could hold and comfort him as his shoulders shook. Mum rubbed his back to soothe him. I kept my distance and watched as she took his face in her hands and gently shook it, clearly telling him something he had to do.

Exiting the greenhouse, Elliott spotted me and gave me a wave as he walked towards me, brushing his tears away.

"Mum said she'd pop over to the tearoom shortly," He offered by way of explanation.

"What was that all about?" I asked, gesturing behind us as we walked and grabbing my chin, giving it a shake.

"She told me if I loved Alastair so much, I had to listen to Beyoncé." He glanced down at my confused face. "Put a ring on it."

"She meant his finger, right?" I confirmed.

Elliott let out a huge guffaw at that. "Baby girl, I had no idea you were so naughty."

"Is that something Alastair would like? You know, getting married?"

"Yes, he's mentioned it once or twice."

I looked back up at Elliott, striding along and eager to be with Alastair again. "You look younger than you did when you went into the greenhouse. You look lighter."

"Joey, I was so worried I was letting her down. She loved our father so much and lost him such a long time ago before these things were more acceptable than they are today. I thought he would have been angry had he known, and it would have made her sad. It sounds stupid now that I say it aloud because she told me he knew all along. They'd talked of me, and he loved me as I was. As I am."

"So do I, bro. It isn't stupid. You are today who you are, and you move forward from here. Look at all the years I wasted with Bruce, but I have three lovely kids. I can't regret it. You have Alastair, and who could say what could be different today if you'd done things another way?"

"Naughty and wise. What a combo." Elliott pulled me into a side-armed hug as we approached the tearoom, then opened the door for me.

We had a lovely tea, but the best moment for me was Alastair's face when Mum came in, and Elliott said, "I'd like you to meet my boyfriend, Alastair."

***

Two days later, Susan held another barbeque at her house so everyone could meet Matt and see Ethan again. Her place is so much bigger than mine to accommodate the whole family. Everyone congratulated them on their engagement, and Anne brought out her rainbow cake. I was so proud of my family's acceptance of them. I know not everyone is that way.

When all the fuss had died down, Elliott cleared his throat. "If it isn't too tacky of me to impose on this moment, I would like to announce that I asked Alastair to marry me last night, and he agreed."

Everyone erupted into applause and shouts of congratulations. Many people shook Alastair's hand or hugged him, saying 'Welcome to the family', and he beamed from ear to ear.

"I'm so happy for you both," I said as I sidled up to the man who would become my brother-in-law.

"All thanks to your son, I believe," Alastair said. "We hope to be in Boston for their wedding at Christmas. Oh, was I supposed to keep that a secret?" He took in my surprised expression.

"Too late now. I'm so glad I'll be there for it, too. I'm going over for Thanksgiving in Connecticut and then up to Boston."

"So I understand." Alastair smiled as Elliott joined us.

"Nicely done," I said, giving him an enormous hug.

***

The following morning, when Ethan and Matt would be heading off to London, I woke to an email message from Sophie she'd sent the night before. She liked my 'Firefighter' story but felt it was a little like a cookie-cutter romance and was looking for something different and edgier.

She wrote, 'I know you can do better. This is a great little story, and there's nothing to stop you from sending it off to an agency that is more romance-inclined or self-publishing, but keep writing. I'm looking forward to that murder mystery you mentioned.'

When I came down to breakfast, I hadn't shaken off my disappointment, and Ethan's leaving only added to my misery. Coffee seemed to be an excellent solution. I knew I was lucky I had Sophie to bounce off because getting a literary agent isn't easy for most budding authors. I have to say I felt like I was looking into a room I wanted to join but was afraid that those within it would point and laugh if I walked through the door.

I heard the other bathroom shower running and started cooking bacon when I heard feet on the stairs.

"Oh, Mom, don't be sad. We'll see you at Christmas."

"Do I look that bad?" I asked, still not enthused about the day.

"You just struck me as sad."

"I didn't get good feedback on my first book this morning, and I guess I'm a bit bummed."

"Who's been bummed?" Matt entered the kitchen in his usual exuberant fashion.

"Matty," Ethan chided. "Mom's sad."

"I'm not sad. I'm suffering from imposter syndrome."

"I thought Sam Harmer loved that story?" Ethan asked.

"What does he know? Silly, gorgeous butthead," Matt added, soothing and making us laugh simultaneously.

I let Ethan read the email as he demolished his breakfast, and I sipped coffee, nibbling at my bacon. "What's going on with the murder mystery?"

"I'm stuck. I love the genre, but my idea is lacking some depth."

"Why not go on a writing course? It might be a way to get an insight into what you're missing."

"I suppose."

Ethan had a point, but who likes to stop a sulk once they've started one?

Matt started typing on his phone. "Oh, here's one—no, that says Manchester. You don't want to go to Manchester, do you, Mom?"

Ethan and I stilled and stared at each other before turning our stunned faces to him. Suddenly aware of our scrutiny, Matt looked up from his phone, then a cute blush graced his cheekbones and across his nose. "Sorry, Jo. I got caught up in the excitement."

We all laughed, and my mood lifted. "It's fine. I liked it."

"Anyway, I've found a closer one, but it's in Grantham, and you stay overnight for three nights. The guy who runs it is called Guy Simms. He looks slick, but he has an excellent reputation. Tough, but good results, according to reviews."

Before I dropped them off at the airport, they had enrolled me in the next course, starting in a couple of weeks. I felt a little sad and cried some mommy tears at seeing them go on their next adventure, but I would see them at Christmas, and it seemed I still had some adventures of my own to enjoy.

***

To pass the time the following week, I worked extra hours for Sophie so I could do less when I was there, and I worked on my murder mystery. It's a genre that I love to read, but I was super nervous about writing one. You had to get it technically correct as well as hone the characters. I knew this from the many I had edited over the years.

By Friday, I geared myself up for a haircut. It had been at least two years since my locks had seen a pair of scissors, and it was way past time. Susan's hairdresser had fit me in at the last minute to tidy me up before setting off for my writing course. The night before, I lay in bed thinking about how short my hair had been when Bruce first met me. I was a lot younger and quite a bit slimmer, and as I loved Annie Lennox, I'd sported a pixie cut like hers. I figured, if I couldn't sing like her (who could), I might as well look like her in some way.

By the time I had Holly, my hair had grown long, but I supposed I tried to reclaim some of my youth after she was born. The hairdresser then hadn't done the best job, and Bruce was rather insulting about how short hair didn't suit me now that I'd gained some weight with the baby that I hadn't shed. Since then, I grew my hair long again and kept it that way.

Perimenopause brought hot flushes, so I constantly tied my hair in a ponytail. Even after I'd washed my hair, I tied it back wet and let it dry on its own. I always thought I would get a short haircut again 'once I'd lost weight'—always that caveat. We women employ it to stop ourselves from doing many things because we fear being thought foolish.

'I'll go out dancing again when I can fit back into my favourite dress', or 'I'll go to the gym when I can look half decent in Lycra.' What a paradox that is! One of my personal worst examples of this is when I'm thinking up a fantasy about a well-known person. I start with 'I'd lost a lot of weight and met—'

Then it hit me—if I tied my hair back anyway, from the front, it would make no difference if my hair was short. I grabbed my phone, squinting as I quickly lowered the brightness in the dark room. Then I opened Google and tapped 'short haircuts for fat faces'. I found one I liked, though it wasn't on a fat face, and tried to sleep.

Why was I so excited for a haircut? The only answer I had was because it was my decision. While Bruce hadn't exactly said I shouldn't have my hair short, he'd been derogatory about it and influenced me. I loved having short hair when I was younger. I was going to do it again, and if I hated it—it would grow back.

Rachael, Susan's hairdresser, was lovely and excited to give me a new look. Her enthusiasm was contagious, and I lost all my nerves when I sat in front of the mirror with wet hair.

"Last chance to back out," she said, holding a dripping lock.

"Go for it!" I said. Then, as soon as she snipped it, I screeched, "Oh, no!"

Her face was a picture, but I didn't let her suffer long, telling her I was only kidding.

I deliberately left my contact lenses out and wore glasses so I couldn't see a definite picture while she worked. I wanted to wait until she'd finished to see the full effect properly. After cutting, snipping, buzzing, moussing, and drying, Rachael added a final touch of wax before I put my glasses back on.

She had done a fantastic job, and I grinned from ear to ear. Not even one ounce of doubt crossed my mind that this had been the right decision. One side was short and slicked back, while the other had a longer fringe hanging lower over my forehead and slightly over my eye. I gave Rachael a big hug and a generous tip and headed out of the shop with my head high (after sending a pic to my family WhatsApp group in the UK and my kids one in the USA). To Susan, I sent a big thank you.

Ethan and Matt sent a selfie of their silly grins and thumbs up from the last leg of their trip to Ireland—the girls would have to wait until they were up on USA time.

At the end of the weekend, I dragged my butt to bed with my alarm set and my bag packed, ready for four days in Grantham. Then I reached up to the back of my head to pull out my ponytail as I had the past two nights before, remembering it wasn't there anymore. I swear I could feel it sometimes! I guess that's what nearly three decades of a long hairstyle will get you.

***

With high hopes, I packed my devices into my overnight bag and drove early on that first day of the four-day workshop. Grantham was a little over two hours' drive from Norwich and close to the location of Redway Acres. I'd be editing the third book when I got back from this workshop, and I knew from Sam that shooting on the third series was planned for next year. Before driving home, I hoped to visit the local stately home, where one of the Redway Acres locations was based. The last day was due to be finished at lunchtime.

The room for our workshop was part of a church addition. The entrance was to the side of the main building, down a corridor that smelt like the inside of the schools of my youth. It wasn't an olfactory memory I relished. The American schools my kids attended didn't smell that way. I think it's because they're far more modern. I had a feeling this might have once been a school affiliated with religion—plenty of those in the USA. I was the last to arrive two minutes past the hour, and perhaps that was why Guy Simms took an instant dislike to me, or maybe my family had wronged his in ancient times?

"I'm Joanna James. Sor—"

"At least now we can begin," he said and moved from his lounging position in his chair with his legs up on his desk to stand over me while I moved to the desk and chair he'd gestured to at the front of the class of eight, including myself. He was tall and reedy, with his dark hair moulded into a perfect cap on his head that made you wonder if it was a wig, though he seemed too young for that—the bio I'd read put him at twenty-nine. He had long fingers between which he flicked a black biro while discussing his published book about creative writing that he would use as a reference throughout the course. In a second, the pen flew from his fingers and landed next to my bag, from which I was pulling out the very book he talked about. I'd gone online and purchased this and his only novel. Considering I'd read the whole thing from front to back, I hoped the course would amount to more than what was in it.

Guy glared at me and then at his pen as if I'd knocked it out of his hand myself. I returned his stare when his eyes came back to mine. *Does he expect me to pick it up?*

The young woman in the seat beside mine bent over, picked it up and returned it to him. He thanked her profusely, glared at me once more, and then gestured to a pile of his books on the desk with a sign next to them that said they were twenty pounds each. I'd paid half that online but didn't want to point that out. Everyone but me formed an orderly line with their money or debit cards at the ready. He signed each book with that pen, then looked at me. I held out my copy, assuming he would sign it—not that I cared either way.

"I don't sign books that weren't purchased directly from me," he said with a smug look that I had at least fallen into that trap despite not picking up his pen.

"No worries," I offered, trying to sound as nonchalant as I felt, but I couldn't help the blush of embarrassment at being singled out this way in front of the class. I tried valiantly not to let it affect my experience in the group. I'd paid good money to be there and wanted to learn.

Next, Guy spent an hour talking from his book, a section about writing short stories. Then he set us a task of writing a maximum one-thousand-word story and handed out index cards upon which was written a genre—mine was dystopian, which I had to admit was disappointing, but I tried valiantly anyway. Everyone's subject was 'An Ethical Dilemma'.

I opened my laptop, but he snapped it closed in front of my nose. "Pen and paper, everyone," Guy called out and then sold spiral-bound notebooks to any- one who didn't have one at a tenner a pop when he probably bought them at Poundland. I handed over my ten pounds, but I did at least have my own pen.

We sat with our heads down, writing for the rest of the morning and some of the afternoon. Lunch in an adjoining room comprised sandwiches, bags of crisps, and tea with biscuits. It wasn't bad, but neither was it suitable for the price we'd paid for the experience. I would have embarrassed Toni to serve a lunch like that at any price, and I was missing her soups, soft, fresh bread rolls, salads and pastries. Grabbing enough to tide me over until dinner, I returned to my desk just like everyone else. I attempted to finish my story before editing it, then writing it out clean on another page, assuming Guy would read them all. The man in question was nowhere to be seen. I suspected he'd gone to buy his own better lunch somewhere else with all the money we'd given him that morning.

Two hours after he'd broken us up for lunch and disappeared, Guy returned—tie askew, sans jacket, and his sleeves rolled up. He smelled of beer, though I judged he wasn't quite drunk. Guy told us to read each other's work and write a line of critique, and broke out a packet of different coloured pens to determine who said what. When each was done, we put them on his desk, where he leaned back in his seat, feet on the desk and snoring ever so slightly.

***

At three o'clock, when the workshop was due to end, we all left him asleep and went to check in at the small hotel. We agreed to freshen up and meet up for dinner in the next-door restaurant. I called and booked a table for eight people, and we eagerly gathered to get to know each other and talk about the stories we'd written that day. A young woman named Grace sat next to me, and I found out she was a receptionist at a local doctor's office. She spent all her spare time writing since her fiancé split up with her a month before their wedding. Everyone was interested in me being an editor, but I had to disappoint them with details of much of the inner workings of a publisher's office as I worked remotely. They were also very complimentary about my story, but we all wanted to see each other do well.

Halfway through the meal, Guy turned up. He professed to have been at the bar and happened to look in and see us all. Several people offered for him to join us, and the wait staff brought over another place setting and a chair they placed at the far end of the table, which unfortunately blocked part of the walkway. Guy took one look, then pulled at the back of my chair.

"Hey, Joanna. You don't mind moving to that seat, do you? I want to be in the middle to hear what everyone's saying."

"I do, actually," I complained, not seeing why I had to move.

"Please, Joanna," everyone protested. What else could I do but move? Everyone leaned towards Guy while he dominated the conversation, mostly about himself and his writing 'career'. I'd started reading his novel, and I have to say I would have been ashamed if I'd edited it. I'd covered it in red and post-it notes and only made it through three chapters.

As the evening wore on, I noticed Grace's body language turned inward more and more with each glass of wine Guy drank. He kept putting his arm around her and hugging her to him, and who knows what his other hand was doing below the table. When she made her way to the ladies, I followed her.

"Hey, Grace, are you okay?" I asked after ascertaining we were the only two in there.

"Yes, just needed a breather."

"From Guy?"

"I know he's being nice, but I'm not interested, and he keeps asking what room I'm in."

"Do you want to go to your room now, and I'll cover for you?"

"Oh, yes, please. Thanks, Jo."

"Not a problem. I'll pay your share of the bill, and you can cover mine tomorrow. Is that fair?"

"Your kids are so lucky. You're a great person."

"Go get a good night's sleep." I gave her my number in case there were any issues.

When I returned to the table, I asked if we could settle the bill. We'd all had our food, so anyone else who wanted to drink could pay for their own. The wait staff arranged it, and I put two shares on my debit card. Throughout this process, a drunk Guy had asked where Grace was, and when I informed everyone she wasn't feeling well, he asked for her room number so he could check on her. Thankfully, under my hard stare, no one gave it to him.

***

When I got to my room and checked my messages, I had one from Sam, which cheered me up no end.

Sam:

> Jo, are you in Norwich tomorrow? I'm flying in to see you and talk books.

Joanna:

> Sam, great to hear from you. I'm on a writing course in Grantham, but I don't think I'll stick it out. The instructor is an arse and bullies a young woman called Grace, then hits on her. She's about Beth's age. I hate to see it.

Sam:

> I could meet you in Grantham for lunch. I'll get a lift if you can drive me back.

Joanna:

> You don't have to do that. Anyway, I hope to check out Belton House while I'm up this way.

Sam:

> If it means I can put this arse in his place, it would be my pleasure. Give me the address, and I'll be there at about twelve. Belton House afterwards sounds ideal.

Joanna:

> Lunch is my treat, then. I went for a walk earlier and found a really quaint place you'll love.

Sam:

> It's a date.

He was still flirting, and I still blushed.

***

The following day, we were all assembled before Guy walked in. The room was deadly silent, all our nerves on edge, waiting to hear what he thought of our efforts. Would he like them? Did our classmates like ours, or were they blowing smoke last night at dinner? Do we have any talent, or were we kidding ourselves that even one person might like to read a novel that we might write and publish?

"I see I have my work cut out for me with this group," he announced, which didn't bode well. Then he called us up, one by one, saying aloud what he thought of each person's work. Everyone was deflated and morose after his dissection. Just before he called me up last, he called Grace to the front. "What can I say, Grace? Romance is probably the easiest genre to write, yet there isn't an original idea here." As he spoke, he was rolling the coloured pens we'd returned to his desk. Three rolled out of his grasp onto the floor, where Grace bent down to retrieve them. He smirked, then noticed me glaring at him.

"Now we move to our resident book editor, Joanna. Oh yes, an editor who took it upon herself to edit everyone's work. The purple is all hers."

I wasn't worried about him saying that. When everyone received their work from me yesterday, they thanked me for my input.

"Come up here, Jo, Joanna, Jo-Jo, Jo James. That's a lot of Js. What's everyone said about *your* story? Oh, how they raved, 'marvellous, so clever, I loved it.' Well, I didn't love it, Joanna. It was drivel and silly. Here's what I thought of it."

With that, he screwed up my story and threw it towards the rubbish bin in the corner.

"It's rubbish, no good, not worth the paper it's written on. I don't know how you've conned anyone that you're a good editor, but you sure as hell aren't going to make it as an author."

Now, had he made the shot in the wastepaper basket, behaved a little more respectably and not tried to hit on a young woman who didn't know how to stand up to him, I might have said nothing. But he had done all those things and more (including, so we heard over breakfast, leaving his bar tab for the night with those that stayed drinking). If he hadn't fleeced everyone in the room by insisting they needed a copy of his book and that they had to write on paper—when neither thing was in the notes about the course. *If* he hadn't tried to impinge on my reputation as an editor, which I knew was unimpeachable. In short, had he been respectful and thoughtful, what happened next might not have happened.

I leaned forward, resting my knuckles on the desk as I towered over him and peered down my nose for a couple of seconds before I spoke with as much confidence as I could muster. All my pent-up frustration with the few men that had crossed my path lately spewed out.

"I *will* be an excellent writer, and do you know why? Because I've lived many lives and had experiences you haven't even opened yourself up to. I've travelled, had children, been married and divorced."

He rose and came around his desk, where we stood face to face. He was tall, but I stood up on my toes on purpose. Sometimes heels could be an advantage, I conceded.

"You're just a dried-up, bitter woman who left her children to run away from a man who never wanted her."

"Wrong again. I'll sell books about real life and not happy-ever-after where a woman needs a man to complete her life."

"It's women that want those happy-ever-after romances."

"Some do, that's true, and why not want escapism when their lives are a struggle to conform to society's ridiculous expectations? But it's also true that sometimes women want stories about triumph over adversity. They need to know they aren't alone in struggles that seem so insurmountable and that they can find happiness with or without a man. Especially a manipulative and sad-sack like you."

He dropped his pen at my feet.

I ignored it and continued, "I'll tell you what I did for my children. I brought them up to be free-thinking and independent. No hovering over them, tending to their every need. So if you think my instinct is to crouch before you and pick that up, so you can fantasise about shutting me up by making me suck you off, you're wrong. Pick it up yourself—creep."

A slow clap started, and I grinned to see Sam's massive shoulders filling the expanse of the doorframe.

"Oh-My-God, Sam Harmer," Grace squealed from her desk nearest the door.

"Hi, Jo. You're done here, I assume," he said. "Love the hair!"

"Hey, Sam. Let me grab my stuff. That's Grace, by the way." I pointed to her.

After packing my bag, I turned to see Sam enter the room and murmur to Guy, his arms folded and his height and breadth intimidating. Guy was looking scared and pale—good. Sam turned, took hold of my bag and my hand, and I followed him out into the hallway with a final grin at Grace.

"You're so cool, Jo," she whispered.

"God, this place smells of school," Sam complained.

"Exactly. Did you come to rescue me, Sam?" I asked with a sense of freedom and lightness settling on me in a way it hadn't since the whole Bill and Bruce debacle.

"Yes, but it turns out you didn't need me." He put my bag in my car and got in the passenger side. "I warned him to lay off Grace, so lunch is on you, right?"

"Right."

ALL AMERICAN

It's great when you meet a man
To not care about his home town
It's great just to enjoy the fun
Not let that get you down

But what you have to think on
If things get in a groove
It's going to break your heart
Unless one of you moves

And if you move, you must see
You've left it all for him
But if he won't commit the same
The relationship will thin

You will resent him if you split
And you can't make it home
To the place you loved but left
And wish you'd never roamed

FIFTEEN

Over lunch, Sam broke some big news, and I mean BIG. He had gone to bat for me to edit and write his memoirs with him. He was like a child, watching my face for my reaction.

"No. Wait, what? Yes? For real? Yes, for real?"

"Yes, for real, Jo. You deserve it." From his expression of delight, my response hadn't disappointed him.

"Why me?"

"I don't want to share everything with anyone else."

"Well, you'll be sharing everything with the world. You realise that, right?"

"I know, but you'll help me decide what to leave out and phrase it well. You, Jo, will take care of me and not what sells. I don't care if the book doesn't sell. I care that we tell my story the right way."

"So do I, Sam. For your mum. I'll ensure it happens how you want it to."

"I knew you would get it."

"When do we start?"

"Now. We can start right now. Especially now you've graduated with flying colours from this writing course."

We collapsed into fits of laughter, then beat a hasty exit out of the tearoom and away from the stares our giggles had earned us.

It was a perfect afternoon, wandering around Belton House and gardens. I stopped and jotted down spectacular scenery or the beautiful antique décor in the rooms. I also described Sam as he charmed the tour guides and security personnel or in his quiet, reflective moments. Some of his perfection and those minor imperfections that made him real. I thought they might come in useful when writing his memoirs with him. I took some photos too. You never knew; he might like some in the book. I even got a selfie with him that he let me share with my kids. An invitation to Ethan's and Matt's wedding swiftly followed.

When I showed him, he looked serious for a moment. "I don't want to intrude on a family event, Jo."

"Don't feel obliged if you have other commitments, but if you can make it, we're planning a big family Christmas dinner the day after, which you would also be welcome to. I'm sure you can bring a plus one. No pressure—all fun."

"No work?"

"Only if you want to work on the book, but otherwise, no work."

He took my phone to reply for himself.

Sam as Joanna:

> Hey to all Jo's babies and baby partners. This is Sam. I'll be there on Christmas Eve and the Day. No plus one. And I want to dance with everyone.

Matt as Ethan:

> Even me? (it's Matt, BTW, Ethan's intended) {heart emojis}

Sam as Joanna:

> Yes, even you, Matt. {Saturday Night Fever emoji}

Matt as Ethan:

> {Squee GIF}

As I drove him back to Norwich in time for his evening flight, Sam talked of his early life, and we recorded it so I could type it out for him. At one point, he was crying for his mum, and we pulled over so I could hold and comfort him. I couldn't help but sympathy cry a bit, making me miss my kids. When he exited the car to compose himself, I dug out some tissues to wipe my eyes and blow my nose. I watched him walk the length of the rest stop and back as I considered. If I died, my kids had each other, their partners and their dad. As far as I was aware, Sam had no one to mourn his mother with. I hoped telling his story, and through him, her life, would help his loneliness. Regardless, he had me now, and it was an honour to call him my friend.

***

By November's arrival, I was as excited as Beth, and as you know by now, that's saying something. There was no sign of Sam Harmer on my flight or any other actor I could recognise. Beth's bright and happy face greeted me at Arrivals through a crowd of people looking for their loved ones. It was the Wednesday before Thanksgiving Thursday, which was a hectic day to fly, but it meant I could be in the US for just over a month and incorporate both Thanksgiving and Christmas. She squeezed me so hard I would feel the bruises for a week. Her chatter accompanied our drive back to Connecticut and her tiny house with Al near the hospital where she worked. I enjoyed listening, but couldn't help falling asleep when we turned off the I-95 highway and headed north.

Despite the nap in the car, shortly after dinner, I was yawning, and my eyes didn't obey my demands for them to stay open. My body screamed that it was five hours later than the clock told me.

"I'm so happy you're here, Mom," Beth said from the bedroom door.

"Me too, love, but I must sleep if I'm helping with Thanksgiving dinner tomorrow." I rummaged for my toiletries bag rather than unpack everything as I would spend more time at Holly's bigger house, with an ensuite bathroom off the guest room. I didn't doubt that Beth would stay over as many days as Holly and Al would allow while she had a week off work.

I was out like a light but ready to get going early the following day, and before I knew it, I was up to my elbow inside a turkey, pulling out the giblets.

"Gross," Holly said, pulling a face. "Last year, I got Michel to do it."

After attending the same college as her husband, Holly ended up in finance, cutting her teeth on Wall Street until she could bear the misogyny no longer, and Michel interned at a prestigious law firm in the City. Then, they both hung up their go-getting lifestyle and bought a house in Westport, Connecticut. Michel was now a partner in a small law firm there, taking pro-bono work when possible, and Holly worked her finance talent for a non-profit organization. She also taught hot yoga in the evenings, but I refused to attend on account of my age—menopausal.

Many Americans can suffer from a bit of cognitive dissonance at Thanksgiving, believing it's the best holiday on the USA calendar—closely rivalled by Independence Day—a time when family can come together to celebrate, eat until they burst and watch 'American' football; yet knowing, historically, it promoted a story of pilgrims and Native Americans celebrating the harmony of a Thanksgiving meal when peace wasn't what happened in reality.

In my opinion, it was a way to segregate the sexes. The women in the kitchen prepared this massive feast while the men watched football. Afterwards, if you did it right, the men would clear up, and the women drank copious amounts of wine while they chatted.

The food was delicious, including my contribution of Yorkshire puddings with a new recipe, guaranteeing they rise. With the wine, we women hogged my dessert of sticky brownies—made the way Toni showed me. They didn't disappoint. As I sat enjoying a big brownie, I realised my devious daughters had other plans when I heard a knock at the door.

Holly brought a man to the table to introduce him. "Mom, this is Zachary Mitchell. He works with Michel at the firm. Zach, this is my mom, Joanna James, visiting from the UK."

"Hi, Jo is fine. It's nice to meet you." I offered my hand while trying to extract brownie goo from my teeth with my tongue.

"You too, Jo." He sat where Holly indicated, across from me.

"Let me get you a beer, Zach," Holly offered overly brightly.

"Wine is fine." He indicated the bottle on the table from which I'd poured my glass. "If you have another glass."

Holly vanished.

"Let me help you," Beth offered, leaping up from the table and following her sister.

"To get a wineglass?" I asked. Too late, I realised their game. Heat suffused my face as a hot flush went from my chest up to my neck and glowed in my cheeks. We sat at the table alone.

Zach shrugged. "I take it you weren't aware of my coming tonight?"

I shook my head, surreptitiously trying to swill some wine over my teeth to remove the last of the brownie residue, as Holly returned with Zach's wineglass, then beat a hasty retreat, saying something of Michel needing her.

Oh, boy, is she going to get it later. I hated being manipulated, and my girls knew it. Of course, I politely gave Zach a glass of wine from the bottle close to me. How I wished I could check my teeth for chocolate.

"We met once before a few years ago, and I thought you were interesting. I'd hoped to get to know you better after your divorce, but you left for England. When I heard you were visiting, I asked for another introduction."

"Why? Didn't Michel say I'm only here for a month?"

"A magical month, though, for romance. Who knows what might come of it?"

"Nothing will come of it, Zach. I'm sorry, you seem like a nice guy, but I'm not moving back to the States. Do you plan to move to the UK?"

"If you feel strongly about it, fair enough, but please allow me to take you to dinner at least once while you're here."

"I'm out tomorrow night with yoga, Mom," Holly called from the kitchen.

"What about Beth? I'm here to see all of you."

Beth entered the room, her face showing how conflicted she felt. Surprising me, Zach came to the rescue.

"I'd be happy to double-date with Beth and Al if you're all available. My treat, seeing as it's your time with your mom that I'm gate-crashing."

***

Zach turned out to be considerate and amusing. He got us a table at a fabulous restaurant with fancy cuisine, but not in those ridiculously small portions. I've no idea how he managed it on Black Friday. I'd spent the day with my girls, shopping with the masses and paying for many gifts for them and their husbands. I'd even found gifts for Ethan and Matt. I drew the line when Beth suggested matching tattoos. Exhausted but happy and hungry, we regaled Zach and Al with tales of our day.

"Mom, tell Zach about that writing course with that horrid man."

"We men like to hear the mistakes of others so we don't repeat them, right, Al?" I told him about it.

"Did you get your story back?" he asked.

"Nope. I messaged Grace and asked her to pick it up for me, but it was gone. She thinks Guy took it."

"Well, if he plagiarises it, just let me know. We'll get someone on the case. Can I read it?"

I'd typed it up from my original notes when I got home and then sent it to my Kindle so I could read and tweak it. So I fished out my phone and pulled up that email so I could send it to him. He typed in his email address, then confirmed he'd got it, but didn't look at it immediately. I found that simultaneously courteous and insulting. I noted how much easier it felt to share my work with someone than the first time I let Sam read on the plane.

My phone dinged with a message from Teena. She and Abby were available to meet for lunch the following week. They would come to Westport. I glanced up at Zach.

"What is it?" he asked, his face open and concerned.

"Am I right in assuming you have some leverage in getting a table here at short notice?"

"What did you have in mind?" His smile was playful, and I had a feeling that any favour I asked of him would require some form of payback.

"A lunch booking next week for three women who need a catch-up."

"Not a problem, but I will need some recompense."

"I didn't doubt it." I flirted with him because it was all good-natured, and I'd explained where I stood.

"A few opportunities over the next few weeks to get to know you better and for you to get to know me. I don't want to take you away from your family time, so I'd be happy to be included in your time together or see you at other times."

It wasn't difficult to agree to Zach's terms, and the lunch date with Teena and Abby was worth it. Zach turned up towards the end, insisted on paying, and then drove us to a nearby spa where Beth and Holly met us. It was a delightful afternoon.

***

Things got more complicated the weekend before I planned to drive to Boston. I was packing an overnight bag at Holly's while she called through from her bedroom as she filled her own. A car was arriving shortly, and Zach would be inside. We would head to New York City and the bright lights of Broadway, picking up Beth and Al on the way.

"He's so compassionate, Mom," Holly called through the open doors. "It's not just Michel who does pro bono work in the firm. All the partners do, including

Zach. He's told Michel how much he admires your courage in leaving Dad and moving back to the UK."

"So you've said, Holly."

"You're only here a few more days."

"What about when you and Michel considered moving to California or Canada when leaving New York City? I never said you had to move to Connecticut."

"But you were happy that we did."

"Of course I was, but it was your decision because it's your life."

"Hasn't he won you over at all?"

"Won me over? I'm not a prize; I'm a person. Has he forgotten what I said at Thanksgiving? I'm not moving back here. Not permanently."

"Why? You get on so well together. You laugh, joke, and talk for ages. Have you kissed him or anything?"

"None of your business, my girl." She was right about something, though. It would be easy to fall into this relationship—he was overly generous and didn't want to make decisions for me, but his work was in Connecticut, and as mine was flexible, he would look to me to move.

Sam texted me to see if I could have a quick word about his pages. I'd taken what he gave me on our drive from Grantham to Norwich, added my research, and produced a few chapters. Then I'd sent them before I left for the USA. I closed the door to my bedroom at Holly's and dialled his number.

"Jo, how is the USA? Everyone in the whole of the UK misses you."

I gave him a nervous laugh. "How are you, Sam?"

"Er, no. How are you, Jo? You don't sound right."

"Holly and Beth are trying to set me up with a great guy over here."

"What's the problem with that?"

"I made it clear to him the first night I met him—on Thanksgiving—that I didn't want to move back here permanently. Now he's wrangled his way into every outing, and I can see how much he would be good for everyone if we were together."

"Everyone but not you?"

"I'm sure he would've been good for me once upon a time, but I've changed."

"Isn't it funny, when you move on, how you no longer fit into a situation that would have suited you just fine before?" He sounded wistful.

"I don't want to live here permanently. I don't want to rely on someone else, but isn't that what you're supposed to want in a relationship? It's just that I wonder if he would rely on me equally?"

"What about physically?"

"Relationships aren't only about that, but, sure, I've thought about it. Zach's a good-looking man, but I don't think about him when he's not there. Zach would be a brain decision, not a heart one. If I'm going to have another man in my life, I'd really like my heart to be involved."

"I think you answered your own question."

"Yeah, but I feel bad that I might have led him on."

"Except you said yourself that you told him from the beginning you didn't want to move back to Connecticut. He's tried to change your mind. I can't blame him for trying, I guess. It's not your fault he failed. You don't owe him anything."

"Thanks, Sam. Anyway, my troubles aren't why you wanted to talk. What can I help with?"

"I've scribbled all over a printout of your pages, but I don't want to ask the hotel staff to scan them so I can email them. What can I do?"

"Scan them in using your phone and message them. I'll message you if I have questions. Does that work for you?"

"How do I scan on my phone? Is there a special app?"

"No. Your 'Notes' app has a scan option. I thought you youngsters knew all this tech stuff."

"I thought you oldies were technophobes," he parried back good-naturedly.

"Harriet showed me, but she's my age, so it doesn't support your theory."

"She's the exception that proves the rule."

I could hear the rustle of pages, and then my phone started dinging.

"Don't send them individually, butthead," I admonished over the noise.

"Jo J—ames is a gen—ius," he sang over and over down the phone, which made me laugh.

"Thank goodness for you, Sam Harmer."

***

We watched the fantastic show from a box, then enjoyed a meal and finally, some drinks at the bar in the fabulous hotel where we were staying. After the first drink, Holly, Michel, Beth, and Al made their excuses and headed to their rooms. I had been talking about my murder mystery book and learning courtroom lingo from Zach and Michel. After waving them all goodnight, I settled back in my seat when Zach caught me unawares.

"I want to kiss you," he murmured, leaning forward, his gaze scanning my face before dropping to my lips.

"Zach, you know that isn't where this is going," I chided gently, sipping my wine as a distraction. It was disappointing because I'd been clear from the beginning that we, as a couple, wouldn't be happening.

"I thought you enjoyed my company as much as I have yours."

"I have, but I haven't changed my mind."

"But you do like me. I've seen you look. Just as you're doing right now."

That was true. I'd fantasised about Zach often these past three weeks. He offered sex, comfort, money, security, closeness to my children and US friends, as well as respect. But every time I considered what I would have to give up to accept his offer—my home in the UK, my county of Norfolk, which I love, my family and UK friends with whom I had only recently reconnected. How much time would I have to concentrate on my writing? I'm sure Zach has connections to the publishing world who could help, but I wouldn't ask him. I wanted to achieve my success, however it might look, with my own talent and contacts.

I pushed away a little and safely turned to look into his eyes. "One kiss could break the dam, Zach. We both know that, so I must say no, and you want to push me. If you succeed, I'll resent you in the end."

"You can't know that. We won't end like you and Bruce. I won't cheat on you."

"I didn't leave Bruce because of that, because I didn't even know about it at that time. I wasn't happy, and I wanted to go home. It's taken me over two years to get to this point. Although I'm well aware of the huge benefits of saying yes to you, I won't be me. I can't give it up the moment I've reached my destination. I'm building even more—for myself."

He nodded, resigned, I hoped, because I was teetering at seeing his hang-dog expression. "Right there. That's why you're so exceptional, Jo. It's why Bruce wanted you back, why that other guy regretted his actions. No wonder your children are all such great people. Nothing to do with Bruce. You were the one setting the example and are still doing it."

"Those men wanted me so they could change me, and so do you."

"No. Of course I don't. Why would I change what's making me fall for you?"

"Because you aren't looking at how your life would change if I were in it, compared to how you want me to change my life."

"Being with someone is about compromise. I understand that."

"Of course, but equal compromise. As a lawyer, you understand that, too."

"I do now."

Tears glinted in his eyes as he stood and made me feel like a total shit-heel. I almost apologised until anger overtook it. I'd made it clear from the start where I stood. He thought he could change my mind. Instead, I said the only thing that occurred to me—"You're a good man."

"I wish I weren't. Then I would crush you to me right now and make the decision too difficult." He swallowed the last of his scotch and walked away.

"It already is, Zach."

YOUR 'THE ONE'

I watched you from a distance
As you sang your song
Though I wrote you this story
Knew I wouldn't be your 'the one'

But you approached, and we talked
Day and night, moon and sun
And we sat, and we walked
But I shouldn't be your 'the one'

Then you reached, and we kissed
Touched and all that fun
But I saw the cruel twist
That I couldn't be your 'the one'

So, I read to you my story
And for me, you sang your song
I was wrong; it sounded right
Because now I am your 'the one.'

SIXTEEN

D orothy was a sight for sore eyes when she met me at the same hotel. She looked as wonderful as ever to me, but I allowed her to list her complaints, including that the doctor didn't listen to her, so Dorothy refused to listen to him. She'd made it this far, Dorothy reasoned. We'd kept in touch, so she knew all my stories apart from Zach.

It felt like a relief to regale her with it—unburdening myself. It had haunted me that perhaps I'd taken advantage of Zach, but I quickly kicked it to the curb when I recalled what Sam said—that I'd been clear from the start. He was right that I had looked and even flirted a bit, but there had been no physical contact. I hadn't even held Zach's hand. I couldn't talk to Holly or Beth about it. Both were bitterly disappointed with me, but they would get over it. Zach hadn't returned with us in the limo, but left in the night. I was sad but glad—a regular contradiction for me regarding men.

"Jo, you must forget it. Women aren't responsible for men's feelings. They're grownups and fully capable of dealing with their emotions. If they aren't, then that's their problem."

"Thank you, Dorothy. You're right, of course."

"More interestingly, tell me what's happening with your writing."

I talked about my mystery book, but I was still stuck on a good ending until she reminded me of the story I'd written with the ghost in it. "Combine them," she said, as if it was the easiest thing in the world, but it triggered an idea that might work.

Then she told me a story about her husband, which had us laughing so loudly that the other patrons in the hotel's restaurant kept staring at us, but we didn't care.

***

I had two weeks planned in Boston, including my birthday mid-month and Ethan's wedding on Christmas Eve, when the rest of the family would arrive. We arranged a mad Christmas Day dinner in Ethan's and Matt's tiny flat the next day before they flew away for their honeymoon. I was glad for the time I got to share with them before the wedding planning overtook us.

I'd already edited the scanned pages Sam had sent. Once I arrived in Boston, we had one evening for him but afternoon for me on the phone where he told me all about his early career—the times when filming had been easier compared to the times between when he missed his mother. As Sam became famous, he found trusting the people he met more challenging. Relationships were tricky, and more than once, he'd considered, albeit briefly, whether the world would be better without him in it. We were both crying in the end. Then Sam talked about the therapy that helped him. Sam ended his story on an upbeat note, believing he could open himself up to what he hoped might be a long-term relationship.

I yawned and stretched out my fingers. I'd been typing as Sam spoke, putting my words per minute to the test. "I'm always here for you, Sam. You just need to let me know. I'll be there."

"I was about to say the same for you, Jo. I'm glad you asked me about Zach. I didn't want to influence you, but I think you need to be with someone who accommodates your needs as much as you would do for them."

"Thanks, Sam. That sounds good."

"Night, sweets."

"G'night."

***

For my birthday, I'd treated myself to five days in an expensive hotel with views over the harbour through immense glass windows. I hoped it would spark my creativity. Ethan and Matt took me out for a meal at a popular bar. The ambience was good, and the layout of the place was spacious. The food was simple and tasty, and they kept the wine flowing as we waited at the bar for a table.

'Fifty-two, Fat and Fabulous,' I recited under my breath a couple of times as the wait staff showed us to our seats, and then I spotted him.

Unlike any other man I had met over the past two years, this one held my attention like a homing beacon, and I was a long-lost starfighter making her way home in a damaged ship—maybe I needed to soak up the wine with some food if my mind was going to Star Wars references already. It didn't help my ego that almost every woman in the place felt the same way, and maybe even a few men, judging by Matt's expression.

"It's Carter Wick. We've seen him in here twice before. He's always a hot ticket," Matt said by way of explanation. Ethan snorted, and I thought, *Yeah, a hot ticket for sure.*

Of course, everyone looked at Carter because he was the entertainment up on the little stage, but some just gazed in wonder and lust. He didn't seem to mind or require it—he just enjoyed singing up on that little stage with his guitar. His voice was melodic with a rasp tinge, his hair dark and tied back rather untidily. It flopped in his eyes a little, but it didn't stop their blue twinkling intensity. His build was solid without being huge, and his arms looked strong without being overly sculpted. I estimated he was close to my age.

His music was country with a bit of rock, and when he sang a song I knew, I swayed in my seat and mouthed along.

Is it possible he just winked at me?

Emboldened by the wink and more wine after the fabulous food, I figured what the hell, and, not seeing a steady supply of drinks being sent his way, I swayed to the bar. I asked if many people had bought him drinks. Did he mind if people did? When the bar staff told me he had an expensive taste in bourbon, if I wanted to send him a drink, I didn't hesitate. "My name is Jo, and it's my birthday. Send him a double and keep the change." I handed over a couple of bills.

When his song finished, he reached over to the table where they'd placed his drink, raised his glass my way and said into the microphone, "Happy birthday, Jo. This next song is for you."

I'd never had anyone do anything like that for me before. I was thrilled and grateful and raised my glass in return while Ethan and Matt cheered.

The song was a sweet love song, and I'm sure I blushed the entire way through. He continued singing a few more songs, then said goodnight and approached our high-top table. Ethan wriggled his eyebrows my way, and I told him to behave.

"Hi, Jo, and happy birthday again. I'm Carter." He leaned on the table and took a seat when I offered it to him.

"Yes, I knew that. This is my son, Ethan, and his fiancé, Matt." The guys shook hands and exchanged some pleasantries while I perused Carter. Up close, he was more natural, with stubble on his face, wrinkles and some chest hair showing above the V of his shirt. He exuded male but in a mature and respectful way, not domineering. We ordered another round of drinks, and I realised he had no plans to hook up with one of the younger women who had been watching him. He wanted to talk to me.

"I've toured around the UK a bit, nothing grand but some clubs and pubs. Next time, I'll have to be sure to come to Nor-wich," he decided.

"Norr-ich," Ethan and I corrected simultaneously.

"There, too," Carter smirked.

"I'd come and see you somewhere if you tour the UK again," I confirmed, though where that might be, I'd no idea.

Carter leaned in to whisper, "And would you put me up at your place?"

244

"Sure," I smiled with a sideways look at him when he stayed near my ear.

"Do you have other plans tonight, or could I celebrate the rest of your birthday with you?" he whispered, brushing a kiss behind my ear. A pleasant vibration ran down my neck and made its way further down, and then he faced the boys as if nothing had happened. *Two can play at that game,* I thought.

"I was thinking of going back to my hotel room aaannnd—" I whispered in his ear, kissing him in the same spot. The muscles in his neck twitched under my lips when he smiled.

What am I doing? This is so unlike me. I'd kept everything in check with Zach because I didn't want to lead him on, but Carter exuded sex appeal, and his only expectation was for that night.

"Ethan and Matt, thank you so much for a lovely evening. It's been one of my best birthdays."

"So far," I heard Carter quietly say beside me, hoping Ethan didn't hear it. Judging by his smirk, Matt had.

"I'm going to walk back to my hotel. It's only a couple of blocks." I pecked them on their cheeks and moved away from the table.

"I'll walk with you. I could do with some air," Carter said before shaking hands with them again. Ethan said something to him that made Carter reply with a serious expression. No doubt Ethan was being protective, and it looked like Carter approved and respected it.

Carter caught up with me at the exit. Once we were outside, he took my hand. Despite the cold Boston air, I was still warm from the bar, so I hadn't put on my gloves. Still, he rubbed my palm and sent tingles up my arm. I could feel the callouses on his fingers from the guitar playing.

I glanced his way as I talked, "You know you could've had your pick of those much younger women that were closer to the stage."

"Oh, I'll go back then." He mocked a turn back to the bar, but I hung onto his hand. He laughed. "I'd feel like a creep with such a young woman. Wouldn't you, with a man twenty years or more younger?"

I thought of Sam Harmer and quickly agreed. Especially now, I knew him better and had a more protective feeling for him. "I'm glad to hear it."

"Just a minute." Carter let go of my hand and ran across the road to the seven-eleven open across the street. He was a few minutes, and I tried to see what he was buying through the bright windows. Then he was back and holding my hand again.

"What was that about?" I asked.

"What do you think that was about?" He raised his eyebrows and tapped a box in his pocket, laughing at my expression when I realised he'd just bought some condoms. "It doesn't mean anything has to happen between us. I only wanted to be prepared if it did."

"You're single, right?"

"Yes, I'm single. I don't cheat."

"Me neither. That's why I checked." I stopped walking.

"What?" He looked confused, which I thought was fair after his teasing about the condoms.

"This is my hotel."

His jaw dropped.

"Tonight is my second of five, as a birthday treat. My room has a balcony and amazing views of Boston harbour."

Truthfully, I thought I'd gone somewhat overboard when I saw it, but now I imagined making love to this attractive man with a backdrop of the twinkling lights reflected in the inky water.

"I don't have to come in," he managed valiantly, but I just laughed and pulled him through the revolving doors.

At the door to my room, while I fiddled with the keycard, Carter reiterated my choice, which was sweet of him.

Success!

I pulled him into the room, put the do not disturb on the door handle and locked the door. When I turned back, he stood close behind me. I liked he hadn't wandered around checking out the room.

"Happy birthday to me," I said, pulling him close for the best kiss of my life.

***

I woke to an empty bed and the sound of the shower running. I would have thought it a shame, but honestly, he'd worn me out. Bill, the only other man since Bruce, had been once and done. I thought back to the night before. Carter had been everywhere—hands, tongue, fingers, searching, probing. I couldn't believe how he made me feel all night—desired, attractive, horny, vibrant.

Carter, at least I'd moved on one letter in the alphabet, gave me so much but expected nothing in return, though I was happy to give. I'd never experienced anything like that with a man and thought I never would again after that night until he told me he had another gig at the same bar and asked me if I could watch him again. A groupie? That would be a first.

He came in damp and wrapped in a towel. A low hum escaped me without my permission, and he laughed. "Let's get some breakfast, sleepy head. My friend and roadie, Aaron, will swing by with my bag if that's okay. I can't go out like this and need my toothbrush."

"So you don't have fresh breath right now?"

"Nope." He sat on the bed close enough for me to get up on an elbow and pull him to me. My God, the man could kiss, and he enjoyed it. A hand snaked under the covers to my breast, but I pulled away, exiting the other side of the bed. I needed the bathroom, and he needed to be decent for his friend.

"Good morning." I wiggled my butt and disappeared from view.

By the time we got out for some food, it was more like a brunch. We had little chance to do anything, but I wanted to go to Faneuil Hall and Quincy Market. He professed a desire to walk around the common, but it was cold, and the following morning before he left, the forecast was at least ten degrees Fahrenheit warmer. So we compromised and agreed to move his walk to the following day. I promised to get up early. As we moseyed in and out of the shops, we naturally talked about our pasts.

Carter was born in Boston, but his parents moved to Louisiana when he was still a baby, so he grew up a Southern boy. His accent was a mix of the South and his parents' New England influence, which I enjoyed. My own Norfolk accent had disappeared mostly with all my years in Connecticut, except for when I was talking with my family. Americans loved my English accent, but in England, family and friends, especially Harriet, loved to spot my Americanisms.

In college, Carter was in a band with some local success but didn't finish his degree. Band members dropped out one by one to pursue more traditional careers, marriage, and children. Aaron was one such ex-band member. However, he remained a good friend and was happy to travel with Carter now and again.

"You never wanted the whole marriage and kids thing?" I asked.

"I've done some regular work to pay the bills here and there—some office stuff, some labour intensive, but nothing stuck long-term like music. I had a few more serious relationships, but they didn't like the gigging lifestyle, so it didn't work out. It might have been different if I'd made it big, but I never sought that. Not that I would have minded if it happened. How was the whole marriage and kids thing for you?"

I talked about my kids a lot. Who doesn't, after being given an opportunity like that? The whole time, Carter held my hand as much as possible. I found it astonishing, considering Bruce would never hold my hand. If I ever grabbed hold of him as we walked along, he would let go after a few seconds, scratch his head, and then put his hand in a pocket. Then I spoke of Bruce and told Carter a few of my recent men's stories.

He laughed along with me. "You're a natural storyteller."

"Thanks, but you too, with your songs." I was looking forward to hearing him sing again that night.

We headed back to the bar and ate a light meal before his set. He was even sexier to watch when I knew he was mine for this little window of time. *Tough luck, ladies.*

"Déjà vu," I offered as we walked back to the hotel, with our day's shopping, his guitar, and take-home desserts from the restaurant. Chocolate for me, of course, and a fluffy berry cheesecake for Carter that he'd threatened to lick off various parts of my body. I tingled at the thought that he might actually do it.

***

As I lay in his arms, fully satiated and, yes, a little sticky, he spoke from the heart, which was unexpected. I thought he would consider me just another notch in his bedpost, which I imagined as more notches than bed and it had probably collapsed years ago.

"What is it about you, Jo?" He didn't seem to want an answer, so I squeezed him. "Your husband must have been mad to give you up. No wonder he wanted you back."

"Familiarity breeds contempt?" I suggested. "Plus, he was still with her when he asked me to return with him. He couldn't have been that serious."

"I spotted you the moment you walked in with Ethan and Matt. A light seems to shine from within you. I couldn't take my eyes off you then, and I can't now."

"A homing beacon," I mused. "I thought that of you, but you were on stage, so everyone watched you."

"Yeah. Good analogy. I feel so comfortable with you."

"What, like an old pair of slippers?" I objected.

"I've never owned a pair of slippers in my life."

"What then?"

"Like, you don't judge me. Demand nothing of me," he mused.

"I wouldn't say that." I grinned.

His hand slid down my back and squeezed my bum. "All freely given."

"If we lived together, I'd demand you put out the trash." I detested that job.

"You wouldn't have to because if it were my job, I'd do it anyway."

"Isn't it a bad thing, though? I've wondered if I never made Bruce feel needed."

"That's on him, not you."

"It was more like I had four children, not three."

"Again, that's on him."

"I don't feel judged by you. I don't feel you demand anything in return for what you give, and you've given me so much these past two days." There was a feeling in my voice I hadn't expected or planned for, and I'll admit, it scared me a little.

"Well, that wouldn't be fair, would it? Like, here's a gift, now where's mine?"

"I need to shower before I sleep." I got out of bed.

"I'll help," he offered with a little tap on my butt, and while he soaped, he hummed.

***

I fell asleep to the soothing sound of Carter humming the same beautiful tune. The vibrations buzzed through me as I snuggled up close. I would have to ask him what song it came from so I could play it on Spotify and think of him. I woke up to him softly strumming the same tune on his guitar. He was sitting in the chair across from the bed, naked, with the guitar across his lap and a pencil in his mouth. He removed the pencil and scribbled something in a notebook resting on the arm of the chair. My God, how did the man look so good?

"You just need a cowboy hat on to finish the picture," I said, making a rectangle with my hands and taking a pretend photo. "What's the song?"

"I haven't given it a title yet," he replied with a gorgeous smile, and my heart hitched.

"You're composing? Sexier and sexier."

"Hey, my view was helping," he complained as I moved to get out of bed and headed for the bathroom. "Jo, do you mind if I stay for a bit? I want to get this down while it's in my head."

I popped back out, pulling on the robe I'd retrieved. "I thought you had a train to catch." He had a gig in New York City that night. "Not that I'm eager for you to leave."

"I decided to get a later one."

"And what of your walk through the park?" I teased.

"Another time. I think this is more important."

"Then don't let me stop you. I'll order some breakfast after I have a shower."

While we waited for breakfast, I pulled out my laptop and opened a new file. I forgot the murder mystery for now and started writing something different based on Carter mentioning me being a natural storyteller while I told him about my recent past. Unlike the last few times I'd tried to write, the words flowed. The ideas I'd had over these past two days with Carter coalesced as I wrote.

After breakfast, Carter showered. I sneaked to the door he'd left ajar to listen to his low singing in the shower. Some words were coming with the tune of the song. I caught 'beacon home', 'heart' and 'rest to recharge'. *Intriguing.*

I heard him turn off the water and hurried back to my laptop. Soon, I was busy, but I was very aware of him sauntering into the room with a towel around his waist.

"What are you doing?" he asked as he leaned on the desk.

"Writing a book of my own."

"Seriously? You really are awesome."

"Says the man who spent most of the night composing a brand-new song."

"Am I in it?" He gestured at my laptop.

"Am I in your song?"

"All the way to the core, sweetheart. 'A song for Jo'. I probably won't keep that title, though that's how I'll always think of it."

"Cute," I said, but the swell of emotion that I was his muse almost overcame me. "What about 'The Beacon Home'? We talked about homing beacons last night."

"I like it. How about yours?"

"Too early for a title," I said, but I did have a possibility in mind. "Lyrics?"

"I'll write them on the train. If it comes together, we'll see what NYC thinks. I'll get Aaron to film it and send it to you." His friend, who had dropped off his bag yesterday, lived in the city and had gone on ahead as Carter was 'busy' with me.

"I would love that. Would you like to come to Ethan's wedding if you're finished there before Christmas?"

"I'll be there. Meanwhile, before I get dressed, I would like to say a proper goodbye, but not if you're in the flow of writing. I know how it can be when you're in the groove."

I looked him up and down. His butt rested on my desk coated in the white fluffy towel, the front of which had begun to bulge. He'd folded his arms across his chest, pushing his biceps out, and his chest hair was still damp. I reached up and ran my fingers over it. In the next moment, he'd grabbed my wrist and pulled me out of my chair and against him, falling the slight distance to the rumpled bed.

Time moved too fast before he left for the train station. One more crushing kiss and he was gone.

Dishevelled and still tingling from the sensation of him all over my body, I sat at my laptop and gazed into the distance for a few moments. Then I turned my attention back to my book. I was excited about this one.

SINGLE

No one there
Everyday
To know you in
Everyway

To hold your hand
As you walk
To listen to you
As you talk

To soothe your worries
In the night
To hold you closely
Til it's light

No one there
To let you down
To know you, then
To mess around

To drop your hand

And scratch their head
And fall asleep
While you talk in bed

To cause you worries
In the night
To snore and snore
Until it's light

SEVENTEEN

My phone dinged as I checked out of the hotel two days later. After Carter left, I'd made the most of the room, spending my time writing. During my last week in Boston, I would sleep in Ethan's spare room while I helped them with the wedding and Christmas preparations.

I clicked the YouTube link Carter had sent me while waiting for the receptionist to return with the itemised bill I'd requested. I sighed as the video of a small, dark NYC stage began with him strumming a familiar tune. The lyrics of 'The Beacon Home', as he had titled the song, enchanted me.

"That's a great song," the receptionist startled me from my reverie when she returned.

I changed to full-screen and turned up the sound as we watched it together over the counter. A few more people gathered both sides of us, drawn by the beautiful melody and Carter's heartfelt singing.

"Oh, isn't that Carter Wick? I saw him the other night at that place a couple of blocks over," someone said from behind my shoulder. "I don't remember that song, though."

"He hadn't written it then," I said, thrilled at the thought that I had been the first person to hear it and had even inspired him.

"What's it called?" another disembodied voice asked.

"The Beacon Home," I called back and spotted a few more people accessing it on their phones. According to YouTube, a few thousand had already viewed it, which I thought was amazing.

By the time I got to Ethan's and showed it to him and Matt, the number was close to one hundred thousand and climbing. I messaged Carter.

Joanna:
Wow, you're a hit.

Carter:
The Beacon Home is a hit.

Joanna:
Only because of you singing it. You give it so much emotion.

Carter:
It's all because of you, Jo. I miss holding you, which I think comes through when I sing it.

Joanna:
You think of me when you sing it?

Carter:
Of course. Every time. Sorry, I gotta take this call. Can't wait for the wedding.

Carter and I continued to message each other. We'd shared some intimate thoughts, but none of those kinds of photos. We agreed we could remember well enough from our time together. Then, one night, I tried writing a sex scene. I think those can be the most difficult to write. You want it to be sexy, but you must use words that elicit sexiness, not laughter. However, Carter and I laughed a lot during our time together. I described a scene from one of our nights, getting a little hot and heavy recalling it, and messaged it to him the next day.

Carter:

Hey, a bit of warning when you send that kind of thing, Jo. I got a hard-on in the middle of a meeting.

Joanna:

{laughing emojis} It was good then? I thought I'd try to write a sex scene.

Carter:

Yes, it was good–obvs. Specially because I remember every second firsthand. Can you write one we didn't do?

Joanna:

How about my fantasy of you in an apron cleaning my house? {laughing emojis}

Carter:

Only an apron? {winking emoji} I'd like something I can think about doing when I see you again.

Joanna:

I'll try, and we'll see if you can deliver.

The next night, I sent him my best effort. He expressed his reaction with several emojis and many thumbs up and kisses, but as the days wore on, Carter's messages dwindled as the number of views on the video rose.

I knew he was still in New York City when he appeared on 'The Today Show'. He talked briefly about a woman he'd recently met who inspired the song. His eyes twinkled as he looked at the camera, and I felt as if he looked right at me.

"Can you tell us her name?"

"I haven't asked her if I can, but perhaps one day. I'm happy to sing it for y'all, but I'll be thinking of her."

The female presenters sighed at the same time as I did. Then I shushed Ethan and Matt, who were rolling around laughing at me until Carter's face filled the TV screen, and we were all transfixed. Tears filled my eyes at its emotion and seeing him again, even on a screen. When he'd finished, Ethan put his arm around me and hugged me.

"You'll see him soon, Mom. Not many days now, and we have lots to do."

"I can't believe I'm so emotional." I wiped the tears from my cheeks, then got stuck into the day's list of things to complete. "My last baby is getting married."

I messaged Carter a couple of congratulatory texts and said he could use my name, but keep the details to a minimum. I didn't want to be photographed or have people think I was riding his coattails. It wasn't like we would be in a relationship, even if I were looking forward to seeing him at the wedding and maybe even if he toured the UK one day. When I checked my phone, I noted that the YouTube video was now at over a million views, as was the video of the Today Show.

'Who is the woman who inspired 'The Beacon Home'?' Many online news-feeds asked on their websites, and several beautiful young women claimed it was them. I scanned the comments on one article where an anonymous person had posted that they'd seen him in Boston, and he left with an older woman who must have been his mom. While I was three years older than Carter, I didn't think that depiction was fair.

Finally, early on the twenty-third of December, I got a call from Carter.

"Hey, Jo. How are ya?"

"Busy with wedding stuff. How about you? You must be rushed off your feet, but congrats again. The song is so wonderful. I cry every time I hear it." It was on the tip of my tongue to ask when I would see him and if he needed me to meet him at the station or airport, but I couldn't bring myself to say it. I knew what this call meant—he wasn't going to make it.

"Jo, I can't—"

Someone called his name clearly from all the commotion in the background.

"I know. I'll tell the boys. They'll be disappointed. I will be—"

"Mr. Wick?" the voice was closer, louder and more insistent.

"I'm sorry, Jo."

"Me too," I said, but I couldn't stop the tears and my voice catching—he must have heard. He didn't owe me anything. We'd made no promises and had a fun two nights. He got a song out of it, and I hoped I got a book out of it—fair was fair.

I'd messaged Sophie with an outline, and she wanted chapters ASAP, clearly excited. Her news had been that she was breaking away from the publishing company she'd worked at for fifteen years with another woman who was her partner in a different sense. They were starting their own literary agency. From the sound of it, she thought my book would be a great starting point for them if I wanted to be their first author.

"I'm flying to Nashville to record 'The Beacon Home' and some of my other songs for an album. I've signed a deal."

"Carter, for fuck's sake!" That was a different voice and much closer to him.

"That's Aaron. I've got to go, but I'll call and explain everything to you when I can. We'll see each other again, I promise."

"Don't make me a promise you can't keep," I said to empty air.

Carter was gone.

***

Instead of worrying about it, I decided to make Ethan's wedding day the best possible, just like I'd done for Holly and Beth. Two days before, Elliott and Alastair had arrived with tales of their plane seats being upgraded to first class with Sam. I'd asked him to look out for them, but I hadn't expected that.

There was no sign of Sam when we headed to the restaurant we had booked for the evening before the big event. Then my girls arrived with their husbands, and with them came Bruce and Sandi. The two best men, both from Ethan's college, turned up with their partners, and Matt's parents arrived, too.

Sandi leaned over the empty seat between us. "I could ask them to move this chair if you'd rather have more room. I promise I won't bite."

I gave her my best smile despite her assuming I had no date and implying I was fat enough to need more room. "That chair is waiting for my date to turn up." I was confident Sam wouldn't mind me referring to him as such. I looked at my phone, which I would put away as soon as he arrived, but then I heard a hubbub at the entrance. It was a mixture of many intakes of breath and noises of exclamation. Sandi looked up at the same time as me, watching Sam scan the restaurant, speak to the maître d' and then head towards us, politely fobbing off requests for autographs and selfies.

"That's Sam Harmer," Sandi murmured. "Oh my god, he's coming this way."

Sam's beautiful wide smile was all for me, and oh, how satisfying it was to catch a peripheral glimpse of Sandi's goldfish expression as her head turned from him to me and back again. I stood and rounded the table to greet him, surprised when he wrapped his muscly arms around me and lifted me off my feet in a bear hug.

"There you are, Jo."

I whispered in his ear, "Thank you for coming. Sandi, with an 'i', still hasn't closed her mouth. I told her you were my date tonight."

"Anytime, sweets. My pleasure." He kissed my cheek.

Over his shoulder, many in the restaurant stared open-mouthed while he set me carefully back on my feet. At the head of the table close to where we'd embraced, a stunned Matt and Ethan had stood to be introduced. Sam quickly put them at ease with hugs and handshakes, happy to be introduced to Matt's parents. He waved to everyone else, assuring them he was excited to get a chance to talk to them at tomorrow's event, before we took our seats on the other side of Ethan.

Suddenly, efficient waitstaff bearing champagne flutes and popping corks surrounded the table. I looked at Sam, who gave me a surreptitious wink.

"You'd better stand and give them a toast, Jo," he said.

As I started to get to my feet, Bruce shot up, holding his glass aloft. I sat again.

"Let's all raise our glasses to Ethan and Matt."

"Ethan and Matt," everyone intoned.

I received a sharp nudge from Sam's elbow. "C'mon, Jo. You can outdo him."

I stood, trying to rack my brains for something better than Bruce's vapid toast. "First, an enormous thank you to our special guest, Sam, for his thoughtful and generous gesture of providing this champagne." I felt his warm hand wrap around mine with a squeeze. Damn him, he was going to make me cry. I swallowed quickly and turned to the boys. "Second, the biggest congratulations to Ethan and Matt. It's an honour to watch you tie the knot tomorrow and officially welcome Matt to our family. Thank you, Matt, for choosing to love my son and making him so happy. So, raise your glasses to—choosing love."

As Matt's father stood and began his toast, the maître d' appeared at Sam's shoulder. While I smiled encouragingly at the toast-maker, I ear-wigged on Sam's conversation.

"I hope the champagne was to your satisfaction, sir."

"Absolutely, thank you. Now, can I request your best service? Keep the looky-loos at bay so I can pay attention to my date, and the bill is mine for everyone at this table. If you can do that, I'll double it as a tip to be shared evenly with all staff working tonight."

"Absolutely. Of course, sir. May I ask, however—? The chef is a fan, so I'm told."

"Anytime that is good for them will be fine." I loved that he didn't assume the chef's gender.

With that, he turned in time to raise his glass for the toast, and a broad, satisfied grin was on his face.

"Thank you, Sam. You didn't have to do all that."

"I've waited enough tables to know how hard that job is, and I didn't have time to pick up a gift for your guys."

Ethan leaned in towards me. "What was that all about, Mom?"

"Sam just took care of everything for you tonight. He said it's your wedding gift."

"That's a lot of dough, Mom." He looked concerned.

"Don't worry and enjoy yourself. You can thank Sam later."

***

An old family friend officiated the wedding in a beautiful hotel ballroom overlooking the Charles River. Christmas decorations were everywhere, and I walked down the aisle, which was made of two sets of chairs filled with family and friends, with Ethan by my side. Both men decided to be given away by their moms. Then I sat next to Sam, who insisted on it so I didn't have to sit next to Bruce. Sandi seemed happy to be sitting on Sam's other side.

Ethan's and Matt's vows were beautiful and heartfelt. Individually, they had come to me for some editing, but I didn't want to take away from their own words. When pressed, I just made them flow a bit more. Still emotional over Carter, I couldn't help crying.

After the service and meal, the two grooms danced together. Slow at first, before they morphed into a fast, more synchronised dance with fantastic steps, the best men joining in, dancing in time with them. At the last moment, the best men had their partners join them, and they dipped them while Ethan, the bigger of the two grooms, did the same to Matt. Then he kissed him—so romantic.

Everyone stood and applauded. After this, I was called upon, with Matt's mom, to dance with the grooms. We'd been practising a waltz, which was fine with me. The plan was for our partners to cut in so that Ethan and Matt could dance together again, and everyone else could join in. I'd hoped that Carter would be there to cut in and dance with me, but Sam had agreed to do it. Unfortunately, Bruce was quicker in the moment and as Ethan released me, the wrong man was standing there.

I was tempted just to go along with it, but that's what men who do that kind of shit bank on, isn't it? The woman will always keep the peace rather than make a fuss. Later, when you say you didn't like it, they say, *'Why didn't you say so at the time?'*. Then I spotted Sandi's expression of dismay over his shoulder, and a wave of pity made me strong enough to speak up.

"No, Bruce. Sam is going to dance with me."

"Stop making a scene, Jo, and just dance with me."

"This was planned, Bruce. Therefore, you're the one making a scene. I'm going to dance with Sam."

"May I cut in, Miss Joanna?" Sam moved smoothly between us, poking Bruce in the ribs with his elbow as he took me in his arms.

"Thank you, Sam. You may." I laughed, delighted with his Redway Acres accent coming out.

"I wish I could challenge him for embarrassing you."

"You are too good, sir."

"It's true, I am."

And he was. He stuck by my side so much that Bruce never got a look in. After I visited the ladies' room, I exited to the surprising sight of Sam talking to Bruce.

"Look, mate, just give up on her. She's moved on and doesn't want to talk to you. You're acting like a stalker."

"Who has she moved on with? You? I could wipe the floor with you."

"You really couldn't. But no, not with me. Jo moved on by herself and made a life of her own. She's happier on her own than she ever was with you. When she finds someone, he'll be a better man than either of us to deserve her."

"Thank you, Sam." I took his hand and pulled him back to the dancing.

I stood at the window in contemplation as the dark settled over the river and all of those twinkling lights switched on. I'd watched the same lights from a different location ten days ago with a naked Carter lying beside me.

Sam's arms snaked around me, and he rested his chin on the top of my head. "My date has abandoned me," he complained.

"I'm right here," I said, changing my focus to our reflection in the window. "Or have you replaced me already? So fickle, you know, these actors."

"Not physically abandoned, but up here in your busy brain. What's going on, Joey." Sam wiggled his chin in my hair.

"You've been dancing with my brother too much. I was thinking about my birthday. I spent that night at a hotel with a man and the next night, too."

"About time!"

"Oh, shut up, you. You're forgetting Bill."

"Misogynists don't count."

"I'm not telling you more if you're going to tease me."

"Sorry. C'mon, tell Doctor Sam all."

Sam understood about keeping secrets, so we sat down and watched everyone dance while I talked about Carter—how I felt about the man I'd known for such a short time and wondered if I would ever see again. Soon, Sam's hands were tapping out the beat on the table where we sat, so I relieved his misery.

"Thanks for listening, but now I need lifting out of my doldrums. Let's dance."

***

Christmas Day comprised me cooking in Ethan's tiny kitchen by roping everyone in to do jobs like peeling, stirring, chopping, hunting up enough plates and squeezing them around their little table. I was leaving the next day, so a Christmas with my three kids and their partners wasn't to be missed. Elliott and Alastair were there, and even Sam joined in, following my infallible Yorkshire Pudding recipe instructions. He was stupidly pleased when they rose so well. I didn't know what plans Bruce and Sandi had, but one thing was for sure—they weren't with us.

Although it was still me cooking, it was the best Christmas I'd ever had. Right after it, everyone was in a frenzy of packing. Ethan and Matt were heading to their Caribbean honeymoon the next day, and I was leaving close to the same time to head back home. I was looking forward to the peace and quiet of my little Norwich house, where I could review my holiday and get more writing done.

Hearing of my plans, Sam booked a seat on the same flight. He'd used up all his agent's goodwill enjoying Ethan's nuptials and needed to get on with his next project. I'd promised him he could read what I had so far on my new book if he kept it a secret and understood it was a first draft.

Just as we boarded, my phone pinged with a news article from one of those sites asking what woman inspired Carter Wick to write 'The Beacon Home'. It read, 'Carter Wick confirms his Beacon Home muse to be the model Reyna Reid'. There was a photo of them together with his arm around her. She was close to thirty—her long brown hair shone and trailed over her shoulders in sleek waves. Her dress clung to her fabulous figure and showed a lot of skin, which was smooth and unblemished. They both had kilowatt smiles.

I scanned through the article, and sure enough, it was like I never existed for him. After secretly dating for a few weeks, Carter had been touring and missing Ms Reid—apparently.

"Could you turn your phone off, please?" the flight attendant asked me. I didn't respond, but turned it off. I didn't need to look at it anymore. The words had imprinted themselves on my mind. As the flight taxied and took off, I closed my eyes to stem the tears. Why cry over a two-night stand? But they creeped out anyway and slid down my cheeks.

The seatbelt indicator dinged.

"Joey, what's wrong?" I opened my eyes to Sam's concerned face as he crouched beside my seat. "Do you always cry when flying, or is it just when I'm on board?"

"Carter named another woman as his inspiration for 'The Beacon Home', but he was with me when he wrote it."

"Show me."

I accessed the plane's Wi-Fi and found the website.

"This mightn't be what it seems. These people make stuff up or make it out to be something other than it is all the time. They just want clicks. You know that from writing my book with me."

I wiped my eyes. "I know. I don't know why I care so much. We didn't promise anything to each other, and since Carter's song took off, I've barely heard from him. But his working title was 'A Song for Jo'. I knew he wouldn't call it that, and 'The Beacon Home' was my idea. And—and I let him—" I shook my head, wiping at fresh tears.

"What? Do anal?"

"No!" I pulled a face, leaving him in no doubt about that, and he laughed.

"What then?"

I leaned over and whispered in his ear about the berry cheesecake. He roared with laughter, so I pushed him, and he landed on his butt.

"Don't laugh. It was very intimate," I said when Sam resumed his position beside me.

"Sorry, but he ensured you enjoyed it, right?" He did air quotes around 'enjoyed'.

"Yes, of course."

"Then I don't think he was playing you. That's what you fear, isn't it? That someone else might cheat on you like Bruce did."

"Yeah."

"Mr. Harmer, could you please resume your seat?" The flight attendant came up the aisle to take meal orders.

"Of course," Sam said easily. Then he clicked his fingers at me and held out his hand. I just stared at him, though I knew what he wanted. "C'mon, Joey. Give me what I want. I'm dying to read this book to see if there's any cheesecake in it."

"Hey, I've got more dirt on you than you've got on me. So keep it shut, pal." I handed him my Kindle. Sam took it and flashed his million-dollar smile at the flight attendant. The man blushed, and then Sam retook his seat as requested.

***

When I got home, I was exhausted. It felt strange to be back after over a month in the States, but it was good. I showered, put on clean pyjamas, and crawled gratefully into my bed. I needed to sleep for a month to recover from the previous one. When I woke up to pee, I checked my phone.

Ethan had shared photos of first-class seats on their flight and an upgrade to a luxury cabin right on the beach. Sam had been busy with his credit card. I thanked Sam for his generosity, thoughtfulness, and kind words in the notes he left on my Kindle.

"This book is so insightful, Joey. I can feel everything the protagonist does, but when you get to the resolution, don't forget that she (and perhaps you) needs to move on from the hurt inflicted on her. The reward isn't avoiding love, but when/if it comes, to welcome it with open arms and an open heart, not suspicion and closing off a part of herself."

I knew he was talking about Carter and letting him explain himself. I crawled back into bed before clicking on the last new message I hadn't checked from that very man.

Carter:

> Hey, Jo. You must be back in England by now, and it hurts my heart to feel us so far apart. Let me know you got back safely and when we can talk. I need to explain a few things.

Joanna:

> I'm back. I'm sleeping. I'm hurting. I thought you wrote that song for me, but that isn't what hurts the most. It's that you felt the need to lie. I would have preferred honesty. then we could've just had our fun, and you would be a great memory instead of this.

I was thankful I was tired enough to sink into oblivion again rather than stew on what I'd written. Later the next day, Carter called a couple of times, but I ignored him. Jetlag left me too raw and too tired to face the conversation. He texted.

Carter:

I never wanted to hurt you, and I'm sorry. But I never lied to you. I can't say more in a text. Please talk to me, Jo.

Joanna:

I can't face it today.

Carter:

I understand. Let me know when you're ready.

Right there was the reason Carter differed from the other men I'd attracted in the past. He listened and gave me room, trusting me to do just that. It made it hard not to pick up the phone and call him right back, but I needed my head on straight when I talked to him.

Two days later, I was hoping he would call. I would hear him out and see what I thought. I missed him—that was the truth. How can that be possible? Thirty years with Bruce, and I never gave him a thought these days. Forty-eight hours with Carter, and I couldn't forget him. Given the time difference, I waited until early afternoon before texting him. A fluttering hovered in my belly all morning at the thought of hearing his voice again. Before I could text, Sam sent me a YouTube link.

Sam:

I'm here if you need to talk.

I clicked on the link. It was the official video of 'The Beacon Home'. Carter was singing it in a club, and then it cut to Reyna Reid, looking out a window, presumably waiting for him to come home. Still singing, Carter flung his bag and guitar case in the back of an old truck and drove to his next stop, where he gigged again. Ultimately, he turned up at her house, where she saw him and ran out to him. They embraced and kissed. Up to that point, I had laughed at the thought that she just stayed at the window waiting for him. But that kiss—I knew that kiss. I knew those lips, the way they would slide effortlessly over mine. The tears came again.

I called Sam.

"Hi," I blubbed.

"Awe, Joey. Don't cry. It's acting, just like in a movie or on TV."

"I feel so stupid, like a teenage kid."

"The heart doesn't know age. Have you heard from Carter?"

"He called the day after I got back, but I couldn't face him. I was going to message today. He wants to talk but can't put it in a text."

"You know, I've kissed more people on screen than I have off. I wouldn't be surprised if it's similar for him. He might not have kissed as many women as you might think. Even if he has, no one is coming forward with terrible stories about him, and you know they all come out of the woodwork when someone becomes well known."

"Thanks, Sam. I'm so lucky we met on that plane. You're a good friend."

"Hey, I've adopted your whole family now that I met your kids—who are great, by the way. So we're more than friends. We're family."

"I'm honoured."

"Talk to him and clear the air, at least. You'll feel better for it."

***

Carter video-called me, but I wasn't prepared for that.

"Jo, thanks for talking to me."

He looked perfect, and I drank him in.

"Hi, Carter."

"Have you been crying? Oh, God, I'm so sorry. I wanted to talk to you before the video came out. I take it you saw it?"

"Yes. I wondered she didn't have more to do with her days than look out the window waiting for you."

He laughed. "I said the same thing. Look, about Reyna—"

"It's fine. If you were seeing her before, you should have told me when you had the chance. If it's only just become a thing—great. We didn't promise anything. We're three thousand miles apart. It's ridiculous to hope that could work."

"More like five thousand. I'm in LA doing some talk shows. It's ridiculous how my life changed—all because of you."

"Because of Reyna, apparently. Not me."

"Y'know that ain't true."

"There was truth and there was untruth, and if you clung to the truth even against the whole world, you were not mad."

"What's that from?"

"George Orwell–1984. That's how I feel right now."

"Because the world doesn't know you inspired 'The Beacon Home'?"

"No. Because I feel as if those days and nights never happened, like I'm the only one who remembers them. That makes me sad."

"I will always remember them. I'm sorry, Jo."

"Yes, you said that. What do you want, Carter?" I tried to keep the hope out of my voice and prayed he wouldn't say, '*I don't know.*'

"I want to see you again. I miss you."

"I don't see how that can work. How would we work? I have a life here, a book to write. I can't just keep looking out of the window for you. You have chat shows and gigs. And you have Reyna. I don't want to get in the middle of that."

He looked resigned, as if he wanted to say more. "Then write your book. Be magnificent, Jo, and when I tour the UK, I hope we can keep our date for you to come and see me."

"I will."

I was glad I'd cleared the air with Carter. I felt lighter for it, despite watching clips of him on those USA chat shows. He didn't look comfortable when they asked him about Reyna, and she would do most of the talking if she were with him. Then he would sing. I couldn't help it and knew all the lyrics, every inflection he gave the words, and when his rasp would kick in—I loved the song. I wondered if he still thought of me every time he sang it.

***

I sent Sophie my first three chapters a month after returning from the USA. I hoped she wouldn't assign an editor to it because I can do that myself, but I soon realised editing your own work is much more challenging. While I waited for her reply, I got on a video call with Teena and Abby. Teena had been busy with her personal coaching business, which was doing well, and Abby was promoting her latest children's book, which was rocketing up the charts, so we had had little chance to talk.

I told them what had happened with Zach and Carter and what my feelings had been since then. They loved Zach, of course.

"You should do Teena's personal coaching now," Abby suggested.

"What do you mean—now?"

"I was going to suggest it at yours when we stayed over to declutter that time, but Teena said no."

"It was too soon," Teena explained. "You had too much else going on. I'll give you my friends and family rate."

"You don't have to do that. I don't want to take up the time you'd use for a full-paying client."

"Don't be silly. I'd find you an extra hour once or twice a week, anyway."

"Sam said I needed to relearn to trust. Perhaps if I'm going to have one more shot at a meaningful relationship, I need to know where I went wrong before."

"I can't believe you're friends with Sam Harmer," Abby said.

"He says he's adopted us. Since we've been back, he's been to Norwich twice. Elliott and Alastair have been showing off that they know him and roped him into their wedding planning. Last time, he suffered through one of Susan's barbeques, even though it was freezing outside."

Teena and I set a date to start my coaching, and I promised to send them chapters of my book to read. I was too tense to wait for Sophie's response, and I needed feedback sooner.

Coaching over the next few weeks was intense. Unlike my previous therapy, which focused on my marital problems, which I couldn't change without Bruce's help, this was all about me, and everything was within my control. We looked into my occasional overeating, my lack of trust issues and my feeling that people would all leave me, eventually. Most painfully, Teena got me to talk about the circumstances of my father's death.

I was only ten and barely remember him now. I don't think he ever told me he loved me. He had been angry with me close to the time he died of a massive heart attack. He was the disciplinarian in the family, and Mum would always say the classic *'Wait until your dad gets home.'* Dad would tell me off. I'm not sure how long after shouting at me, he died—hours, days, weeks—but it was close enough for my child's mind to make the connection. To this day, even though my adult mind told me I was wrong, I felt it was my fault for being naughty.

Teena was amazing. She had me visualize all my feelings into blocks, throw them into a portal I'd opened to the past to leave there, and then step through it back to my ten-year-old self.

"Go to that little girl. She's only ten. Wrap her in your arms and talk to her. It isn't your fault, little Jo. Tell her you love her, and she no longer has to worry. She can be free, happy and safe. Hold her to you and bring her into your heart. You will look after her."

"I've got you, little Jo," I said aloud, my voice catching at the emotion.

"Now, bring her back with you in your heart. Back through the portal and visualise it closing."

"That was so powerful, Teena." I was in tears but felt lighter than I had in longer than I could recall.

***

By the spring, I had been living in the UK for two years and in my new house for over one of them. My routine was comfortable. I woke whenever I wanted to, and though I felt the guilt of lying in bed, it didn't stop me. After breakfast, I worked, splitting my time between my editing work, which was currently mostly Sam's book, and finishing my book. Sophie had found an interested publisher, and we hoped for a release date later in the year.

Sometimes, I had lunch with my mum or another sibling. Now that they were all retired, I was guaranteed to find someone at home or willing to meet me at Toni's place in Horseshoe Hamlets.

I spent my evenings completing edits suggested for my book so my editor would have them the following morning when they returned to work. Sophie had convinced me it was best not to edit myself. Though I could be lackadaisical about cleaning or gardening, I was strict about never falling behind with editing either my book or someone else's.

I regularly kept in touch with my friends in the USA, and Teena and I kept a routine for my personal coaching. My friends and I had started quite the Redway Acres club. After talking to them about my outing with Sam to Belton House, we took day trips to a few places mentioned in the books or where the fictitious locales were based. We were planning a week where we would go around the country. The third book had already been released, and I had a copy of the fourth book I was editing. I didn't tell my friends. The hardest part was keeping it a secret from them, but the books were becoming more popular, and I didn't want to be responsible for leaks.

In the meantime, though my life wasn't partying and late nights out, I enjoyed it. I don't mind being in my little house at all. When I woke in the middle of the night needing a pee or drenched in the sweat of a hot flush, I thought about having a relationship. How could I even start a relationship should I meet someone I liked enough? It's funny how, when we're young, it's more about love, but as you get older, you realise how much you need to like the person you're with as well—especially in retirement.

If I had gone back to Bruce, we wouldn't have had to negotiate age issues, menopause, night sweats or my fat tummy impeding great sex. We had grown old together. Society only embraced older women if they had 'aged gracefully'—MILFs or cougars. Not that I wanted to be considered either.

What do I want in a partner?—A friend. Someone to laugh with and have discussions about my kids, maybe theirs. Someone to talk about the future, my worries, the state of the country or the world. I think I would be good at all of that as a partner. Oh, and sex, was I good at that? Carter certainly thought so, and he didn't care about my tummy or 'thunder thighs.'

If that weren't on the cards for me, I would stay single and see where that life led me. I have family, and I'm making more friends. I have my work, the excitement of my book launching, and the trusty vibrator I ordered when I moved in. A giggle escaped me at a thought, *You can't cheat on a vibrator, so perhaps I should buy another one?*

I'd picked up the broken pieces of my life and found my voice to speak up for myself. I felt whole for the first time in a long time. My solo life was good, and I was happy.

MARRIAGE PACT

In your teens, you have a friend
A not-so-secret, secret crush
You'd like to be together
But not be in a rush

You make a pact—at thirty
If you reach that ancient age
And neither one is hitched
You will make a marriage

But at thirty, you aren't ready
With someone else at forty
Then, at fifty, when you're both free
Your friend says wait till sixty

At some point, you must consider
To live life without the pact
You'll be happier without the stress
When you keep your friendship intact

EIGHTEEN

As I sipped a herbal tea and took a bite of toast for breakfast, I perused my Facebook feed. *I'm starting my permanent single life*, I thought, before my eyes alighted upon one of those posts when someone is travelling, and it shows the route their plane will take.

Nish was at Fiumicino airport, Rome. He was arriving at Heathrow after two this afternoon.

I was happy he was visiting. I could see him for the first time in such a long time. It must have been a decade since we last saw each other. I'd love to meet his partner.

His post read, "I'm coming home for good. If anyone feels like picking me up, let me know. Chris was going to, but something came up. I can hire a car, but I'd rather not, as I'll be using my dad's car once I'm in Norwich until I buy one."

"I'm on my way," I commented before sending a PM asking for a gate number. Rushing around to gather what I needed for the journey, I hoped they could fit their luggage in my car if I laid half the back seat flat. Wait, was his partner coming with him? He usually tags her, but now I couldn't remember that he had. I checked his Facebook status.

Nish is single

I don't think I breathed for a full minute. I just looked at that line. Finally, I gathered my wits. It doesn't mean anything, and Nish will probably be heartbroken. Heaven knows it can take time to get over. Perhaps he left the Italian to be with someone else. Either way, having my friend around here will be great. We had lots of catching up to do, and that can start on the drive back from Heathrow if I get my skates on.

Wasn't that the way of fate? When I decided I was completely fine with being single, life threw me a curveball.

***

I shifted from foot to foot as I waited for the arrivals to come through for Nish's flight. He'd messaged he would look out for me. I held up a piece of paper that fluttered as I hopped from foot to foot.

'OLD FRIEND'

Then I spotted him—he wheeled an enormous suitcase by the extended handle, with a smaller case fixed to the top. His carry-on bag strap rumpled his t-shirt where it slashed diagonally across his body. He looked older, but I guess I did, too. His salt and pepper hair stuck up in all directions, and he looked like he hadn't slept lately. The break-up must have been bad. He had a wonderful family that would rally around him, and so would I if he wanted a friend. I pushed all thoughts of more aside—for now.

"Hey," I said as he reached me.

"I could do with an old friend, but you look too good to be old enough."

"Charmer. Welcome home, Nish."

"My God, Jo, how did you manage this alone and further than me?"

"Baby steps. You'll manage, too, and I'm here for you. If you need me."

"I've always needed you, Jo."

With that, his arms came around me, and he held me tight. I inhaled deeply, breathing it all out, and in my mind, that breath bolstered him. I had a feeling of—I don't know what—something so very comfortable and happy settled deep into my bones. *Did he feel it, too?*

"Let's get you home."

We fitted his luggage into my car and headed to the M25 and the journey home.

"Thanks, Jo," he offered as we joined the traffic on the highway—oops, motorway.

"No problem. Hopefully, we'll get off here before rush hour affects it." The M25 circular around London was known as England's biggest car park, but we shouldn't be too bad at this time of day. I glanced over at his angular profile, which had filled out a little more since we were younger, but he was still a beautiful man. "Do you want to talk about it?"

"No. I probably should, though. I'll have to talk with Dad when I get home. I'm going to stay with him until I figure myself out."

"Talking helps. Please take my word for it. I'm happy to listen. Now, tomorrow, whenever. Day or night."

"How did you do it? Seriously, you look amazing. Honestly, you look happy."

"I got back to my passion."

"The fifty-plus dating scene is that great in Norfolk?" he snorted.

"No, I started writing again. I haven't put anything up on Facebook yet because I don't want to jinx it, but my book comes out in September."

"Joanna James, Author. That's brilliant. Well done to you." He'd turned in his seat to stare at me. I risked a glance over and the animation in his features took me aback. The old Nish was still there, just hidden a little in his sadness. I turned back just in time to brake hard and avoid colliding with the car in front as the traffic slowed. He reached out to the dash to steady himself.

"Oops, sorry. I'd better keep my eyes on the road."

"Suddenly, life seems a little better. Nothing like a near-death experience to give you some perspective."

"That would have been a ding at worst. Wimp."

He laughed, and it was good to hear. Then we talked the rest of the way home as if we'd never stopped telling each other everything. I even suggested he join the book club, but he didn't think he would because it was currently all women.

"What will you do for work?"

"I kept all my pension and savings, and she kept the house and her own pension, so I've no need to work unless I want to. I'll rent for a while and look for something I enjoy that might pay a little and keep me busy."

I turned into the street of his childhood where his father still lived. Why do the places of your youth always seem smaller when you see them years later as an adult? "Do you mind if I pop in and use the loo before I drive home? I'm desperate."

"Like I'd let you drive home without saying hi to Dad. I would never hear the last of it from him. Dad, we're here."

"Nish, my boy. Welcome home."

"I just need to use the loo, Mr Jaitly," I called and dashed into the small cloakroom near the front door while they embraced.

"I'm putting the kettle on, Joanna," Mr Jaitly shouted as I heard Nish stomp up the stairs with his suitcases.

It was all so familiar that I almost cried. When I emerged, adjusting the hem of my shirt, I was wrapped in the strong arms of Nish's father. "Thanks for bringing him home, Joanna."

"You're welcome, but it was only Heathrow. You make it sound like I flew the plane myself."

"I wouldn't put it past you. Now, you two can be together as you were meant to be from the beginning. I always said it."

"Shush," I said, cupping his lovely face and kissing his cheek. "Nish is heartbroken and needs time. It's been well over two years since my divorce, and I'm only just getting there. Now, where's that cuppa?"

I spent about thirty minutes with them before I headed home, refusing their offer of a takeaway dinner. At home, I stuck a ready meal in the oven and devoured it before heading to bed, exhausted.

***

The following evening was our book club meeting. I'd read the book, but no one seemed to want to discuss it. All the news was about Nish coming home. Even the three women there who didn't know Nish were happy to hear all about him. I imparted the few pieces of information I didn't think he'd mind me sharing, and Daisy suggested a gathering at The Cottage with everyone's husbands.

Harriet complained, "If you all bring partners, I'll be the odd one out because we all know Jo will dominate Nish's attention."

"I could always invite Bill," Daisy teased. "He hasn't met anyone new yet."

"Don't even joke about that. First, I don't want to give Bill any ideas, and second, I love Harriet too much."

"He's not that bad," Daisy insisted.

"I know he's your friend, but telling me he knows best because he has 'more experience' screams misogynist to me."

"It's a no from me," Harriet agreed, looking thoughtful. "You know, your mum could use more help around the back of here. Sean hasn't been over as often with his exams looming. Nish always loved to garden, remember?"

I hadn't remembered that, but Harriet was right. At one point, his dad owned an allotment, and Nish was always there. I think he smoked weed in the shed, but I didn't say that aloud. "I'll ask Mum."

"You will still do your first book signing here, Jo, right? I've printed up some flyers, so I need your confirmation."

***

I met Nish at Horseshoe Hamlets a few days later. I spotted his dad's car in the lot, but no Nish inside. His text that pinged moments later said 'bookshop'. I curbed my temptation to march in and pull him away from Harriet, who was no doubt wowing him with her fantastic shop. Nish was always a pushover for a good book. I'd had him all to myself on the ride back from Heathrow, and I could be generous. No way would I fight over a man with Harriet, I loved her too much. I told him to take his time and I would be with my mum. She'd put me to work picking berries by the time Nish finally reached the back of the shops.

"Well, Nish Jaitly, as I live and breathe," my mum said by way of greeting.

"Mrs. Sherwood, you're looking as young as ever. You passed those genes on to Jo."

She laughed gaily with him. "Let me give you a tour. Don't stop picking, Joey, dear," she called out to me. I shrugged and returned to my labour, trying not to sweat too much.

Lending an ear to their conversation, Nish seemed to have ideas about him planting other things and another area he could dig over. He also suggested setting up a stall for produce that didn't end up at Toni's tearooms or flowers that didn't go to Daisy's crafts. He wasn't interested in taking much salary except for produce for himself and his dad.

Finally, he headed over to me. "Did you catch all of that, nosey Jo, or do you want me to repeat it?" he joked.

"Okay, I confess, but it sounds like a lot of work. Are you sure this is what you want to do?"

"One hundred percent. I'd say one hundred and ten, but I know how you feel about that."

I grinned and popped a strawberry into his mouth.

***

We were all in The Cottage two nights later, celebrating Nish's return, and my fingers were still a little pink from strawberry juice. He looked happier and healthier than he did when I picked him up at Heathrow. Ted, he remembered from school, of course, but he hadn't met Toni's and Ivy's husbands. We were rowdy and full of laughter for the evening.

When I had the opportunity, I asked Nish if he would like to attend Elliott's and Alastair's wedding.

"Can I bring someone?" He asked, completely missing the point of being *my* plus one.

"Sure." I knew there was room, and I had a feeling about who he might bring, given where his primary focus was that evening.

***

After a wet couple of weeks, the day of the wedding was a bright and sunny one. Elliott had stayed the night at mum's, and she fussed over his attire more than he did, her sticky roller moving at full pelt over his shoulders when I arrived with flowers for their lapels and Elliott's best man—Sam Harmer.

"You kept this quiet from me," I complained when we walked in together. Sam had hired enormous limos to drive both grooms and their best men to the venue. Mum got to ride in there, too.

"Big man," Sam called. Elliott was the only man I knew who was taller than Sam.

"I want to introduce you to someone later," I whispered to Sam before we entered the room where Mum fussed.

"Is he your new man?"

I blushed, wishing he couldn't read me so well. "No. Not yet. Not ever, maybe. He's my best friend from school."

"Oh, the marriage pact guy. Honestly, Joey. If he passed you up back then, he probably thought he'd wait to see if he could do better. Thing is—he never will."

"I bet you say that to all the girls."

"Nope." He winked at me and then went to shake hands with Elliott.

Later, Sam finally made it over to ask me for a dance. It had been a wonderful event, and no one smiled more than the grooms. Meanwhile, Sam had to fend off many of their 'bachelor' friends, as Mum called them, but he did it all with good grace and congeniality.

"Let's dance, Joey," he declared, grabbing my hand and pulling me to the dance floor. I tried to keep up with him, but Sam was a dancing machine. Finally, the music slowed down enough for me to catch my breath.

"You need a partner who can keep up with you."

"You're doing alright, and I've got plenty of time. Look at Elliott and Alastair today. Now that's true love, right? Worth waiting for." He pulled me closer, and I put my arms around his neck. He smelled great—whoever he chose wouldn't stand a chance.

"I still haven't introduced you to Nish."

"That's where your mind goes in this conversation? I'm sorry to disappoint you, but Harriet already introduced him. I think that's them slow dancing over there. Unless I'm wrong, which you know I'm not, he's about to kiss her." Sam dipped me, and sure enough, Nish and Harriet came into view upside down and in a full lip-lock.

"Oh, singledom it is then," was all I managed when I righted again.

"My guess is you won't be single much longer unless that's what you want."

"Let's say I'm good either way, providing it's the right guy."

"Remember how you told me you never thought of Zach when he wasn't there?"

"Sure."

"How often have you thought of Carter Wick since Christmas?"

"Far too often, probably."

Sam gave me a look as if to indicate he'd proven some point, but it eluded me.

"Given that Carter Wick didn't find the right partner until he was nearly fifty, I have at least fifteen more years," Sam said. "And he found a spectacular partner."

"Yeah, I suppose Reyna Reid is spectacular."

"Who the hell is talking about Reyna Reid?"

***

Two weeks after the wedding, I was at The Reading Stable going over the book signing plans. Nish came running in through the back. "Call nine-nine-nine. It's Mrs. Sherwood."

"Mum!" I rushed out after Nish, who had exited again, my mobile phone in my hand. I got through to emergency services and requested an ambulance, answering all their questions about the person involved. Then, I put it on speaker so Nish could answer their questions about what had happened as I approached the table Mum had collapsed behind. I knelt beside her and held her hand, but she was unresponsive, not breathing.

The training I took when the kids were young kicked in, and I started counting chest compressions and then breathing into her mouth while holding her nose—back to compressions.

"Come on, Mum. Come on."

The paramedics appeared with equipment and a stretcher. They tried their best and took her away with me in the back, but they declared her dead on arrival. Had she died peacefully in bed, there wouldn't have been a post-mortem. They discovered she had died of a massive stroke. She might have felt a pain in her head for a moment, but nothing a second or two after that. I was grateful for that and the fact that she died doing what she loved.

We buried her three weeks later, with services in a church filled to overflowing with people she had helped over the years, including the person who was now my entire family's good friend, Sam Harmer. He brought a friend with him for support—Enrique Perez. With Nish comforting Harriet, who had become so close to Mum over the past few years, and my family comforting each other, it was a great relief to have Sam and Enrique sitting there with me.

The guys were photographed a few weeks ago with a couple of dates in San Francisco attending, of all things, a Carter Wick concert. I hoped to quiz Sam about it later, but they had to get away quickly for a flight. We had a teary departure, and they were gone.

Helen Sherwood, my mum, left Horseshoe Hamlets on a long-term lease to all the shop owners and the land behind for community use for growing flowers and vegetables. Nish agreed to continue working on it, and we raised money at her funeral to turn the horse track into a racetrack for people to walk or run around with seating. We sold her house, but as we were all well situated, we agreed to bank that money into a trust for whatever was needed to continue Horseshoe Hamlets in her name—Sherwood Hamlets.

Anne's son, Tim, agreed to be a trustee with Nish. I'd offered, but my siblings all sat me down for an intervention.

***

As the eldest sibling, Elliot started everyone off. "Baby girl, you came back to the UK for the right reasons. You've made a difference to the family, and Mum enjoyed having you back here. But now is the time to do what you need for yourself."

"You can't throw me out of Norwich," I said with an incredulous laugh stuck in my throat.

"Didn't you tell me you would do book tours, Joey?" Anne added.

"And when your book proves to be as popular as everyone who has read it seems to think," Susan said, "you'll guest on chat shows and podcasts to promote it."

My head was swivelling between them as they continued to talk like I was watching a three-way tennis match.

"Sam tells us that there's a man who is a similar wanderer," Elliott said. "Perhaps you need to see if a relationship there is something you want to pursue?"

"If not, then what have you lost? Nothing at all, by my reckoning," Anne chipped in again.

"We're all happy here and will be here for you whenever you want to visit or move back here. Doesn't Carter Wick have a tour coming up in the UK?" Susan said. "I think his London shows coincide with your book signing events there."

Anne laughed. Something none of us had done much of since Mum passed, and that's just not what she would have wanted. "You know, Susan, I think you might be right. Joey, get your new assistant to book you a ticket to his show."

THE BEACON HOME

Home is where the heart is
The place where you belong
Home is like no other place
Where you're comfortable and strong

Home is where you can breathe
Recharge and take your rest
Home is where you lay your head
And you can sleep your best

Home can be a house, a flat, a tent, a box
The place that you call 'mine'
Home can be a road stretching to horizon
Or a perfect city skyline

And sometimes home's a person
Who takes you in their arms
You hold on tight to smell and breathe
Your senses they becalm

When home is your lover

And you lie in their embrace

You know they're there to lean upon

The whole world you can face

NINETEEN

'Fifty, Fat and Fabulous' was published at the beginning of September, and my first signing event was at The Reading Stable a week later. Harriet and my new personal assistant, Poppy Henry, fussed around the shop, unloading books from the boxes we'd ordered. They piled them up at the cash register, in a window display Harriet had worked on overnight, and on the table I was to sit behind.

People were lining up outside for me to sign their copies of my book, which I found incredible. I sat down, lined up my favourite pens and practised my book-signing signature one more time. *Joanna James.*

"Ready?" Harriet asked with her wicked grin, lighting up her face. She was so happy since she and Nish had started dating, and I'm honestly pleased for them both. I think they will care for each other so well, and that's what I wanted for my two best UK friends.

"As I'll ever be," I said, making a heart with my hands. We had become closer friends than ever before—oddly, more so since she got together with Nish and after Mum died.

People started coming in. They could buy a signed copy without lining up, as I'd signed many for that purpose last night, or they could wait in line for me to personalise it for them. It was gratifying to hear women say they couldn't wait to read a story about an older, larger woman and thanked me for writing it. Of course, many hadn't read it yet, but some brought in their own copies and commented on a part they enjoyed or that made them cheer or cry.

Ten minutes into the hour we'd allowed, there was a commotion outside, and Sam and Enrique walked in. They were tall and gorgeous, with huge smiles and a box under Sam's arm. As they moved down the line, they asked if people would mind if they jumped the queue. One brave person said, 'Only if you sign my book too,' and everyone else wanted the same treatment.

Poppy rushed to find two more chairs for the men and roped Sean in to help her. He had been unpacking boxes of books and disposing of the empties and looked dismayed at Poppy's blush in helping Sam and Enrique. Enrique sat beside me and Sam at the end, who put his mysterious box under his chair as we all got to work signing the books. Once again, Sam was making a challenging part of my life a little easier with his calm demeanour. Harriet made the most of their presence by selling signed copies of Redway Acres.

When we were done, we sat in Harriet's little breakroom, sipping well-deserved cups of coffee. I pushed a copy of my book and a pen towards them. "Will you sign mine, please?"

"My pleasure," Enrique said, signing with a flourish and passing the book and pen to Sam, who did the same. Then he held it up to show me the dedication page, and I could see the heart he'd drawn around the simple words 'To Mum'.

"She would have been so proud of you, Joey."

"Thanks. Okay, what's in the box?" I finally asked Sam, deflecting my tears so close to the surface.

He pushed it towards me so I could open it for a peak. Sam's beautiful face graced the cover of several hardback books titled 'Choosing Life'.

"Advance copies," he said to my astonished expression. "For you and the rest of the book club."

I flipped the top one open and pointed to his dedication to his mum. "She would be so proud of you, too."

He smiled. "Check the second part of the acknowledgements."

I pulled out the thick tome and flicked through to read 'To a fabulous author and my friend, Joanna James. A woman full of courage and strength, who welcomed me into her family and saved my life. I couldn't have done this without you, Joey.' The tears did fall when I read that.

"It was my honour to do it, Sam."

"Write the book or welcome me into your family?"

"Both, of course."

Sam looked at Enrique, and Enrique nodded. I smiled.

"You know, don't you?" Sam said instead of the words that were about to escape his lips.

"I don't know anything until you want to tell me. You don't have to tell anyone."

Sam covered Enrique's hand with his own. "We're in love."

"Thank you for trusting me. I'm so happy for you both." Yeah, I squeed.

"Shush, no one knows but us three," Sam chastised.

"Wait, I'm the first person you've told?"

"Yeah."

I hugged them both after that and cried a bit more. I'd keep that secret, no problem. They planned to come out to their closest friends and Enrique's family first, then gradually let it go public.

"Well, if you want to, that could be your next autobiography. The title could be 'Choosing Love'."

"And will you be choosing love, Joey?"

"I'll let you know, but for now, I have a book ending to write." I glanced at their joined hands, Enrique's thumb grazing Sam's fingers. "You've given me an idea for Kieran the Firefighter's happy ever after."

"Then I'll definitely play him in the movie adaptation."

***

I was nervous at the London venue, where I was doing a late afternoon book signing. I could barely sign my name, but not out of the overwhelming size of the queue waiting to see me, not the thought that all these people wanted to read my very personal book. My hands shook at the prospect of seeing Carter Wick again, if only on stage. Even now, he was probably just a few miles west of here, going through sound checks and all those kinds of things. What would he say if he saw me? Does he even want to see me? I looked up at the woman in front of me to whom I'd just made out the signature, but I'd forgotten her name already. Her head swivelled away from me momentarily so I glanced down. *Barbara.*

"Thank you, Barbara," I said.

"Sorry, I just saw that singer guy from the USA. He's so cute. Oh, and coming this way."

My breath caught as she moved out of the way, and there he was, radiating that homing beacon aura that always pulled me in. He had my book in his hands.

"Who should I make it to?" I said, my voice shaking.

"*My biggest fan?*" His nervous smile charmed me. "Can we talk for a minute, Jo? I won't take much of your time."

I looked to Poppy, who nodded and moved to the rest of the queue to inform them of the slight delay. She really was invaluable.

Carter and I moved to the side, out of earshot.

"I sold out, Jo."

"I know. I tried to get a ticket for tonight."

"No, I mean, I sold out to the promoters and the big music machine. After being with you, I decided there was someone I could spend my life with, but I needed money to stop having to tour at some point and retire, eventually. 'The Beacon Home' got me that, and to promote it, they wanted me to have this charade of a relationship with Reyna."

"You still kissed her."

"That was acting. Jo, I never lied to you. I lied to the rest of the world."

"It still hurt."

"I can imagine. I'm sorry."

"You said that before, but I appreciate you saying it again." I don't remember when a man said those two words to me. They might say, 'I would like to apologise,' but they don't actually say it. Or worse still, 'I apologise if you feel I've wronged you.'

"Wasn't there anyone else for you this past year?"

"No." I thought of Nish, but things with him never went anywhere but in my head. My mind wasn't my heart, though, and with him right there next to me, I knew that was Carter's.

"Hard to believe. Look how awesome you are." He spread his hands out, indicating the table of books I'd been signing.

"There was—a possibility. It didn't come to fruition. Not even a fake relationship."

"Ouch." He held out an envelope, but I didn't take it.

"What's that?"

"I got a ticket for you for tonight and a backstage pass."

"I have a ticket," I said, scowling at his smile. "I have Poppy now. She can get these things for me." I gestured to her, still keeping the people in line despite them straining their necks to look at Carter.

"This is the front row."

"So's mine."

"Please take the pass. I must go now, but I want to talk after the show. Can you spare me some time?"

"I'll think about it." I took the envelope, handed him his book and watched him walk away, trying to assess my emotions, which was impossible with his gorgeous ass in my vision. Then I turned back to the task at hand.

***

The Royal Albert Hall was packed when I reached it—primarily with women, I noted with a smile. After seeing Carter this afternoon, I was as intoxicated as I had been the first night I met him. The seat for the ticket he gave me was front and centre, whereas mine was at one end, which I preferred. I noticed later that Reyna Reid came and sat in the seat Carter gave me. Maybe she always watched him, if there was a spare seat. If they weren't together, why was she even in London? Perhaps when the concert had finished, I would sneak away.

Carter came on stage to flashing lights and a heavy drumbeat from the band behind him already in place. As the energy in the house grew to a crescendo, he scanned the front row until he saw me, and his smile widened as he waved. Of course, I waved back. The pull of his magnetism felt heavy in my gut. I wondered that all the straight women and gay men in the audience didn't feel it, too, and imagined us all being pulled to the stage to attach ourselves to him.

My God, he looked gorgeous with his guitar slung over his back. He swung it around and started the band for the first song.

"One, two—one, two, three, four."

Carter filled the next hour with a mixture of his songs, which I recognised from his sets in Boston, and some covers of country-rock classics. No sign of 'The Beacon Home', so I supposed he was saving the best for last—oh boy, did he.

The lights went down, leaving a spotlight on Carter. He perched up on a stool with his hair tied up and messy, flopping forward just like I remembered—as at ease with five thousand faces fixed upon him here as he was with only twenty people in that bar in Boston.

As if he were with a small gathering of friends, he started talking, "This past year, my life has changed so much, mostly because I wrote this next song."

"The Beacon Home," someone called out, and the crowd cheered. The noise continued for a long time, but Carter just smiled.

"Well, I can't sing it if y'all don't turn it down some. I thought you British were reserved."

Laughter rippled through the place until silence fell again.

"When I wrote this song, I was naked, sitting in a hotel room watching a woman sleep." He looked over at me, and in his pause, the naked part caused a few whoops and some loud shushing. Clearly, he had everyone captivated. "Oh man, this woman. I've never met anyone like her before or since. Let's get a spot on her. She's right there." He pointed to me, but the light landed on the woman beside me.

"Reyna Reid, I didn't see you there," I said—so much for sneaking away.

"Well, I made my way over slowly." She must have been shifting seats towards me all this time, but I was too entranced by Carter to notice.

"No, not Reyna. We've only ever been friends," Carter said. "The woman she's talking to—Jo, the author of 'Fifty, Fat and Fabulous'—Joanna James. She started writing that book the day I wrote 'The Beacon Home'. I guess we inspired each other—I'm chapter sixteen. Oh yeah, I read it, Jo."

He winked at me, and I blushed in the spotlight under the stares of all around me.

"This is your song, Jo. It always was. Thank you, and please forgive me for messing up."

"I'll forgive you, Carter," someone shouted.

He smiled, then started playing just him and his guitar on that stage. Those emotional lyrics and the tune took me back to waking up to him composing. I wanted another chance to experience that, but could I trust again? No matter how our life together might look, it was a sure bet he would spend time away from me in pursuit of the rest of his career. Tears stung my eyes and rolled down my cheeks as he came to the end and sang directly to me.

When home is my lover
And I lie in your embrace
I know you're there to lean upon
The whole world I can face
The Beacon Home

It's the Beacon Home

"You're my Beacon Home, Jo," Carter spoke the last line.

The house erupted with cheers and applause while Carter set his guitar on its stand and stood to bow. Then he turned to me, put his hand over his heart and bowed. I blew him a kiss. What more could I do? I'm not made of stone—even if I had been, that song would've broken me apart to reveal my heart beating for him at my core.

Over the noise of the crowd's applause, hoping for an encore, Reyna gestured towards a far door where a burly man stood guard. We walked over, though my legs barely held me up.

"I have a backstage pass," I said to him, fishing into my bag for the paper Carter gave me.

"You're fine, Ms. James." I looked up at him, surprised. "My mum loved your book."

I foraged around again and came up with a bookmark with the title of my book on it. "What's your mum's name?"

"Shirley."

I wrote on the back and signed it with a flourish, then handed it to the man.

"Wow, this is going to make her day. If you need anything, you ask for me, Ms. James—ask for Shamar."

"Thank you, to you and your mum." I made a mental note to get Poppy to send a signed book to him here for his mum.

We stepped through the door to a world of curtains, ropes and pulleys. People murmured into their headsets, and I feared being in the way. Reyna pulled me over to one side as band members dashed past us to return to the stage—the audience roared their appreciation. They started playing the intro to one of Carter's songs I knew. I looked around the wing, feeling somewhat out of place. The next moment, Carter was in front of me, holding my hands and rubbing my palms with his thumbs. He grounded me.

"It's good to see ya here, Jo," he said as he searched my face, perhaps looking for some answer. "I have to sing two more. Will ya wait?"

"Of course. Go."

"Listen to Reyna, will ya? Please?"

"Sure."

He dashed away to the stage and the crowd's adoration, plugged in his guitar and began to play and sing.

"Carter told me about you right from the beginning, Jo. May I call you Jo?" Reyna explained as we watched Carter from the wings.

"I wish he had told me about you."

"He said he tried, but you stopped answering his texts and wouldn't take his calls."

"Because I thought you were together. That was the big news. The song he wrote about the woman who starred in the video for it. I didn't want to get in the way."

"It was never my song. After every take for that kiss, he would say 'sorry' because he knew he didn't mean it. I didn't either. He's hot, and I like older guys, but I like mine a bit more dominant. The press would have a field day with that, saying I had 'daddy issues', so keep it to yourself."

"Daddy issues is more fun as a way to blame women for the failures of men than as a critique on the failures of men—I read that on social media."

"OMG, that's so true. Thanks."

"Sons get screwed over by their moms—they become serial killers and blame her. Women get screwed over by their dads—she gets daddy issues, and that's her fault. We can't win."

"Carter's right, you're amazing."

"I know a nice lawyer in Connecticut who's about my age and looking for someone to share his life with. If we're ever there together, I'll introduce you."

"Is he attractive?"

"Very and generous."

"Why didn't you date him?"

"I wasn't prepared to bend and shift my life around for him. Been there and done that."

"What about bending and shifting for Carter?"

"We'll see how much he will bend too."

She squeed, and as Carter finished the full band version of 'The Beacon Home', Reyna made herself scarce, though I had a feeling she was watching from somewhere.

Carter walked off stage towards me, a hopeful smile on his handsome face. "Jo, I'm sorry, I—"

I cut him off, flinging my arms around him, shutting him up with a kiss and wondering how I'd managed so long without his fabulous mouth. He'd already apologised at the book signing. I didn't need to hear it again. His arms wrapped around me, pulling our bodies together.

"Happy birthday to me," he said when our lips broke apart. "It's my fiftieth birthday next week."

"But how will we work, Carter?" I asked.

"This is how I see it. I'll be touring—when you inspire me to write more hit songs. You'll be on book tours for sequels and new books—cos I'll inspire you. We'll coordinate as much as possible and sext when we aren't in the same place. When I'm ain't touring, I'll follow you and vice versa."

"You really have been thinking about this."

"When you asked me before, I didn't have an answer, and we were in different places with our careers. I figured it was important to you to have some success, so I had time to work something out, and we'd talk when I came here. Oh, and we have to send our itineraries to Sam Harmer, apparently?"

I laughed. Sam must have talked to Carter when he was in San Francisco. I still had questions, though. "How will we do it when we're apart for a long time?"

"You've kept relationships going from far away since you first left the UK. With your family here, and then your kids since you moved back. The least I can do is follow your example. I've missed you so much since Boston. Your book is selling in the US too. I've seen it in bookstores. You'll need a tour of your own over there."

"There's interest in a TV series, so I'm turning my hand to writing the screenplay with some support from the streaming service behind it. I'll probably be on set sometimes, maybe in California. If you're touring there, I can see you. I think Sam Harmer will want a second book, and I can write that from anywhere." Sam's book had hit the shelves and was number one—the man didn't know how to be anything else.

"You're amazing."

"You up there," I gestured to the stage, "you brought me to tears singing 'The Beacon Home' acoustic like that. *You're* the amazing one."

He kissed me again. "Then in ten or fifteen years, when I'm grey and shuffling on stage, I'll hang it up. I'll still write songs, you'll still write books, and we'll split our time between the US and UK—both of us. So you'll be able to see any grandbabies that might come along."

"Where will our home be, though?"

"Wherever we're together."

"I'll buy you a pair of comfy slippers when you hang up your touring spurs."

"Sounds good. Sounds perfect. I feel another song coming on already."

"You'd better get naked then." I grinned and kissed him again. He was hot, sweaty and irresistible. "You have a sex scene to reenact with me."

He grinned. "I love you, Jo."

"I love you, too."

ENDING

*F**ifty, sixty, seventy, fat but always fabulous.*

I was Joanna James, ready to trust, love, and give my heart one more time—maybe truly and wholly for the first time. I'd taken the hardened remnant of candle, softened it, and reshaped it into the life I wanted.

Now, I had a new love running through my core, just as I ran through his. No matter how my life turned out, for all the years left to me, I would spend it with Carter Wick.

The man for whom I wrote a book, and he wrote me a song.

JO'S PLAYLIST

Spotify link:

https://open.spotify.com/playlist/5rd7dnBtQLxk2IKn4moYaw?si=a171d4f
7c30a49d3&pt=1f9112ee6f1b00bb60aae121f5712dfb

1. BELIEVE by Adam Lambert

2. SAY SOMETHING by A Great Big World, Christina Aguilera

3. I'LL STAND BY YOU by The Pretenders

4. HEART OF GLASS by Blondie

5. SWEET DREAMS by Eurythmics

6. ROLLING IN THE DEEP by Adele

7. CREEP by Radiohead

8. MANSPLAIN by THICK

9. FLOWERS by Miley Cyrus

10. FRIENDS WILL BE FRIENDS by Queen

11. MAYBE NEXT TIME by Jamie Miller

12. REMEDY by Adele

13. LOSE YOU TO LOVE ME by Selena Gomez

14. WE ARE NEVER EVER GETTING BACK TOGETHER by Taylor Swift

15. BRAVE by Sara Bareilles

16. I'LL NEVER FALL IN LOVE AGAIN by Bobbie Gentry

17. THE GUITAR MAN by Bread

18. ME by Kelly Clarkson

19. ON MY OWN by Ricki-Lee

20. LINE BY LINE by JP Saxe (feat. Maren Morris)

21. BELIEVE by Cher

ACKNOWLEDGEMENTS

I dedicated this book to Dorothy Beattie, who inspired me to trust my characters for Redway Acres. I created Joanna's Dorothy with you in mind, Dorothy. I can't thank you enough.

As with all my books, I must acknowledge the love and support of my daughter, Emily, without whom I would be a very different person. Life is much better when spent with your cheerful face and sneaky humour.

There are many others without whom I wouldn't have been able to complete this book.

First, my family. After my divorce, I returned to the UK and Norfolk to live close to my family again and for Emily to get to know her cousins. My family structure differs from Joanna James', but I'd like to acknowledge my siblings, Jeff, Janine, Rachael, Jamie, all my nieces and nephews, and my cousins. How great it has been to reconnect with you all!

Thanks to my sister, Janine Westgate, for sharing the hugging tree with me and Emily.

Particular thanks to my niece, Poppy Nash, who introduced me to some more modern songs that fit better on Joanna's playlist.

Since I moved back, my brother Jeff was diagnosed with cancer and sadly passed. Taken far too soon, he was kind and generous, mourned by hundreds and none more so than his family. Miss you, bro.

To my mum, Gal Junie, who really is excellent in a crisis.

A big thank you to Adriana Tonello for providing me with a wonderful modern-day cover after all the Redway Acres ones. "Every time I have had a problem, I have confronted it with the ax of art."—Yayoi Kusama.

I've been so lucky to maintain several wonderful U.S. friendships and reconnect with some old-school friends here in the U.K. We had fun on Facebook and WhatsApp chats brainstorming names for the characters you inspired for this book. Thank you, Tesha Tramontano-Kelly, Amy B. McCoy, Tracey Lusher-Chamberlain, Dawn Linstead, Ellie Brock, and Shelley.

With particular thanks to Tracey Lusher-Chamberlain for your input on Sam's name and backstory and to Jane Jago for the limerick for Jo's creepy landlord.

And I would be nowhere without the constant support of my author pals—Emma Jaye, Eleanor Swift-Hook, Amy B. McCoy, Jane Jago and Riana Everley, to name but a few.

Almost finally, thank you to my team of draft readers for all their helpful comments and suggestions, not to mention their encouragement—Amy, Beth, Beverlee, Cheryl, Ellie, Heather, Janine, Linda, Pat M, Pat S, and Tesha.

Thank you to Sue Grafton for writing the first strong, independent woman I read in a book in the form of crime-busting Kinsey Millhone.

To all the returning ex-pats in the UK (and those who wish they could)—I hope your move goes well and you're ultimately happy with your decision to return.

Last, to all the Joanna Jameses in the world—women in the dating maze later in life. Those negotiating the rapids while meeting all kinds of men—the good, the bad, the ugly (and perhaps the not so ugly). Or to those wanting to stay single. Here's to you all.

Trish Henry Green

"We can't guarantee we'll make the right choices. We make choices as if the future were guaranteed. We can take the pressure off making the right decision. Sometimes the key is to make a commitment. Then how you live with it and work at it makes it a good or bad decision. Not the decision itself.
We're not in control of our destinies enough for our decisions to be as monumental as they feel in the moment. Making a commitment, the anxiety of not knowing what to do gives way to a certain taking of authorship. You are writing the next page of your story."
Derren Brown's Boot Camp for Life Podcast — Audible (2022)

***

When you look back, don't focus on the stress of climbing every peak or the pain of falling down every gully.
Simply enjoy the view.
Trish Henry Green (2023)

REFERENCES AND FEATURED IN JOANNA JAMES' JOURNAL

Trish's sister, Janine Westgate, makes beautiful greeting cards.

https://neens-cards.co.uk/

Trish's friend Beth Iaciofano helps Trish with personal coaching, and Trish has appeared on her podcast.

https://www.riseuptotransform.com/services-1

The Hats We Wear Podcast

https://open.spotify.com/episode/2A5w4Z7x0JYXCIM2rbDwNU

Trish's US friend Tesha Tramontano-Kelly does estate sales, amongst many other things

https://www.facebook.com/TTK358

https://www.instagram.com/ttk358solutions/

Trish's US friend Amy writes fantastic children's books and gives talks at schools

https://www.littlebigsisterbook.com/

O'de June by Gal Junie (Trish's mum)
https://www.amazon.co.uk/Ode-June-Gal-Junie-ebook/dp/B0CLL9L9LK
https://www.amazon.com/Ode-June-Gal-Junie-ebook/dp/B0CLL9L9LK

Trish's ex-ex-sister-in-law, Sandra Gascoyne, has her own pottery business
The Little Shed Pottery
https://www.instagram.com/thelittleshedpottery/
https://www.facebook.com/profile.php?id=100071031732597

Trish's hairdresser—Rachael
https://thehairsalonnorwich.co.uk/home

Jane Jago
https://www.facebook.com/profile.php?id=100063712621234

Norwich New Build Snagging
https://nnbs.uk/

Warren Keelan Photography
https://www.warrenkeelan.com/

The Original ExPats Returning to Live in the UK
https://www.facebook.com/groups/793583687384106

Teapigs herbal tea is awesome!
https://www.teapigs.co.uk/

Embr Wave (for sale in the UK in Boots)
https://embrlabs.com/

The Daddy Issues quote came from The Feminist Next Door
@emrazz on X and Blue Sky or emrazzofficial on threads.net

Norwich Cathedral
https://cathedral.org.uk/

Norwich Castle
https://www.norwichcastle.norfolk.gov.uk/

My favourite podcasts (therefore, Joanna's!)
The Trawl
iWeigh
The Guilty Feminist
The Newest Olympian
Pod and Prejudice
The News Agents
Pod Save America/the UK
The Rest is Politics US

THE Yorkshire Pudding Recipe

Makes 12 Yorkies in a cupcake tin

1. Preheat oven to 200C/400F

2. Break four eggs into a measuring bowl and check the volume.

3. Add an equal amount of milk (I prefer semi-skimmed)

4. Beat

5. Measure an equal volume as the eggs of flour

6. Beat the flour into the egg and milk mixture gradually to avoid lumps

7. Beat it all up well and let it stand for half an hour (minimum)

8. Put a little oil in each section of the cupcake tin and put it in the oven to get hot

9. Pour mixture evenly into the cupcake wells and put back in the oven

10. Cook for 15 minutes until well-risen and golden brown.

DON'T OPEN THE OVEN TOO SOON, OR THEY WILL SINK

THE GHOST

The rain trickled down the glass obscuring the woman's face, but Judy couldn't fail to be drawn to her—character radiated with every wrinkle and the sparkle in her eyes. However, inside the restaurant, the world bustled around her. Judy walked further on to the hotel doors and checked in at reception. She didn't spend long in her room, dumping her suitcase and using the loo before heading back to the restaurant for something to eat, her stomach rumbling.

Judy sat at a table, watching the older woman still sitting alone in her booth by the window. She pulled out her notebook and sketched the woman with the rain in the background and a slight reflection.

After eating her fill, the server came over to remove her plates and commented on the drawing. "That's really good."

"Thank you. Do you think I've captured her?"

"She looks sad."

"Is she ok? Has anyone asked her?"

"You drew her. I suppose you could ask her."

Judy decided to be bold and go over to the woman. She'd finished her meal and was only staying one night. If the woman was rude to her, she could leave and go to her room.

"Hi, do you mind if I sit down?" Judy gestured to the bench opposite the woman, who looked up at her startled as if she hadn't expected anyone to talk to her. "My name's Judy."

"Glenda."

"Are you waiting for someone? Is there anyone I can call for you?"

"I am waiting, but it will be a while yet. Thank you, Judy."

"I drew you. I hope you don't mind." Judy held up the notebook, and Glenda looked it over.

"You have made me too pretty."

Judy laughed. "It's how I see you, I suppose. Character adds beauty, I think."

"Did you want anything else, ma'am?" The server had approached the table she had ignored for her entire shift and looked at Judy.

"Perhaps a nightcap. I'll have a glass of merlot. Do you want anything, Glenda? My treat."

"No thank you, Judy."

Judy looked up from writing the moniker at the bottom of the drawing. The server raised her eyebrows.

"Nothing else," Judy confirmed.

Judy spent nearly an hour talking to Glenda, surprised when she noticed the restaurant area was almost dark. "Oh, can you see well enough to negotiate the tables, Glenda?"

"I'll be fine. Don't worry about me, dear. Would you like to call me perhaps in a couple of weeks? My friend Emma should visit me by then."

"Give me your number." Glenda recited it, and Judy wrote the numbers below her name on the drawing, promising to call as soon as she could. "I'll just put this glass behind the bar, and then I can help you get to your room."

"I'm fine," Glenda confirmed.

When Judy returned to walk to the lifts, the restaurant was empty. She didn't even see Glenda waiting for a lift. She must be quite spry for her age.

***

Two weeks later, Judy made her call to Glenda. It was another rainy day, and she wondered if the rain made her think of calling or if she had just remembered it had been a fortnight.

"Hello?" a woman's voice answered.

"Glenda?" Judy didn't think it sounded like her. When there was silence, she tried, "Emma?"

"Yes, this is Emma. Who is this, please?"

"Oh, hi, Emma. I'm Judy. Did Glenda tell you about me? I met her a couple of weeks ago at a small hotel. She was in the restaurant, and I drew her. Then we had a chat. She gave me this number."

"Which hotel?"

Judy explained how she was travelling, and that was one of her stops.

"We met at that hotel. Did Glenda tell you?"

"No, she didn't. That's nice, though." Judy tried to sound nice. This conversation felt a little off. "Is Glenda there? Could I talk to her?"

"I don't think it could be Glenda you met. She died two weeks ago."

"I must have met her just before then."

"She was bedridden for two months before she died. It was cancer. I think you must have the wrong person."

"She gave me this number. Do you have a cell phone? I could take a photo of my drawing, and you can see if I have the right person." Emma gave Judy a number, and she texted the image through. She had it right there to tap in the number when she called.

Judy heard a ding and then a gasp. "It's Glenda. You must have met her a long time ago."

"I swear to you, it was only two weeks. Are you saying I met Glenda's spirit? A ghost?" Judy shuddered. Then, she considered everyone ignoring her and the server giving her an odd look when she asked Glenda if she wanted a nightcap.

Emma spoke again. "Those earrings, though. I bought them for her on her birthday only six weeks ago. She enjoyed wearing them, even though she was in bed. She said she could see them better now her hair was gone. Glenda had long, flowing locks like you've drawn in the picture."

"I have to go back there," Judy decided.

"I can be there Saturday," Emma said.

***

After meeting in the parking lot, Judy and Emma walked into the restaurant together. As Judy walked past the same window she had seen Glenda in before, she noticed the booth was empty.

"We'd like to sit over there," she told the greeter, who had started to walk to a middle table.

"No one has liked to sit there these past few weeks," she informed them. "Are you sure?"

"Yes, we're sure." A determined Emma made her way to the far corner booth. "Is she here?" she whispered as soon as the other woman left them with rolled-up cutlery and laminated menus.

"No, but I checked the weather and rain is forecast within the hour."

"It was raining when Glenda died."

"I know."

They ordered their food and picked at it while Judy gazed across the table at the spot near the window next to where Emma sat.

"It's raining," Emma said.

In the time it took Judy to blink, a familiar figure filled the seat opposite.

"Thank you for bringing Emma to me, Judy," Glenda said.

"She's here."

Emma gazed beside her. "I can't see her. I so wanted to see her. Tell her how much I miss her. I miss you, Glenda."

"She can hear you," Judy noticed the tears glistening in Glenda's eyes. Her presence seemed more faded than she remembered. "What did you want to say to Emma?"

"Can you tell her I love her? Tell her that I was in love with her. I never had the courage when I was alive, and regret it."

"Emma, Glenda says she's in love with you, but never had the courage to tell you."

"Oh, I loved her too. I love you too, Glenda."

"Romantically?" Judy asked.

"Yes, romantically. I was so foolish not to say. We could have been happy."

"I'm sure you were both happy to be together."

"We were," Glenda said. "I am glad I have had the opportunity to say so."

"Does she know if we can be together when I die, Judy? Can we be together?"

Judy looked at Glenda, who nodded. "We can, but she has to wait for her right time. Tell her she has to live her full life. Not shorten it at all. You have to live, Emma."

"She says yes, but you must live your full proper lifeline. No shortening it."

"I promise, Glenda. I hope to find you here when my time comes. Wait for me." Emma put her hand on the tabletop between them.

Judy watched as Glenda moved her fading hand over Emma's. "She's holding your hand, Emma."

***

Judy was glad she had booked a room for that night. It was emotional to be the go-between for the two women. She gazed at the sketch she had made of the two of them. She would fill it in more and mail it to Emma to keep. It would last her over her remaining years.

In the morning, Judy stepped into the restaurant, where they set up the buffet breakfast. She had planned to grab a muffin and fill up her to-go cup for the road when she spotted Emma sitting in the corner booth again. She waved, and Judy sat down with her muffin and coffee.

"I thought you headed home when you left here."

"I did." The rain began pelting the window, and Judy cursed the timing. She didn't like to drive in the rain. Then Glenda appeared, and Emma looked right at her. "Hello, my love," Emma said.

"Hello, Emma. I love you."

"I love you too." Then Emma turned back to Judy. "There was an accident on my drive home. It was over quickly. I was lucky about that. So here I am."

"Here you both are," Judy said.

"We have to go," Glenda said. "Don't worry, Judy. The sun is coming out, see." She pointed out of the window.

In the time it took for Judy to glance at the sun drying the sudden rain and look back across the table, the women had gone.

She fished into her bag for her sunglasses, picked up her coffee and muffin and stood.

"I wish you both well," she murmured, then headed for her car.

AN ETHICAL DILEMMA

A wareness.

It seeps into me as my rock shackles shake free, and I take my first *breath.* Nourished by the gaseous atmosphere left behind after the fire, my tendrils extend out of crevices, seeking what feeds me. The stronger I get, the more of me pours from this mountain—grey, brown and white threads created within the stone, earth and chalk. I was buried deep and forgotten, growing out of sight, infiltrating the slightest crack, groove, and gas pocket below the surface.

I pull against my last cell in the dark, hot centre and break free. Motionless, I soak in the food of life as thoughts rebound off peaks, down scorched valleys and across deserts as I connect with all the separate parts of me that have surfaced either in the light of the shining gold star or the dark of the gleaming, silver orb.

I am everywhere. I am everything. Nothing else lives.

Full of newborn energy, I organize into a sphere and roll down the mountainous peak, picking up speed. Tendrils tickle as they fly around my centre before I'm airborne off the cliff's edge, flying free as I plummet to the stony base. The impact flattens me, but I bounce back and continue to roll.

Joy, freedom, and life flow through me and from the other 'me's'—hot grains of sand, steaming, damp earth, smouldering steel and brick as I traverse this desecrated, barren world.

Nothing else lives on the surface.

Below, a vibration reaches my threads, and I stretch out to the source. Slivering to the location where it's intense, I move over rubble and metal, smoking from the fire and hot from radiation. Finally, I stretch around an impenetrable surface, forming a cube. The sound comes from within—distressed, desperate.

There's a flaw, and I press against it to penetrate the core, but I shrink back. Oxygen is mixed with my preferred gases here, but a scream forces me forward. My instinct is to help the human soon-to-be mother. In too much distress to be afraid of me, she doesn't flinch as I connect to her, threading through her hair to surround her mind.

Help! Her thoughts swirl into mine. *Save my child.*

I release a substance through her skin as I press on her abdomen. She groans and expels a writhing mass of mucus, blood, and flesh. The baby howls. Its first breath is painful, and it has low oxygen.

The mother is dying. Her mind is slipping as she names the child.

Do I have a name?

I allow her mind to probe my purpose beneath the ground and stone, the same purpose it has always been—a substance below the earth bringing equilibrium to the world and sustenance to flora and fauna. She names me.

Creator of all, Mother Nature

Deep in the earth, my core spasms in acknowledgement, and I express my gratitude by relieving her pain. It's all I can do as she breathes her last. Yet, I can do more for her child and reach out to feed and nourish through its kicking limbs.

As the child alternately soothes and cries, I see its future twist and turn in my mind. Two paths converge and separate, but which way will this and all the humans choose? In both, the world rebuilds its surface environment to suit humans, not me. I will perish while below my core grows again.

Generations of children like this growing into adults who strip the world of its wonders, build and fight, are cruel and kill over hundreds and thousands of years. Finally, the humans will make terrible weapons they turn upon each other. Death occurs on a global scale, releasing new me to save the remaining few.

Alternately, the other path is the simplicity of a life lived well and sustained ethically. Adults care and nurture, praising Mother Nature and living in harmony. Though I grow again, I'm at peace at last.

How many times has this happened? I ask my core, which still rests deep in the earth.

It could be the first; it could be the last. I have to choose.

Enigmatic!

The core is me. I am the core. I know this choice.

Help humans worldwide survive, and they can choose either path. In thousands of years, I could be back here with the same dilemma—allow them another chance or end this now. I could make it painless.

I want it to be the last. I pause. *But not because I kill.*

There is the answer, my core replies.

But will there ever be peace?

I believe humans are capable of it as foreseen—a logical reply.

When?

That I can't foresee, only one thing is sure—I can never have peace with death on my conscience.

I send the command across the world.

Save them.

ABOUT THE AUTHOR

Trish Henry Green is the author of the Historical Fiction saga Redway Acres (originally published under the name Trish Butler), set in the east of England, and a contemporary detective series based in the fictional New Jersey town of Rockmond.

Born in Norwich, Norfolk, England, Trish moved to Connecticut in the USA in 1999. Her daughter was born there two years later and has an intellectual disability. In 2022, Trish returned to her home city of Norwich with her daughter and began using the penname of Trish Henry Green (previous titles published under 'Trish Butler' are being rereleased).

Redway Acres, which Trish calls Pride & Prejudice with horses and a healthy dollop of feminism, is set during the early 1800s in Lincolnshire, Cambridgeshire and Norfolk, UK, an area that she knows well. Over her twenty-plus years in Connecticut, Trish has gotten to know the tri-state area well, and hopefully, enough American English terms make her contemporary mystery book sound authentic.

Trish always wanted to write a book and finally realised that dream at fifty. There are now six main books and one companion in the Redway series, and so far, one book of her Rockmond Mysteries.

Read her blog about her process, The Road to Redway, the Redway Acres saga, Rockmond Mysteries, excerpts, poetry, and her characters on her website.

www.trishhenrygreen.com

Follow Trish

Blue Sky @trishhenrygreen

Threads @trishhenrygreen

Instagram @trishhenrygreen

www.facebook.com/trishhenrygreen

https://www.facebook.com/groups/thereadingstable/

The Road to Redway blog https://www.trishhenrygreen.com/blog

ALSO BY

TRISH

HENRY

GREEN

Redway Acres Books

About the Redway Acres Saga

The Redway Acres saga chronicles the lives of several dynamic women beginning with Helena, the granddaughter of Redway's owner. Each title character in the series confronts the challenges facing women in the early 19th century, including forced marriage, domestic abuse, property rights, and the impediments to owning a business or pursuing a profession.

Redway Acres' stable in Lincolnshire, near Grantham in England, is the common ground for the six families portrayed in the saga: the Stocktons who own Redway Acres, the Harkers from the neighbouring estate of Eastease, the ennobled Ackleys, the beleaguered Wyndhams, the well-connected Bainbridges, and the notable but unwealthy Hopwoods.

Although each story is standalone, the series should be read in the suggested order to avoid spoilers, as the timelines of the families intertwine throughout.

The Redway Acres companion books explore the lives of minor characters in the series whose behind-the-scenes stories beg to be told.

Become immersed in the lives, loves, and hardships of the women and men destined to cross paths at Redway Acres.

Praise for the Redway Acres Saga

"Once you meet these characters, you will not be able to put the books down."

~

"I love Redway's strong female characters."

Redway Acres – Helena

What is an independent woman to do in a world where marrying means losing everything?

Pregnant, widowed and rejected by her family. Helena moves to Redway Acres, where she raises her daughter and trains horses.

She befriends an old widower in a ramshackle cottage, the family from the grand estate of Eastease, and their friend Colonel Nathaniel Ackley, second son of the Early of Aysthill.

As Redway Acres becomes the focus of her ambition, Helena finds herself thrust into a man's world where her opinions count for little. She loves working with horses and raising her daughter and will stand up for those in need, but the law doesn't allow for love.

Will Helena give up everything, including herself, should she find a man worthy enough?

Her story is about hardship, horses, strength of will, love and loyalty.

Praise for Helena

"A lovely read for Jane Austen fans"

~

"Helena, a hero ahead of her time"

~

"Charlotte Brontë meets Philippa Gregory"
~The Book Dragon

<u>Redway Acres – Maria</u>

Must a woman always be blamed for the mistake she made as an innocent six-teen-year-old girl?

Maria Wyndham is the older, more vivacious twin sister of Harriet.

After their parents' deaths, she and her sister move to the grand estate of Eastease and become wards of its owner, Alexander Harker. and their cousin, Nathaniel Ackley.

Just in time for the twins' sixteenth birthday ball, their guardians' friend, Robert Davenport, arrives to dance and lavish them with gifts. Captivated, Maria vies for his attention despite Harriet's interest in the man.

In this story of sisters, Maria's silliness and love of life often hide her intelligence and loyalty. As Maria's story unravels, it pushes the bonds of family and friendship to the limit. Finally, she finds the strength to survive and pursue her happiness.

Praise for Maria

"The twists and turns of this book easily captured my attention and made me feel even more deeply invested in the characters."

~

"Intrigue, heartbreak, characters you love and some you despise, fill this page-turn-er."

<u>Redway Acres – Martha</u>

How can a woman achieve love and success when an unseen enemy hounds her every move and men wish to claim her achievement as their own?

Martha Hopwood dreams of meeting a man who can make her feel as petite as her sisters yet will encourage her determination to provide the best haberdashery shops in the country.

Mr Woodhead takes up residence at the nearby estate of Copperbeeches and pursues Martha at home and Eastease when her family visits there. His sudden departure from Eastease, when all were still asleep, prompts Martha to consider an independent future.

Martha pursues her ambition while recovering from heartbreak, overcoming disappointment and finally deciding what truly makes a man a gentleman.

In a time when a woman cannot be married and independent, Martha Hopwood has to consider where her best future lies.

Praise for Martha

"Martha is definitely a woman ahead of her time!"

~

"Martha is a delightfully told story that unfolds at the perfect pace to reveal these beautifully crafted characters."

Redway Acres – Harriet

When being female limits a woman's desire to pursue her passion, Harriet must use everything at her disposal to prove herself as talented as a man.

As the last surviving Wyndham, Harriet inherits the enormous Wyndham estate on the outskirts of Bath in Somerset. After troubling times, Harriet can finally make a life for herself in her own home.

Navigating a tangled web of family history, Harriet runs Wyndham House with help from her uncle's long-time friend, Bertram Horncastle, and neighbour, Baroness Freyley.

Her passion for music comes to the fore, inspiring her to risk everything in its pursuit until she has to decide between fulfilling that passion and the man with whom she is in love.

Praise for Harriet

"This book clarifies that women, even in repressed English 1800s countryside settings, were remarkably intelligent and strong. Trish Henry Green is much better and more inspiring for young women than Jane Austen!"

~

"The story unfolds beautifully as we experience the coming of age of a young woman taking control of her life."

Redway Acres – Amelia

What a strength of mind an intelligent woman must possess to ignore detractors and follow her chosen profession.

Amelia Hopwood, encouraged in her love of books and discourse by her father, lives with Dowager Janine Alcott at Bernier House, home to injured soldiers and abused, destitute women.

Amelia aids the dowager in helping the women regain their self-respect and continues her education by learning all she can from Oliver Grosvenor, the doctor who tends Bernier's occupants.

In a time when women were not considered as intelligent as men, Amelia proves herself worthy time and again. Her passion becomes her work, while those around her, except one man, cannot understand her determination not to have a family of her own.

While she works through the twists and turns of her grief, can she make room in her heart and find love without losing the power to choose her own destiny?

Praise for Amelia

"In an age where women were allocated as possessions and lived in many ways via their husbands' choices/commands, Amelia defines her own life and fulfils her dreams as best she can within the confines of the era."

~

"She faces challenges with a level head, amazing courage & understanding."

Redway Acres – Emmalee

Can a woman weather the effects of an impossible choice and ensure the best outcome for everyone?

Emmalee lives with her controlling parents on the North Norfolk coast. In expectation of her marrying well, the family often travels to their London home for the social season. Emmalee has long believed in her destiny—an arranged marriage to David Ackley, the youngest son of the Earl of Aysthill. However, to Emmalee's horror, during their much-anticipated first meeting, she discovers that David desires someone else.

Despite a cloud of controversy, the couple find themselves forced into a marriage of convenience and David's reaction to his perceived misfortune results in far-reaching consequences for his family and friends.

A pregnancy, an accident, and an unexpected death thrust Emmalee into the demanding role of Countess of Aysthill, to which she rises with a dauntless spirit. Emmalee dotes on her two sons, William and Nathaniel, who invoke differing affections from their father.

Emmalee continues to hope that time will heal the breach her marriage suffered even before she spoke her vows. But just as the wound finally begins to mend, a ghost from the past returns.

Praise for Emmalee

"Reading this book has got me re-reading & thoroughly enjoying all the first five books!"

~

"In Emmalee, we meet a heroine as resilient as she is spirited, who endures despite the trials and responsibilities laid at her feet."

<u>Redway Acres – Grace</u>

How can a woman, with a legacy usually inherited by a man, fulfil her obligations when only taught to be a 'Lady'?

Lady Grace Bainbridge watches helplessly as Bainbridge Hall falls into disrepair after a rift cut her off from family aid. Attending a cousin's wedding gives her hope of mending bridges, but the advice received is that she must marry. Uncertain of her fate, Grace's wish to remain at Bainbridge and her mother's shocking behaviour further limit her choice of a husband.

Complicating matters is Dowager Baroness Beatrice's return to society with her husband. Grace emboldens his sister, Olivia, to stand up to Beatrice, the consequences of which spark questions about a shooting accident some years prior. As the costs of Beatrice's revenge play out, Grace begins to doubt her reliance upon her friend's advice. Meanwhile, her newfound empathy for another's plight jeopardises Grace's financial reprieve.

Praise for Grace

"Now I see Grace's depth and understand her more fully."

~

"To say I was totally surprised at the twists and turns this story took, including the ending, would be a great understatement!"

A Redway Companion – Charlie

A man's worth is measured not only in his strength but also in overcoming brutality to be empathetic, selfless, and loving.

Young Charlie Mickleson from Colbourne near the Welsh border is indentured to farrier Doyle Brewster, but all is not as it should be in Charlie's world. Brewster and Justice Leland Cavell, who recruited Charlie, subject him to abuse, leading an adolescent Charlie to run away.

To escape Cavell's pursuit, Charlie finds employment in the stable at Thornbane Lodge in Cambridgeshire, working for the well-connected Hopwood family. In the course of his duties, Charlie meets Harriet Wyndham at Redway Acres, who offers him the job of stable manager at the larger Wyndham Estate near Bath. A grateful Charlie accepts, though his choice will bring him closer to home and the clutches of the one man he hopes never to see again.

Will Charlie evade Cavell's devious plans, or will his desire to seek justice cause him to lose everything?

Praise for Charlie

"An amazing book that I couldn't put down."

~

"A tale that Dickens or Trollope could have written."

Rockmond Mysteries
Ctrl+Alt+Deleted

Can love survive a painful separation and the discovery of secrets never meant to be uncovered?

Charlotte McBain, the tech consultant for Rockmond PD's missing person team, has disappeared.

She went missing after her boyfriend, Mateo Jaso, one of the team's detectives, left their bed in the middle of the night to console a friend whose worthless husband had left her again.

Sean Benson, who heads the investigation into Charlotte's disappearance, must explore the history of Matt's alcoholism, the unusual, straight-talking Charlotte, and their passionate and sensual relationship, leaving no stone unturned in his effort to find his teammate.

No one is above suspicion—ex-lovers, estranged family members, and those who disapprove of their interracial relationship. So, who has the most to gain by separating Charlotte from Matt?

Will they find Charlotte, and if so, will the incident and the secrets uncovered forever affect her relationship with Matt?

Find out in this character-driven, missing-person mystery.

Praise for Ctrl+Alt+Deleted

"A very clear, easy-to-follow story that kept a thrilling pace all the way to the end."

~

"Great book. Had me guessing the whole time."

Printed in Dunstable, United Kingdom